Butchered Dreams

Hadena James

Acknowledgments

To everyone that makes these books readable. Your attention to detail and persnicketies is appreciated.

Huge kudos to my friends and family who put up with me.

To my readers : Yes, Malachi is a little bit odder than you ever imagine. Just wait until you see the inside of his house…

Also by Hadena James

The Dreams & Reality
Tortured Dreams (Book 1)
Elysium Dreams (Book 2)
Mercurial Dreams (Book 3)
Explosive Dreams (Book 4)
Cannibal Dreams (Book 5)
Butchered Dreams (Book 6)

The Brenna Strachan Series (Urban Fantasy)
Dark Cotillion (Book 1)
Dark Illumination (Book 2)
Dark Resurrections (Book 3)
Dark Legacies (Book 4)

The Dysfunctional Chronicles
The Dysfunctional Affair (Book 1)
The Dysfunctional Valentine (Book 2)
The Dysfunctional Honeymoon (Book 3)
The Dysfunctional Proposal (Book 4)

Short Story Collection
Tales to Read Before the End of the World

I believe these blank pages are necessary for aesthetic reasons, but for the life of me, I can't stand to have blank pages in a book. However, it looks odd to have the "Also By HJ" face the prologue.

Prologue

Patterson Clachan sat in his car. The motor had been turned off for over an hour and the cold was seeping into the vehicle. His mind wasn't thinking about the cold seeping into his bones, it was concentrating on his newfangled phone. Someone in the retirement community had suggested he get a new smartphone. Always intrigued by shiny new gadgets, he'd immediately gone to the nearest cell phone store and bought one. The kid that sold it to him had said it was the top of the line.

The kid was probably right, but Patterson had figured out everything except how to make a phone call. And a phone call was what he really wanted to make at the moment. It was a few minutes after seven in the morning and he needed to check on the condition of Nyleena.

Despite shooting her in the face, for which he was indeed sorry, he felt a compulsion to check on her. Besides, Aislinn was taking his very brief calls to update him. He found this strange and didn't know if she was using the calls as a way to plot against him or allow him some peace of mind. Either way, the contact was not unwelcome.

After several more minutes, Patterson realized he did not want to make a call to Aislinn using this phone, he had a special burner phone that he kept replacing to talk to her on. He put the fancy gadget on the seat next to him.

A tall black man got out of his car and began walking towards the house. The phone call would have to wait. Patterson watched him with interest. His gait was affected by a slight limp, so slight, you wouldn't have noticed it if you weren't paying attention.

Patterson had done his research. James Okafor had been a soldier in The Congo Wars. He was positive he'd been one of the men involved in the Rwandan Genocide. He'd seen a lot of death in his world. It had started during The Great Depression and continued to present day. There were some he couldn't abide; pedophiles and men convinced that genocide was the solution were at the top of the list. He'd heard "I was only following orders" so much that, the very thought of it made him ill.

On the other side, Patterson understood the man's rage. He'd come to the US with his wife and daughter. His daughter had died at a county fair, when the announcer's box collapsed while she sang The Star Spangled Banner. She had been the runner-up to the fair queen. If she had been the queen, she wouldn't have been in the box. It was a tragic accident, but for a man on the edge, Patterson knew why he killed the queens.

That didn't excuse him from trying to shoot down Aislinn's helicopter as she was transported to the hospital. Nor did it excuse him from firing into the restaurant, nearly killing Aislinn and managing to kill Michael.

While Patterson really liked to slice people open, he thought the punishment should fit the crime. In this case, slicing open his victim seemed too easy. This man was killing teenage girls who had won pageants, and federal agents eating dinner.

He waited for the lights to go out in the house. While he waited, he picked up the fancy phone again. He flipped through the photo album until he found the picture he wanted; Donnelly, Myrna, Eric, Isabella, and Aislinn were in it. They were smiling. Aislinn was about six years old. It was the last thing that Donnelly, his son, had ever given him. He'd scanned it in a few years earlier so that he could carry it around with him.

His finger touched the face of his dead son and he dug out the burner phone.

"She's still alive," Aislinn answered without a hello.

"That's good, she's a fighter," Patterson answered. "How are you?"

"Not willing to talk to you," Aislinn's voice was stoic. Not a quiver, not a tremble, nothing to indicate her emotions.

"Aislinn, you do know that I meant to shoot her in her shoulder, not her face." Patterson pleaded his case again.

"You say that like it makes it better. You shot her. You shot your own granddaughter. I get your sister, I found her note, but Nyleena did not ask you to shoot her." Aislinn hung up.

Patterson sighed as he put the phone away. He'd leave it here for the Marshals or FBI to find. The light went off in the bedroom and Patterson got out of the car. He'd already been in the house several times and he had a way in. He went to the backdoor and inserted the key he'd lifted from James at the bar a few weeks earlier.

He carried the cane into the house, instead of walking with it as was his usual custom. The stick was made of gidgee wood from Australia, one of the hardest woods in the world. It was coated to make it easy to clean.

The handle was ornately molded carbon steel with a flattened end. While the cane was fully functional as a cane, it worked even better as a club.

Patterson crept into James bedroom. The man was already asleep. Patterson tried not to become agitated. He had rules. Killing an innocent while they slept was about mercy, their deaths were quick and painless, but evil deserved to know it was going to die. Those rules were why Nyleena had been shot in the face. He couldn't shoot her in the back, no matter how much easier it would have been for her. When she'd turned, he'd just fired, accidentally aiming too high.

"What the fu..." James rolled over, reaching for something. Patterson flipped on the light and interrupted his profanity.

"Now, now, we'll have none of that," Patterson said to him. "I've been watching you for a while James. You seem like a decent enough fellow, aside from killing teen pageant queens and computer geeks working for the US Marshals."

"Get out of my house," James growled.

"I would, but I wasn't done. As I said, you seem like a decent enough fellow, but I have a feeling you aren't. Even without killing the pageant queens, I think you are probably a monster. I've been doing my homework and you served as a soldier during the genocide in Rwanda. So, I checked and you are indeed a Hutu and not a Tutsi. See, I considered letting this minor detail slide, but the more I thought about, the more I realized I couldn't. This is a problem for you."

"I'll give you one more warning because you're an old man," James sat up, he held a long knife in his hands, no doubt pulled from under a pillow. "Get out."

"Now, now," Patterson said, "there will be plenty of time for knife fights later. At the moment, I'm just interested in talking. The killing comes a little later."

"The only one that's going to die is you," James growled again, his muscles tensing. Patterson watched all this and timed his swing perfectly. The knife skittered across the floor as several bones in James' hand broke. James continued forward, weaponless, and Patterson hit him in the thigh with the heavy cane. James fell to the floor.

"I suppose you would just like to get to the killing," Patterson tutted. "That's the problem with modern killers, they never want to talk. What ever happened to the days of civilized conversation? You must have questions about who I am and how I know about the Marshal and the pageant queens or your service in the Congo. Or how about the reason I intend to kill you? That should be of interest at the very least." Patterson walked around James, who was still sprawled on the floor. "No? Nothing?" Patterson frowned.

"Fine, I'll play along," James was moving now. He got to his feet. Unlike most people, he didn't cradle his broken hand or rub at his sore thigh. He stood tall and acted like neither bothered him. Patterson's frown relaxed, he was going to enjoy this. "Why are you going to kill me?"

"Well, that depends. Do you want the honest reason or do you want some bullshit story that will make your death have more meaning?" Patterson asked.

"Honesty," James said.

"Because I'm a killer," Patterson answered. "Like you, I enjoy the hunt, I enjoy the pain, the blood, the screaming and crying and begging. Unlike you, I'm old and I've found random killing just doesn't interest me anymore. It used to, don't get me wrong. There was nothing I enjoyed more than slicing up a Nazi or two, before returning to the front lines with a gun and shooting them. Back then, Nazis were a dime a dozen and expendable. After all, they were evil and who was going to miss a few?

When I came back to the States, after the war, I found killing didn't have the same appeal. So, I stopped for a long time, had a family, a beautiful wife with a brilliant mind and strong will, then I lost all those and killing felt great again. Surprising how that happens." Patterson stepped to the side as James rushed him, knocking the larger man with the cane on the back of his shoulder. "You should stop, you aren't going to get hold of me. We will just continue to dance around until I decide I'm bored. Then the torture starts. The torture will last a long time, because I think you deserve it. If you're lucky, you'll die during the torture. If you aren't, well, you would have my sympathy if I was capable of such a thing."

James showed his first weakness. His fingers found his bruised shoulder blade and touched it gently.

"What did I do to you?" James asked.

"Aside from try to shoot down a helicopter carrying my granddaughter? Not much. My granddaughter is an interesting person. She's a killer too, but she controls the urges better. So, instead of being like you and me, she's a US Marshal with the SCTU. You not only shot at her helicopter, but you killed a friend of hers at the restaurant while they ate dinner. That's when I decided to kill you. Now, five months later, I've learned that you were involved in genocide and that, well, that just creates a bigger problem. My plan originally was to just kill you. Slice you open and pull out all your organs, let you die fairly quick, albeit painfully. But I just couldn't fight off the images of my granddaughter at a funeral, crying of all things and you killing, raping, maiming innocent people just because they weren't exactly like you and that made me change my mind. It made me realize that I was going to have to kill you slowly. So that is exactly what I intend to do." Patterson swung the cane with a quickness that would have made a snake jealous. It connected with James' collarbone. It snapped with an audible popping noise and James grabbed at it. With his attention on his collarbone, Patterson swung again, gentler, hitting James in the head. The man fell to the floor.

Patterson went to work. He heaved and shoved to move James to the bed. It took a few minutes to get the restraints in place, but once they were, Patterson took a break. James was still not moving. He'd have to hoist the larger man onto the bed. Another second and Patterson bent down, grabbing the taller man under the armpits, he lifted and James came off the floor as if he weighed no more than a small child. Once on the bed, Patterson put him into the restraints, then sat down to wait.

James groaned. Patterson hit him in the leg with the cane, bringing a scream from the other man. He was wide awake now. The screaming would be a problem though. Patterson took something from his pocket and affixed it to James' face. The sounds were instantly muffled. While Patterson liked the screams, he couldn't have the neighbors alerted. James made strange noises through the gag. Patterson hit him again, bringing the cane down on a rib. The bone shattered under the blow.

Patterson brought the cane down over and over again until blood began to soak into the bed. Several of the blows had broken the skin. Patterson smiled at his handiwork. James was still alive, although he was badly maimed. Several of the smaller bones had broken under the heavy head of the cane. But Patterson wasn't done yet.

He retrieved James' knife from the floor. The man's chest was bare from sleeping. Patterson heated the tip of the blade with a butane lighter. As it began to glow red, he removed it from the flame and placed it against James' chest. He had to do this eleven times to spell the word "KILLER" on his chest.

James was only making very quiet sobbing sounds now. Patterson was okay with that. He'd given him a good beating, James deserved to be allowed to cry. Patterson sat the burner phone down on the dresser and brought in a chair from the kitchen. He sat down.

"As I said, the problem with your generation of killers' is their lack of communication. They never want to just talk about things. Wisdom has taught me that sometimes, talking is the best weapon. I'm going to sit here and talk to you until you die. It shouldn't take long now. I'm sure your internal organs have been injured, you've already pissed blood all over the bed, a sure sign of kidney damage. I hope it hurts, James. I hope it hurts a lot. While people like you and I rarely think of the pain we cause others, we do cause them pain. Lots of it. Looking back, I know that those Nazis had families and they were probably on the front lines because it was either be a Nazi or else. Of all those you killed during the Congo Wars, how many had families? How many times did you make a parent watch as you slaughtered their children? I imagine it was many. Men like you and I only feel alive when we are killing. For me, it's a genetic flaw or evolution. Were you always a killer, James or were you created by the situation? Were you one of those men that followed orders but found you liked it?"

James made a gurgling noise. Patterson nodded at him and touched the tip of an imaginary cap. He checked for a pulse and found nothing.

"Consider yourself lucky, James. I considered castrating you," Patterson said to the corpse as he exited the bedroom.

One

Machines beeped and whirred. The heart monitor was steady. Aside from the giant bandage, Nyleena looked peaceful. Being in a coma was probably the best sleep she'd had in ages. My own experience a few months earlier with a medically induced coma, had proven that outside noises filtered into coma dreams.

Because of this, I was reading to her for several hours a day. Crappy books that I would never have read on my own, but were her kinds of books. Top of the list was Janet Evanovich. I was hoping that Ranger and Morelli were filling her sleeping mind and not Patterson shooting her in the face over and over.

However, the three days I spent at the hospital weren't doing me much good. The grey walls were claustrophobic. The smell of antiseptic and the noisy machines had created a headache that wouldn't go away. Multiple meals of hospital food was upsetting my normal diet and impacting my digestive system as well as my headache.

The Justice Department was taking the shooting very seriously. There was a cop outside the door at all times. Nyleena had a private room, and they had been courteous enough to bring a bed in for me as well. I also had a special recliner and a chair to allow me to sit in different places and positions.

The doctors believed the coma was caused by trauma to the frontal lobe. While the bullet hadn't penetrated the area, the bone behind her sinuses had cracked causing damage to the brain. Emergency surgery had saved her life. If she woke, the doctors were confident that she might have some amnesia about the event, but otherwise would be relatively unharmed, but that was an "if." People lived in comas for decades and Nyleena wasn't showing any signs of waking up.

If she died, I was going to beat Patterson to death, I didn't care if he was our grandfather. If she lived and woke up, I would just break his legs and make the cane a necessity. If she stayed in limbo, I wasn't sure what I was going to do.

Several minutes earlier, he'd called. I'd hung up on him after updating him on her condition. It had shaken me out of my reading reverie. I stood up and paced.

"That was Patterson," I told my cousin. "He is still apologizing, claiming he meant to shoot you in the shoulder, not the face. I do not know if I believe him. I wish you would wake up."

"Think that helps?" Xavier came into the room.

"Yes, I remember having weird dreams when I was in my coma. I believe they were caused by the external stimuli around me. I've been reading to her, but Patterson's call broke my concentration."

"I brought you real food," Xavier held up a bag.

"If I eat one more salad or cheeseburger, I will die." I told him.

"Guess it's a good thing I brought Chili's and got you their southwest pairings. There's a chicken soft taco and a sour cream chicken enchilada in the box with extra rice and a nice big Mt. Dew." Xavier handed me the bag. I set it down on the table and checked the clock. Patterson had called before dawn. It was now almost noon. I'd lost time. Not uncommon with a migraine, sleep deprivation, or high stress situations for me. "Why don't you take a walk, I'll read to her for a while."

"Why? I'm starting to like the grey," I lied.

"What grey?" Xavier asked.

"The walls," I told him. "Who paints a hospital grey?"

"Ace, the walls aren't grey, they're a pale eggshell blue." He frowned at me. "How often do you see grey walls?"

"All the time. I cannot figure out why the Marshals offices are always grey."

"They aren't. Are you color blind?"

"I see colors," I told him.

"Do you? Do you really?"

"Yes, they tested me for it when I was young because my dad had issues with color."

"What issues?"

"I do not know." I told Xavier. "What does it matter?"

"That is a good question," Xavier pursed his lips. "So, your sensory perception of color is off. What do you think about impressionist art?"

"Those fuzzy representative paintings with color blotches? I dislike it."

"They aren't fuzzy. When was the last time you had an eye test?"

"A while."

"I think it's time for another. I believe you have a rare condition in which color variations cannot be seen when they are near other colors that are of similar hues. It is occasionally inherited, but can also be caused by trauma to the brain or eyes. It might explain why light gives you migraines."

"Another day," I told him, opening the box. The food smelled great. I had a pang of something as I took the first fork full, knowing that Nyleena was being feed through an IV. She loved Mexican too.

"What are you reading?" Xavier picked up my Kindle.

"Janet Evanovich's *High Five*. I've been rereading the entire series to her." I chewed and swallowed. "Shouldn't you be out tracking down Patterson?"

"Yes," Xavier took a seat. "Unfortunately, now that the world knows he's your grandfather, the FBI is handling it. They won't even let the VCU handle it, they have some sort of task force. We are all getting ready for another case, except you. You've been granted a week of leave to deal with your psychological condition now that Nyleena's out of commission."

"How are you going to work a case without Lucas, a geek and me?"

"We have a geek, her name is Fiona Stewart. She started yesterday and the two of you are going to hate each other. Lucas has been released for work, so there's four of us going."

"Where?" I chewed another bite very slowly.

"Tennessee and I'm not to tell you any more. Besides, do you think this is the sort of conversation we should be having around Nyleena? Shouldn't we be discussing happier things?"

I sighed. Xavier began reading from the Kindle. I ate quietly, listening to him. He was good at reading aloud, for some reason, I found that unexpected. When I finished my food, Xavier stopped reading. He looked at me with a frown.

"What?" I asked him.

"I brought you clothes as well. It's been three days, the nurses say you can use the shower in the room. And you need a shower, desperately."

"What if she wakes up?"

"I'll be here, reading to her. When you get out, I'll go," Xavier said. I sat where I was. "Seriously, Ace, you're starting to smell like road kill. Go take a shower."

I gave in. The shower was hot and the shampoo smelled of mint. It tingled on my scalp. It felt good to be under the spray, but my ears were constantly searching for the sound of Nyleena's voice or excited noises from Xavier indicating she was awake. When I got out, I dried off and dressed.

"No magic spell awoke Sleeping Beauty while you were away," Xavier told me as I exited.

"If she was Sleeping Beauty, I'd find a prince to kiss her." I took my Kindle back. "Sadly, she's Nyleena and there isn't a prince in the world strong enough to break the spell she's under. Our own grandfather." I shook my head. Patterson could protest all he wanted, I was still going to hold a grudge over it. "So, what's in Tennessee?"

"Nice try," Xavier stood. He touched my cheek, rubbing away a droplet of water. "Don't read into that, you look terrible, even for you. Are you sleeping?"

"Yes," I told him. "I think the nurses are drugging me at night, but I'm sleeping."

"Paranoid, interesting. Why would the nurses be drugging you?"

"Because I did not sleep the first night. At all. Has it really been three days?" I asked.

"Yes, it has. Do you intend to stay here for the entire week?"

"I can't think of anywhere else to go," I told him.

"We'll check in as often as possible." Xavier left. I returned to the book on the Kindle and resumed reading, but my mind wasn't into it anymore. They had sent regular FBI agents to hunt for Patterson Clachan. Someone in charge was an idiot. Patterson would tear them apart; figuratively, of course, since he really liked to use knives.

Two

There isn't much one can do at a hospital for long durations. When my voice began to give out, I'd put on an audiobook for Nyleena and played video games on my phone. I didn't have a social networking profile on any site, I didn't have anyone to keep up with. The thought of having to find people to "friend" made me slightly ill.

As I had discovered during my long term stay in a hospital, it left a lot of time for thought. I had come to the realization that introspection was a bad idea for a sociopath. My ego tended to inflate and at the moment, I had no one to help humble it. While it seemed like a strange understanding, I knew that letting my ego grow was a negative thing. The larger it grew, the more convinced I became of my own superiority and I didn't need more of that. I needed less. Less was hard to come by.

I also couldn't sit and fantasize about how I would kill Patterson Clachan. It was unproductive because I probably wouldn't get the chance and frankly, the methods were becoming much more brutal. The Inquisition had nothing on me as far as torture methods went, I had already come up with about a million new ones. Some were more disturbing than others.

My phone vibrated. The number was blocked. I answered it.

"She is still alive, still in a coma," I told Patterson. "You know I want to torture you, right?"

"Yes," Patterson answered. "I understand. I would prefer you wait for her to wake up that way I will know that she is going to be okay. Honestly, I didn't mean to hurt her like I did."

"Yeah, yeah," I grumbled. "I still want to torture you."

"I'm sure you've come up with some very creative ways to do it as well." Patterson paused. "I killed someone this morning. For you. I beat him to death so you wouldn't have to. He killed Michael. He knew the bomber, personally, and I watched as the final breath slipped from his body in the form of a gurgling sob. He didn't die quickly. It was terribly painful. I've sent the address where he can be found to the FBI."

"Am I supposed to thank you?" I retorted, angry that I wasn't going to have the pleasure of beating the shit out of Michael's killer.

"Not in the least, I just wanted to let you know that justice had been served. If you had found him, you would have ended up with your brother. We can't have that. So I beat him to death to keep you from doing it."

"Great, now I'm angry about that too." I admitted to my serial killing grandfather.

"I understand that as well. Donnelly was right about you, the rage burns deep and strong. You might be more of a killer than any of us."

"You are not allowed to mention my father's name," I growled.

"He was my son!" Patterson's voice rose and even over the cell phone I could hear a small tremble in it. "I have just as much right to be angry about his death as you do, possibly more because I got to spend less time with him. Only after your incident with Callow did he begin responding to my attempts at communication."

"Liar," I said calmly and hung up the phone. Surely my law-and-order father hadn't been in contact with his serial killer father. As I thought about it, I knew I was wrong. He probably was in contact with Patterson. Maybe that had been part of the change in my father. He had a monster to raise, so he allowed a monster back into his life to give him advice. The letters had started coming to me after my father's death.

I put my head on the portable table. My father had been talking to a serial killer trying to find a way to keep me from becoming one. That was life altering information.

Personally, my father had been dead too long for me to maintain an emotional attachment to him. Worse, our relationship hadn't been very good at the time of his death. His oppressive behavior had driven a wedge between us, one I hadn't had the tools to mend before he meet his fate.

As *Good Omens* played on the iPod I had borrowed from Gabriel, my mind began to think about my real relationship with my father. He had stopped being my dad after Callow, a distinction in my mind that was larger than the Grand Canyon.

However, what teased me now was the question about how much of that difference had been him and how much of it had been me. I had changed as well. Finding the survivor inside had made me feel alive, capable, and awakened the monster as never before. I couldn't even imagine what it had done to my parents. It wasn't just a lack of sympathy, it was a lack of understanding.

I wasn't having children. I would never know the love of a child or know how it felt to love them back. I wasn't even sure I was capable of such a thing. For me, children had never been an option. It wasn't just a lack of impulse to have sex, it was that I was sure I would make a bad parent. I wouldn't be able to connect to a child. They would be a burden, a nuisance, a road block to whatever it was that I wanted to do right that moment. Also, they would provide a weakness if I did connect, another way for the monsters to hurt me.

Suddenly, I realized I needed to make a phone call. The speed dial screen only had seven phone numbers. There were only eight in my entire phone. I had removed Michael finally.

"Good news?" Malachi's voice came onto the line.

"We will reserve judgment on that. I just got a call from Patterson. He's claiming he beat a man to death this morning and that the man was our sniper. He also claims he found him because he was friends with the bomber."

"Is that Good Omens in the background?" Malachi asked.

"Yes, it's soothing, something for Nyleena to listen to when I need a break." I told. "Now, about the dead body."

"I'm not on the case. You're not on the case. I can pass along information, but that's it." Malachi said with a tone. "I have some reservations about it though."

"You have reservations about reporting The Butcher killed someone?" I couldn't stop my mouth from falling open.

"It isn't about The Butcher killing someone, it's about the FBI agents on the case. They're good agents. I would hate for them to get caught up in this and die as a result."

"That sounds a lot like sympathy," I told him.

"It's the right answer," Malachi said and hung up. My mind twirled the answer over in my head. It wasn't a hidden code, I knew exactly what Malachi meant. He was fairly certain he'd be sending them to their deaths. That would be wrong, but if enough FBI agents died, the powers that be would ignore the conflict of interest and send Malachi and his team to get Patterson.

Left to his own devices, Malachi wouldn't have thought twice about it. However, I would and did have reservations. Death was rarely the best solution in my opinion. While Malachi listened to my voice tell him that, I heard it come to me from Nyleena.

I looked at her. Xavier was right, she did look like a fairy tale princess. Her long, very dark brown hair was spread out on the pillow where it had been brushed. With her eyes closed, her lashes looked thick and dark, like a model's. If one could ignore the giant bandage that covered her entire left cheek, she was picture perfect.

Nyleena was a natural beauty, whatever that meant. I had been told it many times by different men that had come and gone from our lives. Her skin was pale and perfect, the only scars were covered by the sheets and she had far fewer of them than I did. It seemed unfair that she would now sport a nasty gash on her face if she woke up.

With the limited range of emotions, I was struggling to figure out how or what to feel about my current situation. Mostly, I was pissed and looking at her made me angrier. What I couldn't voice was why it made me angry. Yes, I missed her to the best of my ability. However, the reason behind the anger was more self-centered. She was my touchstone, without her, I was floating in limbo, searching for something to latch onto and claim as my own. Without her, it was harder to control the monster that lurked inside me. It was a dangerous situation to say the least. If I lost control, I'd kill and it would be Patterson's fault for shooting Nyleena in the face.

"Come on," my mother suddenly hustled into the room. "You have things to do."

"What?" I looked at her blankly, wondering what she was blabbering about. I would never tell her to her face that I thought she was blabbering, but in my head, I could say it all I wanted. There were times I wondered if my mother was losing her mind. This was one of them.

"You and Malachi are going to St. Charles," she informed me.

"My team is going to Tennessee to catch a killer. I'm sitting here, trying to figure out whether to torture granddad before I kill him or not."

"Don't be ridiculous," my mother tutted at me. "You aren't going to torture or kill him. You are going to pack and go with Malachi."

"We are not allowed to go to St. Charles," I informed her.

"That was ten minutes ago," she responded. "Ten minutes ago, there were two FBI agents chasing Patterson. Now, there's one and they think the two of you should advise."

"Did you eat magic mushrooms on your pizza?" I snarked.

"Don't take that tone with me, young lady."

"Fine," I huffed. "Did someone read tea leaves to you?"

"No, Malachi's outside, waiting for you."

"I'm confused. I just got off the phone with him."

"He was in the lobby with me when you were talking to him. He hung up with you and called the agents, one of whom failed to answer, the other one broke into his hotel room and found him dead."

My phone rang. The number was listed as private. I considered not answering it.

"Marshal Cain," I said into the receiver.

"You are not to investigate or touch anything," a voice said to me. "You and Special Agent Blake will advise the FBI agents on the ground. Even with the two of you assisting in a non-investigative capacity, I believe there will be lots of bloodshed." The voice sighed.

"Um, yes sir?" I asked.

"Oh, sorry, this is Director Hugh Newcomb from the Department of Justice. It has been decided that you and SA Blake are needed in the apprehension of Patterson Clachan because the two of you know him. However, you are not to investigate, take the lead on anything or do anything hands on. Do you understand your assignment, Marshal Cain?"

"Yes, sir." I was already standing up. "I believe SA Blake is waiting for me."

"We'll be in touch," he hung up. I looked at my mother.

"Ok, I'm going to go. We are reading from this book, when you finish, you can move to number six. All of them are on my Kindle. When you need a break from reading, there are audiobooks on this iPod," I pointed to Xavier's small mp3 player.

Three

The motel was disgusting. I got the distinct impression it wasn't exactly nice even before Patterson Clachan had gotten into it. The curtains were stained, there was a bleach spot on the floor, and the bathroom toilet didn't seem to flush properly.

The smell of the room was noxious; mold and raw sewage mixing together in the air. I wore a respirator and could still smell it. I didn't gag, although I wanted to.

Malachi stood next to me. He was dressed in a suit that emphasized his long legs and was cut perfectly to meld to his shoulders. A green tie that accented the color of his eyes finished off the outfit. I was in jeans and a band t-shirt. Booties covered both our shoes. One of us was not dressed for the scene. Considering the smell, it wasn't me.

The FBI Agent's name had been Paul Williams. He was a six year veteran of the FBI and had been a cop in Miami for nearly six years before that. Even dead, he looked young for thirty-four. I didn't know what color his eyes or his hair were, both were missing. He'd been slit from his navel to his throat. His larynx had been removed. His organs were laid out on the dresser. I had been told his hair and eyes were in the mini-fridge, but I wasn't willing to open it to look just yet.

"This is all wrong," Malachi said to someone else. We were guests. Neither of us got to be in charge. It was an interesting situation. "Patterson Clachan doesn't kill like this unless he has a reason. If he's killing someone he considers innocent, he fires two shots into their skull; one in the forehead, one through the left eye. And it is always the left eye, never the right." He emphasized the second part. Nyleena had been shot under her right eye. This didn't excuse him from shooting her in the face, regardless of the fact that it seemed to back up his story.

"How do you know?" I asked.

"I've seen it. There are a couple of cases of The Butcher's that Michael and I found where he had slaughtered one person in the house, but only shot the others."

"You and Michael? Interesting." I frowned. That was a fight for another day, but

Malachi could bet his very expensive cowboy boots that we were going to have it. He and Michael had found The Butcher's signature and never told me. I couldn't be mad at Michael, but I could sure be pissed at Malachi.

"I'll explain, later," Malachi told me. "So, why did Patterson Clachan slaughter Agent Williams?"

"That's what he does," the other agent responded.

"It isn't though," Malachi countered. "This was personal to him."

"I thought all serial killers' kills were personal," the agent frowned.

"No, no they're not," I interrupted. "As a matter of fact, few are and most are not sexually motivated either. The Butcher is a great example of a killer not motivated by sex. He's motivated by revenge and a sense of justice."

"This is not justice," the agent said.

"It was to him," I answered, stepping into the room a little further. I still wasn't going to look in the fridge, but I could look at the body a little better. I had a thing about feet and eyes. Eyes creeped me out, feet grossed me out.

"Any disciplinary actions on Williams file? Any black marks? Anything out of the ordinary?" Malachi asked.

"Not really. He was a good agent," the other responded.

"Were you his partner?" I asked.

"For four years," the agent answered.

"Do you remember meeting an older gentleman that looked to be in his fifties or sixties, but seemed older? Walked with a cane, despite not needing it? Had dark hair that was greying only at the temples?" I asked.

"Doesn't ring any bells. I've seen the sketch, I've never seen him." The sketch was a composite drawing from the witnesses at the restaurant where Nyleena and Nina had been shot. I had serious misgivings about it, but since I had never seen him, I couldn't contradict any of the features. His ears seemed abnormally large to me, as did his nose. No one in my family had ears or a nose like his. Nor did it seem possible that the eighty-six year old man could pass for fifty-five or so.

Malachi was doing something on his phone. He had a huge phone, I didn't know the brand, but it wasn't like my iPhone. It looked more like a tablet. His fingers swiped across different areas until he pulled something up and just stopped. His eyes went blank. He opened his mouth and made a strange noise that I was familiar with. He'd just sucked on his teeth. It was a sign of an "ah-ha" moment for Malachi.

Reserved for very special knowledge and revelations.

"How seriously does Patterson take family?" Malachi asked me.

"I do not know, I have never met the man. He shot his granddaughter in the face, theoretically on accident, but killed his sister at her urging. He hasn't killed the other sister, but he butchered his wife because of an argument with her. He's kind of all over the place with his familial connections."

"Ok," Malachi looked at me. "Does he consider me family?"

"I do not know, Malachi. Maybe, maybe not. That could be why he killed Unger. It might have nothing to do with why he killed Unger."

"He killed Unger because Unger was August Clachan's real father. The fact that Unger was a bastard and my grandfather just helped his justification."

Another secret. I didn't bother to hide my irritation. I had been kept in the dark about August being Malachi's uncle.

"Did you have bad dealings with Agent Williams?" I snipped at him.

"Not I," Malachi turned the giant phone around. Before being assigned to this FBI agent, he'd been assigned to another. I recognized the name. It was the agent that had attempted to kill Gabriel. According to the file on Malachi's phone, Gabriel had stated he believed Paul Williams had known about the killings.

"Holy shit," I let out a long breath. "Ok, so if Patterson is considering my friends extended family, the list just got crazy long and out of control."

"I know," Malachi said. "Do you have any idea how many enemies we all have?"

"No, I cannot count that high. No one can." I looked at Malachi. "This takes six degrees of separation to another level. How would Patterson Clachan know that Gabriel thought this guy was complicit in a handful of murders?"

"Gabriel never told you?" He pressed.

"No, I did not know until just now," I answered looking at Malachi. "Someone had to tell him though."

"If it wasn't you," Malachi shrugged.

"You cannot believe it was Gabriel," I told him.

"No, I don't believe it was Gabriel." Malachi answered. "I have an idea, but it's a really bad one and I'm pretty sure you're going to Taser me for it."

"We're standing in a blood drenched room with a dead FBI agent that pissed off

Gabriel and was killed by The Butcher. Any idea is welcome," I told Malachi.

"Michael," Malachi answered. "He's the only person that would have access to both FBI and Marshal files."

"Michael's dead and has been for a few months now."

"That's true, but Michael could have given him the information before he died."

"Why would Michael do that?" I asked, narrowing my eyes, feeling myself getting angry.

"How many cases have you gotten clues from The Butcher on?" Malachi asked. "Five? Ten?"

"About ten," I shrugged, trying to quell the anger.

"That's a pretty high average," Malachi looked at me. "Michael had secrets, Aislinn. We all do. Maybe he saw a way to use The Butcher. And now that Lila and Nina are gone, The Butcher has lost control and he's using the information Michael passed along to suit his own needs before he's caught."

"I'm not buying it," I told him. "Michael was a geek and a good guy. He would not have been passing along files to The Butcher."

"He knew Patterson was your grandfather, we both did." Malachi answered.

"We both knew even before you joined the Marshals."

I pulled out my Taser and shot Malachi with it. He dropped like a stone. I think I caught him by surprise. Points to me.

The prongs of a Taser hit my leather jacket with a thump sound. The barbs stuck into the coat and when I jerked them out, they tore the heavy material. I tossed the wires at Rollins' feet, glaring at him in annoyance at his futile attempt to Taser me. I released my finger from the trigger of my own Taser. I popped out the Taser cartridge and let it fall onto the carpet.

Most people believed a Taser was a multi-use weapon, like a gun. This was incorrect. Tasers required cartridges. The cartridge was connected to the end of the Taser and an electrical current set off a small charge that ejected the prongs up to twenty feet. The prongs were really barbed hooks that set into the skin and delivered the electrical current.

As soon as I popped the cartridge, Malachi stopped twitching. He lay on the ground for a moment longer before standing up. He glared at me. I glared back. It was one thing to tell me Michael might have been feeding our files to The Butcher. It was another to keep from me that both of them had known the entire time I'd been a Marshal that The Butcher was my grandfather. I snapped another cartridge into place, Malachi reached for his own Taser but didn't draw it. The agents in the room stepped away from us.

"You have known this entire time and did not think to mention it? Really?" I spoke calmly, although I wanted to get in his face and shout at him.

"In our defense, we considered telling you," Malachi offered by way of apology. "However, we were unsure what you would do with the information."

My finger twitched on the trigger of the Taser. I didn't pull it, I was waiting to see what other excuses he would make.

"You're supposed to be my friend, my ally, in all this madness and you kept vital information from me. You are a jackass."

"It's because I'm your friend that I kept it from you," Malachi moved his hand away from his Taser. "I was trying to protect you. We found the pattern after the last letter he sent before you became a Marshal. It described the death of a man in Florida. At first, we weren't sure why he had fixated on you, but then I realized that we had gone to school with the guy. You had even gone on a date with him. His name was Tom Fills."

"So, Tom is dead?" I asked. That was no great loss to the world. Our date had ended when he slapped me. I had punched him in the jaw and left him unconscious on the curb outside a restaurant.

"All your ex-boyfriends are dead," Malachi told me. "After Tom Fills, we began searching for others in your past that had died. Patterson Clachan had been picking them off. We combined that with my final letter from The Butcher and the pieces fell into place. We knew then that The Butcher was your grandfather and that he had an MO. It has variables, but he always takes the eyes of his victims and shoves them in a fridge. Unless, they happen to be bystanders, then he shoots them in the head."

"You should have told me." I warned Malachi, feeling the urge to Taser him again. "I know why he takes the eyes. I could have been useful."

"I'm telling you now and I still don't know why he takes the eyes."

"Because it releases their souls." I told him. "My father had this strange belief that if you closed the eyes after a person died, their souls couldn't escape. It was one of his quirks. Knowing that my father held that belief, makes me think he learned it from his father. So, he removes the eyes so that they can't be closed and the soul can be released from the body. My grandmother's eyes were found in the fridge too."

"Why the fridge?"

"To keep them from dehydrating before the soul can escape." I told Malachi. "It's a strange belief, but one my entire family has. They believe it takes a while for the soul to come to terms with being dead and if the eyes are not intact and open, the soul gets trapped on earth. I have no idea where it comes from. I just know that they all have it. Funerals in my family are creepy because they will not let the mortician sew the eyes shut. This means that half the time, the eyes are open and staring blankly, like a dead cod's, at the ceiling."

"Good to know."

"And you would have known sooner if you had told me, jackass," I pulled the trigger. The prongs missed Malachi this time, but only because he was expecting it. He batted them away.

"Stop that," he scolded me.

"Stop keeping secrets," I scolded him back.

Four

The medical examiner placed the time of death for Paul Williams at around eleven p.m. the night before. We still hadn't found our sniper's body, but I was guessing he had died later. This jived with the scenario of events laid out by Agent Jacob Rollins, the agent who had been his partner. He said Paul had been tired and gone to bed around nine. Agent Rollins had gone out for a late dinner and then met some of the officers with the St. Charles Police Department. He'd gotten back to his room about one in the morning.

For most killers, I'd say two hours wasn't enough time to make the mess that The Butcher had made. However, Patterson Clachan had been killing for over sixty years. He was a seasoned professional. I imagined the damage could be done in less than an hour by someone skilled and experienced. That gave him plenty of time to slip out of Paul Williams' room and head over to the house of the sniper.

What I couldn't figure out was where he was getting his never ending supply of clothing. We found a polo, slacks, underwear, socks, and shoes at the Williams' crime scene that didn't fit Williams. They'd also found blood in the bathtub at the motel, lots of it, trapped in the drain and coating the bathtub floor. It had been rinsed off, but not washed away. Water alone couldn't remove all traces of blood and Patterson didn't seem too worried about leaving the evidence.

They'd also found a few strands of dark hair. Looking at it closely, it wasn't black, but brown, a very dark brown, like Nyleena's. Paul had been a light brunette, they certainly weren't his hairs. Of course, considering the state of the motel room, it could have belonged to a previous occupant.

My mind thought about the bleach stain on the carpet. It had been old. I wondered if there had been another murder in the room at an earlier date. I considered calling the motel to find out, but I wasn't supposed to be investigating, just offering advice. Instead, I told Jacob Rollins to check on it. It was most likely unrelated, but I was a curious person and wanted to know.

The VCU and SCTU seemed to have bigger budgets than the rest of federal law enforcement. Malachi and I weren't camped out in some flea-riddled motel with bedbugs and blood stains. We were at a nice hotel with a minibar and view of historic downtown. Our rooms were next door to each other. I had eaten lunch in my room, using room service to supply it. Malachi had invited me out, but I wasn't very fond of him at the moment. My brain kept latching onto his array of secrets and wondering what else he was keeping from me.

I didn't like secrets. I had some of my own, to be sure, but one person knew them all. She was currently in a coma on the other side of the state, but she did know everything. Except that I liked to kill. However, I was sure she had already figured that out on her own. It hung unsaid between us sometimes.

Secrets were like cancer. They ate away at you, tearing you apart from the inside out. They left questions, lots of questions that remained unanswered after death. Like Nina, she had said she would tell us everything, but she had died too soon. Any secrets she had divulged were currently locked away with my own. I hoped Nyleena was dreaming about Ranger and Morelli and not whatever dark secrets Nina had told her.

Now, Malachi was keeping them from me. I didn't expect him to spill his guts every time he saw me, but I did expect that he would tell me anything pertinent that had to do with me or my family. The fact that he hadn't, troubled me.

Another thought occurred to me. Perhaps Malachi's keeping secrets from me was a form of sadism. He knew I didn't like them, so he kept them from me, keeping control and causing me pain and rage when I did finally find out. It made sense. His grandfather had been a sadist, torturing anyone close because it kept him in control and gave him power. August had been a sadist of a different sort. His feeding victims to predators had been both cruel and controlling. He'd been a sexual sadist and murderer, which didn't exactly fit Tennyson Unger's pattern, but it didn't not fit either.

Then there was Malachi. Malachi wasn't a sexual sadist. Malachi liked to inflict pain because pain gave him control, it gave him power. It was the ultimate thrill ride, pumping him full of adrenaline and giving him a high. Sexual sadism was common place, non-sexual sadism was a different monster. It was harder to control and even harder to understand. I only understood because I had been around Malachi most of my life. When he couldn't inflict physical pain, emotional pain was a perfectly acceptable substitute. Sometimes, it was even better than physical pain because it lasted longer and brought out the darker side of everyone.

In comparison, my grandfather was a killer. His goal was to right wrongs and find some twisted sense of justice. Without realizing it, I had followed in his footsteps. I wasn't a serial killer, not using the definition, but there were aspects of my life and personality that suggested it was a possibility. My brother, Eric, was the same. My father and sister were the anomalies in my immediate family, being genuinely good people who didn't kill. Although, I still had some questions about my father. He'd been a cop after all and while this didn't necessarily mean he'd never killed anyone, it raised the likelihood of it.

Perhaps, August had gotten his sadist genes from Tennyson Unger, the man that made Malachi a monster, and gotten his killer genes from Gertrude, a woman I was sure could have easily killed if she had been given the right motivation. There was also the possibility that Gertrude, knowing about her son's proclivities for murder, had killed via surrogate, letting August handle the dirty work and she just enjoyed the rehashing of their deaths.

For the first time, I thought about children. My own children, that is. I had never given birth, had never had a desire to breed, I couldn't even be bothered to have the desire to have sex. However, if I was going to have a child, I guessed that Malachi would be the father. Not because there weren't any other offers, but because it seemed like Malachi was the logical choice. He was brilliant with good physical genes. However, our mental genes would create the ultimate killing machine. The child would go well beyond psychopathic. It would be an unstable creation from the bowels of Hell. No remorse, no empathy, no sympathy, no pain receptors, no feelings, and I was willing to bet it would be alienated even more by a lack of connection with its parents, since neither Malachi nor I could muster much in that department. While August was a perfect pairing of bad mental genes, a child between Malachi and I would be three times worse. Our child would be bat-shit crazy; a sadistic killer with a desire for notoriety and flair. An egocentric monster who only enjoyed pain and death. No one would be safe, ever.

My door made a beep as a keycard was swiped through the lock. It swung open and Malachi came in. He was dressed in a different suit and tie combination and different black loafers. I wondered how many of those outfits he had.

"I'm still really pissed at you," I told the tall figure as he sauntered into my room.

"The feeling is mutual. That wasn't 150,000 volts, it was stronger."

"You do not have a right to be angry with me," I informed him. "As for the Taser, I'm testing a new prototype that will go up to 250,000 volts with stronger barbs for military use."

"Why does the military need 250,000 volts?"

"Beats me, but it works on psychopaths. You dropped like a stone. I will definitely be keeping this one."

"I've come to talk about a temporary cease fire."

"Afraid I will Taser you again?"

"Something like that, and we freaked out the FBI and the St. Charles police. They've never seen two titans go at it before. Agent Rollins told me when you yanked out the Taser, he considered shooting you. It's a good thing you ejected your Taser cartridge."

"That's what I dislike about the model. Does not hold up very long. Truth is, I could not have run the current for more than a few seconds longer. I will be talking to them about it."

"If we were working with the VCU and SCTU, it wouldn't be a big deal. They'd rock back on the balls of their feet and let us get it out of our system, but we aren't. We're working with normal people. When you and I both drop the masks and enter the darkness, they become afraid. Panicked people do stupid things."

"If you can promise me that you have withheld nothing else, I can promise not to Taser you again. But so help me god, Malachi Blake, if I find out you knew so much as his shoe size before today and you did not tell me, I'm going to send you into a world with so much pain, Hell will be calling me for ideas. Do you understand?"

"I can't make that promise," Malachi answered. "I've kept a lot about The Butcher from you, for your own protection."

"That is bullshit and we both know it. You did it to feed your ego and fan the flames for your next power trip."

Malachi stood. He stretched his long arms skyward and his back popped multiple times. He released the stance, letting his arms fall down at his side and stared at me. A lesser man would crack as those vibrant green eyes attempted to search the soul inside the body. I didn't flinch. He broke eye contact first.

"It doesn't bother me that you think I withheld the information for my own purposes," Malachi turned away. "It bothers me that you think I did it intentionally."

"Everything you do is intentional."

"I can make mistakes."

"Yes, you can and this was a doozy."

"You should know, this goes deeper than Patterson. Yeah, he was born with those genes, but he had a lot of help during his childhood becoming the man he is today. He killed for the first time at seven years old, Ace. Sound familiar?"

"I did not grow up to be a serial killer," I told him.

"Yes, but only because your father didn't encourage it. If your father had you tracking down men at eight to kill, you would have become one, just like Patterson."

"You're telling me my great-grandfather created Patterson?"

"It was The Depression," Malachi looked back at me, a quick glance over his shoulder. "I believe your great-grandfather did the killing until he realized that Patterson had a knack for it. Humans were cheaper than livestock."

Blood

Patterson stood in the shower. The hot water ran down his body and swirled a bright pink as it entered the drain. He'd killed three men in twenty-four hours. Despite his condition, it was tiring on an old man. After two of the kills, he'd showered, getting the blood off. The third had been impulsive. It clung to his hair and filled his sinus passageways. He'd used a couple bottles of water in his sinus rinse system to get all the blood out of his nose.

Now, he was washing his hair for the second time since he'd started showering and yet, the water was still pink. He didn't mind the excuse to stay in the shower. The hot water felt good on his skin, his muscles. It had been a long time since they had been used this much in a single day.

So far, they hadn't found anyone but Williams, a despicable man to say the least. He'd been planning to kill one of the two FBI agents, just to get Malachi or Aislinn involved. He never imagined he'd get the chance when Williams decided to go to bed early. After the partner had left, a hooker had shown up. Even through the walls of the motel, Patterson could hear Williams beating the woman.

He wasn't interested in saving hookers, that seemed more like a task for missionaries than serial killers, but he was interested in the wedding ring on Williams' hand. If Williams beat prostitutes to sate his bloodlust, what happened when prostitutes were few and far between?

Patterson stepped out into the main room of his hotel suite. Now that he was older, he was learning to enjoy the finer things in life. For years, he'd been a master carpenter. He'd specialized in creating ornate wooden accents for the homes of the rich.

However, his favorite piece was in storage, waiting for his death. The unit would pass to Aislinn. Inside, she would find a hand carved table. A slab of oak, finely carved with a tree on the surface, then coated to retain its beauty. Four solid legs, each given the utmost care in their design, depicting green men and fairies. He'd worked on it for three years after learning of her interest in her ancestral roots. The chairs had been carved to match, the same oak had donated to each of them. His hands had supplied the details, he hoped she would accept it.

In the room, the flyer on the table caught his attention. It was supposed to be a sketch of him, it looked more like Clark Gable and Danny Thomas had decided to have a child together. They'd gotten the dark hair right, but that was about it. A large nose demanded the attention of anyone looking at it. Large ears, which stuck out from the head, looked ridiculous. The eyes were too small and too narrow. The mouth was too large and the lips were too thin. It wasn't even a good caricature of him.

Disgusted, he turned away. Eyewitnesses were rarely reliable, he didn't need to be a cop to know that. They might be able to pick him out of a line-up, but they certainly couldn't describe the man who had done the shooting. To most, he probably looked like The Invisible Man. No one seemed to report his cane, something he considered strange since it had been dangling from his arm.

A medium sized box sat on the dresser, it had been lovingly created by him years earlier. The details on the top depicted a pack of wolves facing off against a large grizzly bear. Patterson didn't know if such an event would happen in the wild, but he liked the thought. The box was exactly twelve inches long by six inches wide by three inches deep with legs and had a locking latch.

Opening it was always a joyful moment. The treasures inside were among his greatest accomplishments. There were about thirty swastika lapel pins, but only one set of the lightning bolt SS pins. That had been his greatest kill and worst failure. He'd been amazed to have caught the officer off guard. However, the moment had been short lived when it turned out the Nazi storm trooper had enjoyed the pain more than Patterson did. Patterson had to settle for slitting his throat and watching the blood pool around them both.

Into this box of trinkets, he dropped three more items: Williams' wedding ring, a silver chain from James Okafor, and a thick gold bracelet from a thug who had tried to mug him earlier. He also attracted violent, dangerous people. With the thug, he'd plunged a knife into his lower jaw, wedging his mouth closed while Patterson cut out his eyes and then hit him twice with the cane on the head. The second one had broken through the skin and skull. Fluid that wasn't actually blood flowed onto the ground. Patterson jerked the knife free and left the thug for dead. Experience told him it was impossible to survive once the sack around the brain was broken. The would-be robber had only a few minutes to live when Patterson walked back to his hotel.

It had been early enough that no one was in the lobby except a young lady at the front desk. She was busy typing furiously on her phone, uninterested in the old man. Baby wipes had cleaned his face and hands, while the dark clothing he wore hid the rest of the evidence. He'd been careful to also wipe down the bottom of his shoes before entering the lobby.

Patterson crawled into the king-sized bed. The sheets curled around him. He sighed and got up, grabbing the "DO NOT DISTURB" sign from the doorknob and placing it outside in the key card slot. Once again, he returned to bed and climbed between the blankets and sheets.

As tired as he was, sleep didn't come for him. The older he got, the more trouble he had falling asleep. He'd never slept much to begin with, instead he stared at the ceiling. Memories came to him in place of dreams. The memories were unwelcome, they distracted him from his purpose. They were a random jumbling of his past. Flashes of things that had happened long ago mixed with more recent events.

The doctors believed it was dementia. He believed it was his past catching up with him. How many times had he suffered head trauma?

He didn't know. He'd been stabbed in the head once, the tip of the blade stopped by his skull and helmet, during the war. The Nazi had fared worse, his first evisceration. He'd split the man from groin to sternum and watched as his insides had spilled out.

Before that he'd killed, his father finding out that it was easy for Patterson to dispatch the farmhands, but his father had demanded that he kill quickly without damaging any of the body. The preferred method had been a pick axe through the skull. He much preferred his own methods.

Eventually, he gave up and turned on the TV. He found a show about alien conspiracies and put the remote on the bed. He believed in aliens just as much as he did angels. He also believed that if aliens ever found humans, they'd annihilate the species because humans were obviously inferior. He imagined it would be like *Independence Day* without the happy ending.

As he lay there, he realized why he couldn't sleep. His stomach growled loudly. It was past noon. Patterson had few pleasures in life, food was one of them. It was something he could experience with a full range of senses. He appreciated it. He ordered a vegetarian burger made with a portabella top and covered with fresh veggies and a chipotle ranch sauce.

Waiting for it to arrive, he sat at the table. It had no character, no life. The reflective surface reminded him of eyes though. He hated that dead, vacant stare that the lifeless had. As a boy, killing to feed the family at his father's threats, he'd found the eyes to be repulsive. They were even worse when his mother plucked them out and used them in soups. She'd refrigerate them for a day in a glass of milk with some salt and pepper, then take them out, drain them, mince them, and put them in soup.

He ate slowly; savoring the flavors, smells, and textures. Food was a forgotten pleasure these days. It was just something people shoved in their bodies to keep them going.

After eating, he placed the tray outside. His body was starting to feel tired. He knew it was coming as he slipped between the sheets again. This time when he closed his eyes, he slept.

Five

There was another body. Another body missing his eyes, lying in an alley behind a convenience store. Agent Rollins was attempting to get security footage from the store. He hadn't been as brutally slain as most of The Butcher's victims. A large wound under his chin entered his upper palate in his mouth, piercing his tongue. Two hard blows to the head, one breaking through the skull, were the cause of death.

From the looks of him, he wasn't our sniper. He was maybe twenty. Baggy jeans and a shirt that was three times too big clothed him. His shoes were neon green Converse tennis shoes. His white skin had paled with his death. A ball cap lay on the ground near him. Malachi and I both frowned at the body.

"Well, I'm thinking it's obvious," Malachi pointed to the kid's hand. A few inches from the outstretched fingers lay a small pocket knife.

"You would think robbery would be a declining crime," I told him. "When any intended victim could be a serial killer who is badder than you are, why stick a knife to someone's throat and demand money? Senseless."

"No one has ever tried to mug me," Malachi said.

"That's because you're tall and scary looking," I pointed out. "Patterson is not very tall from what I understand, but he is still badder than most people."

"A seasoned criminal wouldn't have picked him as a victim, just like they wouldn't pick you. Victims like you and Patterson are a cosmic joke, so to speak, you look like you should be easy to intimidate, a quick snatch and grab. Only after the would-be mugger gets in close do they realize their mistake. A rookie mistake that results in death."

"I have never killed a would-be mugger," I informed Malachi.

"Yet," Malachi added quickly, "you have maimed a few as memory serves."

"They should not threaten me or," I didn't finish the sentence. Saying her name out loud was a form of torture at the moment. The only person in my life more important than Nyleena was my mom. If it had been my mom lying in that bed, Patterson would have been begging for someone, anyone to kill him.

Rollins kicked the wall as he neared us. Judging by his body language, he'd gotten zilch from the convenience store surveillance. This didn't surprise me. I had never been attacked in an area with a camera.

"So, Williams was most likely killed second," Rollins walked up to us.

"No, first," Malachi said. "Williams was killed before midnight. The Butcher didn't call Aislinn until almost seven a.m., which means he didn't get done killing the sniper until then. This one was probably last. The sun's coming up, he has to be quick. He stabs him under the jaw to keep his mouth closed, then kills him and cuts out his eyes."

"I would disagree," I was looking at the vacant sockets. I had been in hundreds of autopsies, I wasn't an expert, but I had a pretty good understanding of it. "I think he cut out his eyes while he was alive based on the blood pooling around the sockets. He cuts out his eyes, then he bashes him over the head."

"He's never cut out the eyes while the victim was alive," Malachi informed me.

"How many times have you found bodies of muggers that he's killed?" I asked. "See no evil."

"Somehow, she's creepier than you Blake," Rollins said.

"That she is," Malachi agreed. "Ok, so he cuts out the eyes first, he deviated."

"Did he?" I jabbed at him. "I would not know." Malachi let out a long sigh.

"He deviated, for whatever reason, he took the eyes before they died. Any ideas?" Malachi asked, trying to stay composed.

I looked out of our spot in the alley. The road wasn't exactly busy. There wasn't much around here.

"To keep him from getting a look at his car in case he survived," I told Malachi.

"That would make sense," Malachi agreed.

"Worried about his car and not his face?" Rollins asked.

"In stressful situations, witnesses tend to block faces. They do not tend to block car models, colors, or partial license plates," I told him. "When we find a serial killer survivor, we just estimate that about fifty percent of the killer's description is wrong, unless the survivor can prove otherwise. However, when they are describing houses, rooms, streets, cars, or other details, they have good memories. I worked a case over the summer where the woman could remember that a train passed by the window every morning. She did not know the time, just that the sun shined in the window a little before the train passed each day. She could feel it on her skin. However, despite looking at the guy when he kidnapped her, she could not pick him out of a line-up."

"Nina told me that Patterson's first kill came in 1932, he was seven years old. He's been at this for a long time. He would know what witnesses remember the best." Malachi looked at me. "For the record, I didn't know that until Nina called me with the tip a few weeks ago. We'll need to talk after this case is over, there's a lot you should know."

"And you're the gatekeeper of these secrets?" I scowled.

"Some of them. I believe Nyleena is the other gatekeeper." Malachi looked out onto the road. He was envisioning the same thing I was. For whatever reason, Patterson had stopped here or very close. This guy had tried to rob him and Patterson had killed him.

I pictured my grandfather driving a 1943 Ford pickup truck. Baby blue with whitewall tires and in perfect condition. I had no idea why I believed he would be driving this particularly make, model, or color of vehicle or even if whitewalls would fit a 1943 Ford truck.

Since I very much doubted this was the sniper, that meant the old man had made three kills in about 12 hours, give or take an hour or two. Being an octogenarian wasn't slowing him down at all. If anything, an end of life urgency seemed to be making him work faster. But faster meant more tiredness at the end of it. When the adrenaline crash came, it would be swifter, harder, more consuming. The times I'd made it through a fight without an injury, I'd still been zonked out for six or seven hours. It was longer if I was badly injured. After killing the jackass in Alaska, I had slept for nearly fifteen hours. Of course, the crash had taken longer to hit. My adrenaline had continued to surge for a couple of hours after his death.

That meant, if grandfather and I had more in common than I wanted to admit, he was probably curled up somewhere sleeping it off. An adrenaline surge is a powerful thing, it's a high like no other. And like all highs, there's a crash at the end. The crash is slow at first. You feel a little tired, then bam! It slams into you like a freight train loaded with cargo and speeding down the tracks until they glowed white hot. Right up until that moment hits, you think, "this isn't so bad." Then it hits and all thoughts go out the window. Sleep is the only thing that you can think of, sleep and never feeling that way again. Of course, in my world, there is always another high waiting around the corner. Some might call me an adrenaline junky. I wouldn't. Malachi was the junky. When he wasn't chasing serial killers, he was skydiving, bull riding, and drag racing. When I wasn't chasing serial killers, I was watching episodes of *The Flying Circus* and playing video games.

"Ok, so Patterson has to be curled up somewhere sleeping it off," I told everyone. "Canvas hotels. I do not know what to look for except the silver cane and I'm not sure that's a good enough description, but it is a place to start."

"Why is he curled up somewhere?" Rollins asked.

"Ever killed anyone?" I countered.

"No," Rollins answered.

"Killing is an adrenaline rush, even if you do not enjoy it. The fight or flight instinct takes over and as you fire your weapon or beat a man to death with your cane, the adrenaline just keeps pumping. Adrenaline is an endorphin, like a body's natural form of morphine, it creates a high. It has all sorts of side-effects, including a crash. Eventually, it takes more and more adrenaline to cause the high, but the crash stays the same. When I crash, I go down hard, crawling to my bed is a monumental task. This attack was unplanned, meaning the adrenaline surge would have been much higher than the other two kills. He's got to come down from it somewhere, which means he has access to a bed."

"Adrenaline is why little old ladies' find the strength to lift cars off their grandchildren," Malachi clarified. "While it lasts, the brain feels no pain, no pain means no limitations to what you can do. We consider them superhuman feats of strength, but they really aren't. Normally, the person lifting the car suffers all sorts of injuries that they feel only after it wears off."

"Unless grandma is a psychopath," I corrected. "Or rather, grandpa in this case."

"What does that have to do with anything?" Malachi asked me.

"You have not heard Lucas's newest theory?" I frowned at him. "Lucas is using you and me in a case study. We do not suffer those sorts of injuries, because our bodies are used to performing above their accepted capacity. So, when I get pissed and lift a car, I might break an arm or tear a muscle, but it is not going to be to the extent that Rollins is going to have injuries. Same with you."

"Interesting." Malachi looked at me for a moment. "Where is Lucas getting said information, particularly my medical records?"

"From the powers that be," I told him. "So, Patterson is holed up in a hotel or motel. Why would he be here? There are not any hotels nearby. There's this gas station, a few fast food restaurants and some giant cube farms."

"I'm guessing you mean the office buildings," Malachi said.

"Yep, giant cube farms where people wither under florescent lighting, grow obese sitting in office chairs, eat foods from vending machines that contain more processed sugar than the entire country of Ecuador, and develop indigestion and migraines from stress; efficiently removing their will to live until they become numb, mindless zombies who pray for the coffee pot to be full and the supply closet to have staples."

"That is dreary, even for you." Malachi didn't turn around.

"Our offices are cubicles," Rollins interjected.

"And you are dressed in FBI required clothing that strips away your identity." I told him. "The only thing keeping you from being one of those mindless zombies is field work. Check out the desk jockeys in your office next time you're there and then rethink about what I said. You'll find their spirits are broken and they are working very hard just to survive to retirement."

"My office is not a cubicle," Malachi informed me.

"Your office should be padded in rubber," I told him.

"The floor is," Malachi responded. He seemed distant, not looking at me while we talked. His eyes kept scanning the buildings and streets around us. I wondered what he saw that I didn't and began to search too. "This had to be on his way from the sniper's house to his hotel."

"That would require housing," I pointed out. "Patterson's good, but I'm not sure he can keep a man from alerting neighbors in the next apartment while he beats him to death."

"You're absolutely correct," Malachi finally turned back to us. "It would require a house. Preferably an empty house. He doesn't enjoy killing children, he goes out of his way to avoid it. He left a child that could identify him alive once even though he sliced her father open. She said in her statement that he told her to go hide in her closet and not come out until police arrived. She did."

"How did that work out?" I asked.

"The sketch looked like Dracula."
Malachi said. "Literally, it looked like Bela
Lugosi in the black and white movie."

"That means we can all agree that he has
dark hair, but then we already knew that. How
does Bela Lugosi match with our most recent
sketch?"

"Our most recent sketch looks like
someone threw a bunch of pieces from an identi-
kit onto the ground and randomly started
picking them up. Did you see the Dumbo ears?
Will Smith has smaller ears than our sketch.
And if his nose is really that wide, the tip lines
should be ringing off the hook. Since they
aren't," Malachi sighed. "Our description is
basically 'old man, dark hair, has silver handled
cane made of a strange wood that Nina couldn't
remember the name of.'"

"It's not silver," I told Malachi. "It's just
shiny like silver. No way is silver bashing in a
skull like that unless this guy is the Wolfman."

"Trace will be able to give us a better idea
on what it is really made of," Rollins offered.
Malachi looked at him like he was roach that
had just scurried from under a table. After a
moment, the look disappeared and the mask
everyone usually saw was back. Rollins noticed
though, he took a step back from the taller man;
whether he consciously realized it or not.

"Let's go find a subdivision," I announced, breaking the fear that had gripped Rollins at Malachi's icy glance.

Six

We snaked through the nearest subdivision. The houses were all newer. Small, ranch style, single family homes for the working classes, with one car garages and an unsheltered spot for a second car, leaving any husband and wife couple to argue over who got to use the garage.

A few cars were in driveways, but most were gone. The neighborhood occupants off to cube farms to catch office-borne diseases, to factories to work with chemicals that would give them cancer, or to shops where they'd turn wrenches and bust open knuckles leading to tetanus shots and the occasional bout of blood poisoning. This was not a neighborhood for the elite. On the flip side, it also wasn't a neighborhood for those making minimum wage. The house payments were too large, interest rates were too high, and even with energy efficient appliances, and the utilities would be unaffordable.

It was also a neighborhood that was aspiring to be better. Signs proclaimed a neighborhood watch was in effect. The similarity of color among the homes was testament to the neighborhood association enforcing "appearance" codes upon the near cookie cutter houses. There would be no pink houses, it would be offensive. Nor would there be bright red houses with yellow shutters, like the house Malachi had grown up in one street away from me. Flower beds and shrubs were neat, despite being dormant or dead for the winter. Yards weren't littered with fallen leaves, left unraked from the autumn.

Rollins stopped the SUV. He put it in park, glancing up and down the street. His face was wrinkled with frown lines and worry about losing his job or his life. This was not his first choice of assignments, chasing serial killers rarely were. There was money in it, to be sure, the VCU and SCTU were the highest paid divisions of federal law enforcement. When the public stats had been released at the end of the year, I had actually made more than the Director of the US Marshals. Of course, my life expectancy was three years as an SCTU member. His was considerably longer as he sat behind his big comfy desk under crappy fluorescent lighting, talking on the phone, taking meetings, and barking orders at lower ranking Marshals. Malachi and Gabriel made nearly double what I made.

"What are we doing here?" Rollins asked. "If someone had reported a murder, we would have been notified."

"That's why we're here. Maybe the murder hasn't been discovered yet, but I believe Patterson Clachan really did beat this victim to death. That's very messy." Malachi got out of the SUV. I wasn't going to follow. It was cold outside. My brain and body both agreed that the cold sucked. Walking the streets of this neighborhood peeping in windows for signs of blood wasn't going to make me warmer, it was going to make me cranky. This wasn't an area that I needed assistance in, cranky was a state of being for me.

"Do you understand what he's doing?" Rollins asked me.

"Yes."

"Are you going to help?"

"No."

"Aren't you two supposed to be," Rollins paused, cocking his head to the side. I raised an eyebrow and glared at him.

"Supposed to be what, exactly?"

"Like friends with benefits."

"Ah," I frowned. "We are friends, there are no benefits."

"So you aren't romantically involved?"

"I would prefer to drink Kool-Aid with cyanide." I got out of the SUV. Malachi had moved about half way down the street. He was looking for houses with cars still at home, most likely, parked in the garage. I didn't run after him. Instead, I stood in the street and listened to the sounds around me. Traffic was minimal. A single car swung slowly around our SUV. The driver's head pivoted to stare at me as he trudged past, no doubt wondering if Malachi and I were up to something nefarious.

I couldn't blame him. If I hadn't known us and had just seen Malachi running down the street with me standing in the middle of the road and an SUV idling with another man in it, I'd think we were up to no good as well. The car passed both of us. Malachi stopped and watched as he passed as well. The two men were exchanging glares. In our line of work, paranoia is required. I didn't know the excuse the guy in the car had for such behavior.

He parked in a driveway a few houses away from Malachi. The exterior was a dark green vinyl siding with accented shutters. The yard was barren of the customary flower beds and shrubs, giving a clean line of sight to the road. I nodded at the house, hoping Malachi understood.

Even in our neighborhood, people had shrubs and flowerbeds. Not me, of course, that would require me to do yard work. I paid the neighbor kids to mow my yard, rake my leaves, shovel my snow, whatever needed to be done. As a result, I had the worst lawn on my street.

So did this guy. Laziness might explain it, but there were also no trees. My yard at least had trees to drop leaves. Trees helped with utility bills. They hid you from the prying eyes of nosy neighbors. One did not randomly remove all the trees without a reason.

Malachi nodded back and we started slowly towards the house. The man was out of his car now, beating his fist against the front door. He was a large, heavy set man. His face was red, either from the exertion of beating on the door or because he was unhappy with the occupant. The man put his face to the peep hole. Internally, I cringed, waiting for someone to push an ice pick through the small hole and take out the man's eye. He yelled a name.

"Special Agent Malachi Blake with the FBI, this is US Marshal Aislinn Cain, may we help you?" Malachi gave his most charming smile to the man. He instantly relaxed. Malachi could charm a snake out of its skin. That smile made women swoon, I'd seen it. It annoyed me because it was even faker than his usual mask.

"Strange to have a US Marshal and an FBI agent in the same place." The man commented.

"We're looking for something," Malachi picked his words carefully, deciding to say something instead of someone. Manhunts raised hackles; looking for drugs in storm drains, didn't.

"Just a late employee. James was supposed to be at work an hour ago. I called, but he didn't answer. In ten years, the man has never missed work. His car is in the garage." The man shook his head. "I hope he didn't have an accident."

"What does James do?" I asked.

"He's a bartender at Kirley's," the man said. "I'm Wilson Buck, I own the bar. James is my best bartender."

"Let me see if I can find anything for you," Malachi looked at me. Technically, Malachi and Agent Rollins needed a reason to enter the house. If I suspected there was a serial killer or a serial killer's victim inside, I didn't need a reason, I could just bust down the door. However, this situation would need tact, finesse. I lacked both. Instead, I walked around the yard as Malachi attempted to peep in windows.

The trees had definitely been removed. Small impressions were left where they had been planted. One was struggling to resurrect itself and a small trunk timidly peeked from the dirt. Only the truly paranoid removed all their trees. I wondered what James did in his spare time.

"Cain," Malachi said my name softly. Rollins was moving towards us from the SUV. Malachi pointed to the ground near the side door. A perfect shoeprint was preserved. January had gotten brave, allowing a few days of 40 and 50 degree weather during the month. Yesterday, it had been 45. This morning, it had been 40. Right now, it was below freezing again. That was the way weather worked in Missouri.

"It looks," I frowned at the foot print. "It looks small." I placed my foot next to it. I wore a size seven shoe. Malachi required special order shoes at a nineteen. The print was just a little bit longer than my own, but it was considerably wider. It was the only print in the area.

"How tall is James?" Malachi asked Wilson Buck.

"Tall, at least 6 feet 3 inches," Wilson answered, he'd moved around to the side with us.

"Too small for him," I answered. "Ok, Mr. Buck, I'm going to ask you to move your car to the road and stay parked in it until we can ascertain the health of Mr." I paused, I didn't have a last name.

"Okafor, James Okafor," Wilson Buck told me, as he walked away. Rollins was already on his phone, notifying someone.

"I am not supposed to be investigating," I whispered to Malachi. "I think being the person making entry into the home qualifies as investigating."

"Open the door, we'll send Rollins in," Malachi told me.

"That's splitting hairs to a very fine point," I said. "I'm still the one breaking down the door. And if we're right, Rollins should not enter the house alone."

"St. Charles police are on their way, we should have a warrant within the hour," Rollins hung up. I sighed. I wasn't going to stand in the cold and wait an hour for a warrant that may or may not show up. It was possible that James Okafor was sleeping off a bender in a ditch somewhere, but the shoe print made it unlikely. We'd been told Patterson Clachan was a short man. The small print matched that. The removal of the trees was an act of the paranoid, our sniper would be paranoid. It was possible our sniper wasn't just paranoid, but had a military background. Either way, it was the only reason I could think to have the trees literally uprooted from the yard.

"Fruck," I muttered. The first squad car arrived. I shook my head at Malachi. "Rollins, come here."

"What?" His voice was full of indignation that I hadn't considered him a superior. As far as rank went, he probably was, but I had more scars.

"I'm going to break open the back door, you and handful of officers will enter and search the house," I told him.

"We can't do that, we have no probable cause."

"I do not need probable cause, at least not much of it. Okafor has taken the trees out of his front yard, that's a sign of paranoia, a trait often exhibited by serial killers. The shoe print is too small to be his, so someone obviously was walking around his house in recent days, signs of a stalker. He is not answering the door, despite the belief that he is at home. That's all the probable cause the SCTU needs. He displays characteristics of both a serial killer and a victim, which would fit with what Patterson Clachan claimed."

"You can't do that, you're not in charge," Rollins grabbed my arm.

"Neither are you, Patterson Clachan is because he knows who the third victim is and he knows who he is going to kill next. We're just cleaning up his mess. I cannot believe you are so uptight that you will not even let me go jiggle the hand to see if the door is unlocked." I didn't yank my arm away. I stared him down, he released it on his own.

"Fine, go jiggle a handle, nothing more Marshal Cain, do you understand?"

"No, I do not speak English," I snarked.

"Was that supposed to be funny?" Rollins asked Malachi as I crept up to the side door.

"No, that was her being very polite while she called you a jackass." Malachi answered as I tried the knob. It was locked.

"It didn't seem very polite."

"Wait until she Tasers you," Malachi said as I rounded the corner to the back.

Seven

Rollins and Malachi followed me to the back of the house. It didn't take much for me to realize that something was wrong. There were two large doghouses contained within a huge chain-link fence. There weren't two large dogs to go with it. There wasn't a single large dog. There wasn't even a single small dog.

Malachi frowned at the sturdy kennel. He let out a long sigh as his gaze found what I had missed. Blood at the entrance to one of the dog houses. I wasn't much of a pet person, but I still thought killing dogs was wrong.

"There's your proof that something wicked came this way, G-Man," I pointed towards the small puddle of blood. It was congealing into a brown gelatinous goo.

"Stop butchering Ray Bradbury for your odd sense of humor," Malachi was walking towards the kennels. "We do have permission to search dog houses, right? Or do you want a warrant for that as well?"

Rollins made a face and nodded his head. Malachi opened the kennel while I drew my Taser. Of course, at 250,000 volts, it was likely to kill any dog that might be inside, but given the paranoia I'd seen, I wasn't going to take chances with Malachi's life. I already had one person in the hospital.

As he reached the door, he knelt down slowly. His face became level with the hole, after another second, he stuck his head and an arm inside. When he withdrew, he held a Styrofoam container that had been chewed on. The container was dripping a brownish substance that disappeared on contact with the ground. He put his upper body back in the dog house and pulled out a small puppy. I holstered the Taser and moved around the fence to take the animal.

The German shepherd's heartbeat was fast. His chest heaved and fell without much effort. He didn't make noises, like most puppies while they slept. Malachi emerged with a second pup, roughly the same age.

"How old?" I asked Malachi.

"A couple of months, maybe," Malachi answered. "Newly acquired, probably siblings, most likely twelve weeks and picked up from a breeder very recently. There are toys, but they aren't chewed up like most puppy toys. And they enjoyed the Styrofoam just as much as the steak that was inside of it."

"Why give the puppies steak in Styrofoam?" I asked.

"Patterson is a vegetarian, because he has trouble with meat. It's a long story. I'll tell you at another time. I don't think he could stand the steak. He gave it to them in the Styrofoam to keep from having to look at it. I'm not even sure how he got past the smell."

Malachi looked like a nice, good guy cradling the puppy. It was pure perception, he was anything but. It was a good thing he was holding it or I would have Tasered him again. He was keeping more secrets.

"So, he drugs the dogs and goes into the house to kill the owner but he's can't look at a steak?" Rollins asked.

"I once heard that Patterson fainted when the women were killing chickens. People he can kill, animals not so much," I answered. "I'm not sure why, but Malachi knows."

"During The Great Depression, Patterson's father put Patterson's talents for killing to good use. It was his responsibility to kill farmhands, which their mother then cooked to supplement the family's meager food rations." Malachi blurted. I stared at him. "Don't you dare Taser me again. Nina told me. She told Nyleena, too, before this thing started."

I narrowed my eyes at him. It bothered me more that Malachi knew this information and I didn't, even more than the idea that cannibalism seemed to run in my family. Cannibalism I could understand to some degree, keeping information about my family being cannibals from me, I couldn't.

In my head, I heard Lucas tell me to stop rationalizing cannibalism and start focusing on the real problem. We were behind Patterson Clachan with no idea of his agenda. His next victim might be Uncle Joe or it might be someone I had never heard of that lived in another state. I tried to listen to that voice. I wished it was Nyleena's, but her voice had gone terribly silent in the last few days.

Trying to ignore Nyleena's mental absence, I headed for the house. As I reached to jiggle the handle, I realized I was still holding the puppy. It was roughly fifteen pounds, making it strange that I had forgotten about it. I looked at it for a few seconds, trying to decide what to do. A uniformed officer came around the house and I motioned him over using the dog. Without any explanation, I dumped the drugged dog into his arms.

Hands freed, I gently touched the handle. It gave under the weight of my fingers and the door swung open. I had another moment of doubt. Why would someone who was paranoid keep a handle-style door latch? They were easier to break into for starters and any burglar with half a brain could do it. On the flip side, what sort of idiot broke into the house of a serial killer?

The answer was pretty obvious. I was the sort of idiot who broke into the houses of serial killers. It must have been a family trait, because my grandfather also seemed to enjoy it. I stood in front of the door, unable to move. I was having a small identity crisis. I had gone from just waiting for attackers to actually hunting them down. It seemed counterproductive, Nyleena was proof of that.

Thankfully, the smell of blood brought me back to the present. Not just a little, but a lot and beneath the strange, coppery scent was the smell of feces. It was a smell I never got used to. I could stand knee deep in blood and brain matter, but the relaxing of the sphincters in the body made me gag. I fought the urge. It wasn't my crime scene or my victim, although, it was technically my killer. My sniper was dead in the house. I knew that just as sure as I knew I was breathing. I would not get the revenge I longed to experience.

I stepped away from the door, allowing Rollins and the St. Charles Police to enter the house. The officer handed me back the puppy as he drew his gun. Those inside the house were shouting out their identities, like it made a difference to the dead man inside.

"He dead?" Malachi asked, he was scratching the puppy he held behind the ear.

"Yes," I told Malachi. "I feel annoyed that I am not going to get to personally kill this guy."

"Then Patterson really did do you a favor. You should thank him when you meet him." Malachi said.

"Should I also thank him for shooting Nyleena in the face?" I growled.

"No, for that, you should break his arm. This makes twice in a week you've been saved from the dark side." Malachi shrugged. "It should earn Patterson some points, when we finish all this stuff with Patterson, you should really have a sit down visit with Lucas. You've come very close to crossing the line lately and you've been saved from yourself. What happens when no one is there to save you?"

"This coming from a guy that would just as soon torture that puppy as pet it?" I snarked.

"I don't torture animals, there's no sport in it." Malachi answered. "Humans yes, dogs no. I actually like dogs. They're good natured and kind hearted as long as they are treated well."

I considered that. Malachi could love a puppy or a dog. I couldn't. What did that say about me? Was I really beginning the spiral into madness that had consumed men like Patterson? Maybe a sit down with Lucas was in order.

Rollins and several officers rushed out the back door. They were all coughing, a few were gagging. I turned away and put the dog up to my face to block out the sounds of vomiting. I couldn't imagine what was so bad that the police had rushed out of a crime scene to throw up. I knew it happened, but it wasn't common, especially not with a beating death. If Patterson had gutted him or draped his entrails throughout the house, I could see it, but he'd claimed to beat him to death. My curiosity was piqued.

"May we?" Malachi asked, finding someone new to give his dog to. He took mine too and handed it to the woman. She looked stoically blank.

"What's going to happen to them?" I asked.

"They'll be tested for temperament and put up for adoption," she answered.

"Thinking of getting a dog?" Malachi asked.

"What would I do with a dog? I would forget to feed it and it would eat my face off when I got home." I looked at him. "I was thinking of Nyleena. She could use a dog."

"Does she want a dog?" He asked.

"Does that matter?" I returned the question.

"It probably would to her."

"I hear it helps with healing and shit," I told him.

"Even when you are trying to do good things, they come out a little twisted."

"How so?"

"You want to get Nyleena a dog, because it might help her recovery, but she can't have a dog in the hospital and you don't even know if she wants a dog. But you'd get her one anyway, because it would help you."

"You are judging me?" I raised an eyebrow as we entered the house.

"Nope, if it were you in that hospital bed and I thought a puppy would help, you'd get a whole litter. But you're playing with a few cards short right now and the people that keep you somewhat sane are in Tennessee. I feel like I should be trying to help hold you on the sanity train."

"That is rich," I answered, ignoring the smells that were clogging my nostrils and filling my sinus passages with a familiar scent that wasn't entirely unwelcome. Sometimes, even the most morbid things become tied to feelings of being home.

"You should ask your mom about the dog thing before you do anything drastic," Malachi told me. "Where's our booties?"

"What?" I frowned at him.

"Our booties? I forgot to put them on. So did you. We're going to contaminate the crime scene. How could we forget?"

"You sound like Xavier and his stupid gloves. We know who killed him. We know why he killed him."

"But there still might be evidence like where he's been and where he's going," Malachi said.

"Well, Hell," we had only taken about two steps inside the doorway. There was no mud on our feet and our footprints couldn't be seen. We both backed out.

"It's gruesome," Rollins said, dabbing at his mouth, "isn't it?"

"I do not know," I told him. "We forgot to put on booties."

Malachi shrugged at him as someone in a white suit magically appeared and handed us booties for our shoes. I looked at my feet as I slipped them over my shoes. They covered the entire shoe on me. Malachi's feet were a lot bigger, they didn't cover as much of his cowboy boots.

"Is that one of ours?" I asked, as we prepared to re-enter the house.

"One of our what?" Malachi asked.

"Our crime scene people," I was talking in hushed tones, like I might offend the dead.

"I don't know, I've never seen our crime scene people. When they do come into the field, they wear suits." Malachi shrugged and motioned me forward.

I did as instructed. The smell began to grow stronger. I followed my nose into the bedroom. At the doorway, I stopped. Gruesome was a good way to describe it. Hellish would have been better.

Eight

When Patterson Clachan had said he'd beat a man to death, he had way undersold it. Nothing was untouched by blood spatter; from the ceiling to the floor. It was slung across photos, the dresser, a bookcase, the walls, a chair, and everything else in the room.

The skull wasn't just battered, parts were smashed and the bones under the skin looked odd. An eye had come out of its socket and lay on the pillow, the optic nerve keeping it attached. Bones in the legs and arms protruded from the skin, like sharpened stakes.

There was enough blood to make me wonder if he had really died from the beating or if it had been blood loss. Thankfully, the light had been flipped on, allowing all the drying gore to be visible under the naked bulb in the ceiling. One arm and both legs were restrained, but the other arm had been pulled free. The hand was shaped like a club, not a hand.

"His fingers are missing," I said to Malachi.

"I'd bet a twelve pack of Budweiser, that he's a lefty," Malachi said in response. I looked at the left hand, with the missing fingers. Patterson had broken his hand and then plucked the fingers off, pulling and pushing until they broke off. It had created broken shards of bone that poked out from where the fingers met the hand.

"Could you do that?" I asked Malachi.

"Yes." Malachi answered.

"I do not think I could," I told him.

"Your false humanity would stop you," Malachi agreed. "That and you just aren't that big on torture. Sure, you'd rough him up before killing him, but you wouldn't torture him and you wouldn't beat him to death. You'd put a bullet in his brain."

Malachi had a point. There was nothing satisfying in torture. I didn't mind getting in a few good, well deserved blows, but actual torture grossed me out. I would prefer putting a bullet in the skull to breaking off fingers. Maybe I was a little less monster than I thought.

With this revelation in mind, I adjusted to the scene, to actually look at it. Not just observing the brutality and gore, but actually looking at it, with something other than my eyes.

Some killers I got. Others were a mystery.
Patterson Clachan was somewhere in between.

Damaging his sniper's hand I understood.
Beating him to death with this sort of brutality, I
didn't. It wasn't just about the amount of energy
expended, he had literally tortured him. The
victim was restrained, as Patterson went through
the process of beating him. It was very likely
that the weapon was the cane he carried instead
of his fists. It better explained the broken bones
and bruises. It also explained the puncture
marks that could be seen in various places. I
hadn't seen it, but it was possible that the head
had made the puncture marks.

Mentally, I catalogued the injuries. A
puncture mark on a foot, but both feet were
misshapen. One of the bones in the right shin
was poking out, another puncture mark was
near it. The left hadn't faired any better and it
had bones jutting out in two places. I shook my
head and looked at Malachi.

"Why the overkill?" I asked.

"He enjoyed it." Malachi said.

"Patterson is not a sadist." I countered.

"That's true." Malachi looked at the
body. "I'm guessing that after the victim was
restrained, Patterson started at the feet and
worked his way up. Yet, he isn't a sadist, he's a
killer."

"He is a sadist," I argued, thinking back to what he had done to my grandmother.

"No, no he isn't a sadist," Malachi stopped me. "He kills by cutting people open, it's very painful, but it's quick. It's the ritual that causes the pain, not the joy of the pain itself. So, back up. He isn't a sadist."

"If he is not a sadist, why inflict this much damage?" I repeated the question. "If it is not for the enjoyment of his suffering..."

"Enjoyment of his suffering," Malachi repeated the words as if he were chewing on them. "Maybe it was about suffering. Patterson doesn't normally enjoy the pain, but maybe in this case, there was a reason for him to want the victim to suffer. Maybe because he almost shot you?"

"Hundreds of people have almost shot me," I shook my head, still not grasping it. My nose had become blind to the scents in the room. I stepped inside and spun in a slow circle. There was so much blood. None of it was arterial spray, it was all spatter and cast-off from him swinging the weapon.

"His name is James Okafor," Rollins joined us in the bedroom. "A rifle was found in the other room along with clippings of all the bombings, the killing of the Marshal and VCU agent in Kansas City this summer and a news story about his daughter dying at a fair when a stage collapsed while she sang the National anthem."

"Bummer," I responded, still more interested in the blood than the sniper's life story.

"Do you want to hear the rest?" Malachi snapped at me, causing me to focus on what was being said.

"Mr. Okafor was a bartender that was frequented by the bomber that the SCTU was hunting this summer. He was good friends with a guy on the same construction crew as your bomber. He and his buddy are both from the Congo."

"Genocide?" My attention snapped to the walls again. "That's the trigger."

"Why would genocide be a trigger for this?" Rollins asked.

"Patterson served as a foot soldier in World War II. He was part of a group that liberated a concentration camp in Germany. He gets here, figures out that Okafor is part of the death squads in the Congo and loses it." Malachi looked around. "Only this doesn't feel like he lost it."

"He didn't," I looked at Malachi. "I think I understand."

Patterson couldn't eat meat because of his childhood, but even the horror of eating people, couldn't quell his urge to kill. He'd tried to control his urges all his life, but various members of our family had manipulated him into being the killer that he was. When left to his own devices, he tried to fight the urges, when he couldn't any longer, it became a blood bath. However, all that rage was targeted at people that raised his hackles. He hadn't been slaughtering citizens, he'd been slaughtering Nazis. He'd killed farmhands because his father had demanded it. That's why he had been so adamant about catching August. August was everything he abhorred, a pointless killer who preyed on the weak; no better than his father, or a Nazi, or Gertrude, or James the Sniper and possibly, death squad henchman. I'd bet a donut that the buddy was next.

"The wheels are turning," Malachi said.

"Patterson kills because he has to, but that does not mean he cannot direct that rage and make it useful," I told Malachi. "The buddy is next. If they were both in the Congo, then in Patterson's mind, they are both guilty of the ultimate crime."

"Genocide is the ultimate crime?" Rollins asked.

"It is to Patterson," I said. "He kills for a purpose, like a bomber with a cause. But he's a serial killer; this means that while he kills, it is not wholesale. It's just murder, a life to be snuffed out because the world is better without them. Or a psychotic break, like he had when he butchered my grandmother and earned his nickname. His childhood scarred him enough to make him a vegetarian. That means the horrors of World War II would have left an impression as well. Genocide is a pretty damn good reason to kill someone."

Patterson was born a functional psychopath, like Malachi. The urge to kill was there, but Nina and Lila had kept it in check. Now both of them were gone. These three killings were just the start. He was free to sate his blood lust without control and yet, just like I heard Nyleena in my head, he heard Nina's and Lila's. Those voices would keep his kills righteous.

Unfortunately, righteous was a vague word. What I thought was righteous was different than what Malachi thought was righteous. I was sure that Patterson's sense of righteousness was just as different.

My mind brought my gaze back to the blood. That's why there was so much blood. He'd been careful not to hit an artery or a vein.

He'd intentionally beaten him slowly, methodically, torturing him as he imagined James had tortured others. An eye for an eye and all that. I understood, but I didn't agree. At least, I hadn't agreed six months ago. At this exact moment, my agreement was wavering. Perhaps James had deserved every injury. Perhaps he had tortured, raped, maimed and killed without feeling. Perhaps he had committed atrocities for which he had never been punished until now.

This was a slippery-slope for me. When I started agreeing with the monsters I hunted, I risked my own humanity. If I had been a soldier in World War II, I probably would have been a serial killer too. Just hunting serial killers was slowly bringing me closer to that edge. Malachi was right, I needed to sit and have a talk with the resident shrink and I needed my Jiminy Cricket to wake up from her coma and tell me to knock it off.

"There's clothing in the bathroom and they are covered in blood," someone yelled. Any doubts that this kill belonged to Patterson Clachan was instantly gone. I hung my head. I needed to walk away. I needed to pack my shit and go back to Kansas City and sit in Nyleena's hospital room to read to her while she worked up the power to wake up.

Instead, I walked towards the bathroom.

Friends

"They say confession is good for the soul," Patterson spoke quietly. "Do you believe that?"

"Who the fuck are you?" The man spat at him.

"Consider me a debt collector and you have a very large list of debts." Patterson answered. "You didn't answer the question. Do you believe confession is good for the soul?"

"No," the man's voice was curt, but waivered slightly.

"You're probably right, men like you and I, I don't think we have souls, I think that's why we're who we are." Patterson leaned back in his chair. "However, I like a good philosophical conversation and I haven't had one for a long time. Given your background, I'd say you are also a man who likes to discuss philosophy. Am I wrong?"

"What do you want?" The man said.

"That's a long list. I want my granddaughter to come out of her coma. I want my other granddaughter to be safe. They both work in law enforcement, chasing serial killers. The irony of that isn't lost on me, just so you know. Eventually, I'll get caught and they will have to deal with it. The entire world will know that their grandfather is a prolific serial killer. A brutal, insatiable killer, hell-bent on making this world a little bit better by eliminating the scum that infects the gene-pool. Men like you for example, who use your position of power to molest little girls."

"I have never," the man protested.

"You can protest all you like, but we both know different." Patterson answered. "I only stand in judgment of you because I'm not a pedophile. As such, it seems like I should have a little more platform from which to defend my position than you. My victims are never weak and helpless, all yours are."

"Who are you?" The man asked again.

"Patterson Clachan, better known as The Butcher," Patterson answered. "And you are Davis LeVerture, pedophile and school teacher. There, now we've been introduced. Oh, I'm sure you've never actually heard of me. That would be weird, since the press has been staunchly kept away from my cases over the last forty or fifty years. And it's hard to link all my kills together because the victims are so varied, as is the manner of death. Yours will be fitting for your skills. Do you remember a little girl, about six years ago, named Rosa Flores? She was in your class. You raped her after school one day. She was so humiliated that she never told anyone until last year, when she finally admitted it to her grandmother. Unfortunately for you, I know her grandmother. We play bingo together on Friday nights and I'm a good listener, so poor Selena broke down and told me of her granddaughter's confession, seeking comfort. I can't give her comfort, just an ear to listen to the lurid details and justice that her granddaughter will never have because the statute of limitations has run out."

Patterson pulled a hunting knife out from under his jacket. It wasn't fancy or ornate, like his cane. It was just a plain hunting knife, used to skin deer or rabbits. However, it worked well and Patterson kept it sharp enough to split a hair.

"What do you intend to do to me?" The man asked.

"Eventually, I'm going to kill you. That's what people do with mongrels. However, you'll be my fifth kill in thirty-six hours. It's starting to lose its appeal, like a deranged form of aversion therapy. And as a result, while I'm not feeling terribly merciful, I am feeling tired. So all the things I would normally do to a pedophile like you is going to be abbreviated. It will be a fast and painful death, but that beats the long, drawn out version that I had intended." Patterson nodded, as if reassuring himself he was making the right decision. He'd killed four in St. Charles, slept for about an hour and then driven to Sikeston. He didn't intend to stay for long, just enough time to kill the teacher and get back on the road. He'd leave town by dawn, find a motel in the afternoon and sleep until dark. He had a schedule to keep. He didn't believe Aislinn or Malachi would catch up with him until he wanted them to, but better safe than sorry.

A newspaper caught his attention. The headline really, it made him smile. It was amazing what passed as news in a small town. Malachi was going to have a field day with it. It'd be like someone gave him his Christmas and birthday present all wrapped up together.

Patterson stood. His victim was restrained well enough. He preferred them alive, but it would be hard to do everything while he lived. Instead, he started with the important bit. He slipped the knife into the fly of the teacher's pants while shoving a rag into his mouth. This was going to hurt. The teacher was going to scream.

The knife sliced through the cloth with almost no resistance. Patterson did keep it sharp and clean. When the teacher wet himself, the warm liquid washed over the blade. Patterson made a face, disgusted by the teacher's fear.

He'd had lots of practice using the blade. It turned, as if by its own will, and cut a square in the trousers. The city of Sikeston would be missing a teacher tomorrow, but some little girl would be safe.

With the genitals exposed, Patterson laid the blade against the inside thigh, forcing it to break the skin. Blood welled up around the shiny metal and began to ooze down the leg. The first muffled scream welled up from behind the rag. It wouldn't have been heard outside the room. Patterson laughed and set to work.

In a few moments, he'd cut through both legs of the trousers. Patterson pushed the recliner backwards a little more, giving him a flat surface to work from. He laid the blade flat against the upper pelvic bone and began moving it down. The knife was sharp enough to draw blood as it skinned the pelvic area. When it reached the teacher's penis, there was resistance. Patterson had planned for this. The teacher was now screaming as loudly as possible. Patterson guessed there was a fifty/fifty chance that he would vomit and choke on it. Unfortunately for the teacher, he didn't care.

Patterson pulled a length of twine from his pocket. The end was shaped into a miniature noose. He slipped it over the head of the penis and pulled tight. Now, the knife sliced through the skin easily. Blood, urine, and semen spurted out as the organ detached. He didn't touch it. He set it down on the table for later.

The teacher's eyes were wild, more whites could be seen than the darker irises. Tears streamed from them, running down his face, along his jaw line and into the chair. Tears wouldn't be the only thing the recliner would soak up.

Now, there was a decision to be made. He could pluck out the offending eyes now or wait a while longer. The more he stared at them, the more he hated them. The things they had seen as their master had tormented dozens of little girls filled him with rage. Without thinking, the knife was brought to the left eyelid. It cut through the thin membrane, bringing another muffled scream.

Patterson removed the knife, preferring to do it by hand. He placed one finger under the eye, the other over it and began to press and separate the skin. The eye bulged out, with a final push, it popped from the socket. Patterson took the knife and cut the optic nerve, catching the eye as it rolled down the teacher's face. He put it on the coffee table, near the severed penis, then repeated the process on the right eye. Patterson checked for a pulse. It was still there, weak and thready, beating too fast and not hard enough. It wouldn't be long now, Patterson leaned back in his chair, waiting.

He'd quit smoking years ago, but he patted his pocket, looking for the pack anyway. It was an old habit and while he'd been able to quit smoking, he hadn't been able to stop himself from looking for them. A final gurgle alerted Patterson to the man's death. It had taken about five minutes, not the slowest death he'd ever caused, but also not the fastest.

Now, Patterson had a decision to make. It wasn't an easy decision either. He'd never done anything like it, but the news article had brought the idea to the front of his mind. He pulled out a pair of nitrile gloves, not because he cared about leaving fingerprints, but because he didn't really like to touch his victims, especially right now.

Making up his mind, he pulled on the dead teacher's lower lip. The metal sheared it off, revealing the bottom row of teeth. Patterson grimaced, refusing to give into his own revulsion. He steeled himself. It was only going to get worse from here. He pulled on the upper lip, bring it out and away from the mouth and repeated the process. Now both sets of teeth were visible.

Patterson had seen a horror movie once about some weird demons, the leader's head was filled with long pins. However, it was a different demon that came to mind now. One that had some kind of device in its mouth that pulled the lips back, baring the teeth. The teeth had chattered like the demon or whatever the thing was supposed to be, was cold.

He occupied his mind with these memories as he unstrapped the dead teacher. He needed something to keep his thoughts off of what he was about to do. He tried to console himself. The shock factor for the other FBI agent would be enormous, but Malachi would be fascinated. It was rare that something fascinated Malachi. He wasn't sure how Aislinn would react. Disgusted, annoyed, angry, indifferent, any of those were possibilities.

Removing the kill would be a new element too. Somehow he needed them to know it was his. He needed to sign it. He flipped the body over, the legs flapping like curtains in a light breeze. He finished removing the pants with the hunting knife. Then he stopped. Could he do this? He wasn't sure. He was determined to try though.

First, though, he needed to make sure it went to the living FBI agent, Malachi and Aislinn. Even he knew he was stalling, but stalling was acceptable if it meant building up determination. The chair was soaked with blood. He pressed his hand against it, coating his glove in blood. On the wall his finger wrote the words: For Malachi Blake & Aislinn Cain. This required him to press his hand several times into the blood, but it was worth it. When he finished requesting Malachi and Aislinn, he grimaced again and looked at the body. It was now or never.

Nine

"Subtle, like a freight train," Malachi leaned against the wall.

"I think you mean fright train," I corrected him.

"What's a fright train?" He asked.

"I do not know, it just sounded appropriate," I told him. "Maybe it's the train that carries you to Hell."

"You think there's a train to Hell?"

"There should be an express line. It seems silly to pave the road with good intentions. A train, barreling out of control, wheels burning, rails smoking, and a replay of all the deeds that got you there seems like a more appropriate means of transportation."

"You've given it some thought."

"Not really," I told him. "I just think that the road to Hell should be paved with something other than good intentions, especially since everyone says 'it's the thought that counts.'

You cannot have it both ways, either good intentions are bad or they're not. Perhaps it should be paved with the dead wings of the fallen angels; that would also be appropriate."

"Do you two want to help?" Rollins said to us.

"Help with what?" I asked. "We are not allowed to investigate. You do not like us touching things, so leaning against walls, enjoying a philosophical discussion about the road to hell seems like the best way to spend our time."

"You're supposed to be experts on this guy. Give me something useful," Rollins snapped.

"He killed him," Malachi offered. "Not as brutally as James Okafor, but it wasn't an easy death either. I'd say Patterson enjoyed it."

George "Corky" Makanga lay on the floor. His entrails were sitting next to his head. His eyes were in the fridge. His head had been bashed in. And because this didn't seem bad enough, Patterson had carved the word "punished" on his chest.

"Do you have anything useful to add?" Rollins looked at me.

"Yeah, why are two guys from the Congo named George and James?" I asked.

"Sometimes, people change their first names during immigration to something more American," Malachi told me.

"Oh, then I got nothing. I'm guessing that George here died because Patterson believed he was a soldier responsible for raping, pillaging and killing in the Congo. Obviously, he would not have made a very good Viking."

"I've had it with you two," Rollins was turning red and shouting. "You're supposed to be helping me catch this bastard and so far you've discovered drugged puppies and Cain here broke into a house."

"I did not break into a house. I had reason to believe there was a victim inside and the door was unlocked. I did not even enter the house first. If I had opened the door and been greeted by the smell of cookies, I would have closed it and we could have waited for your possible warrant. Unfortunately, I was greeted by the smell of death, so I told you to go inside, which you did. If he'd been alive, you could have arrested him for animal cruelty for drugging two small German Shepherds and leaving them to freeze to death in the cold weather."

"I'm calling the director," Rollins shouted as he walked outside.

"Okay," Malachi shrugged. "Do you magically know where Patterson Clachan is going to turn up next?"

"Nope," I answered. "I would not mind a nap though. His killing streak is making me tired."

Malachi and I exited the house together. We'd seen enough blood and gore for one day. Night had descended upon us, but light pollution kept the stars from being seen. I stared at the sky anyway, hoping for at least a glimpse of a star.

Malachi lit a cigarette and handed it to me. I peeled off my patch without looking down before I accepted it. Rollins wasn't shouting anymore. He looked like someone had fed him crow stew and the beak was stuck in his throat. Malachi lit a cigarette for himself.

"Should we see if we can make his head explode?" Malachi asked as he took his first drag.

"I thought baiting FBI agents was bad."

"Some FBI agents. Others are just pencil necks in suits with badges and guns."

"I take it you feel that way about Rollins."

"Rollins is in over his head. Hell, you and I are in over our head. We can't get ahead of him because we don't know who's on his list. All we can do is try to play catch up, but this one isn't like a normal killer. He has a mission and obviously, little need for sleep."

"That bugs me," I admitted. "If he killed four people in thirty-six hours, how the heck is he still up and walking around? Why isn't he comatose in a hotel room somewhere? Especially after what he did to James Okafor? The guy's like the Energizer Bunny."

"How many people have you actually killed?" Malachi asked.

"Oh no, we are not playing that game," I told him.

"Six?" Malachi asked.

"Sure," I answered.

"Seriously, Aislinn, how many?"

"Seriously?" I looked at him. "I'll tell you mine if you tell me yours."

"Seven," Malachi answered.

"Five," I told him.

"How long did you sleep after each of them?"

"Hours upon hours. Until they put me in a coma for my burns, my longest sleep records were held by those handful of days after the kill."

"Not mine. After my third one, I didn't sleep for four days. It's my longest stretch with no sleep, but not by much. Your crash is faster than mine. I've always wondered why. I think

~ 112 ~

it's because of your migraines. My adrenaline levels off, but it levels off and it's still really high. Yours levels off and it might still be really high, but I think that drop triggers a silent migraine."

"Painless migraine," I corrected.

"Fine, a painless migraine gets triggered because of the drop. That's why you aren't a serial killer. You may not consciously realize it, but when you crash, you have all the symptoms of a migraine except the pain. As a result, you can't become a serial killer because it makes you physically ill."

"Huh," I thought about the theory. It made sense. Going head to head with a serial killer in a fight was a rush and I tended to sleep afterwards for long periods of time, but to kill a person was enormous. It was quite possible that the adrenaline rush gave me a migraine. "What if it's the rush that causes the migraine? Maybe that is why I get so mean when I have the rush."

"You do become super bitch when you have a migraine," Malachi agreed. "This really only tells us that Patterson doesn't have migraines."

"You should point that out to Rollins. It might be useful at some point."

"Just as useful as your bullet train to Hell," Malachi flashed me a grin. It was genuine, which was rare for Malachi. It didn't make him look younger, it made him look evil. If Satan smiled at me like that, it wouldn't terrify me even half as much as Malachi doing it. It made his cold eyes suddenly sparkle, making his impressively green eyes even more dazzling. His normally ageless face, developed wrinkles, making him appear older. His mouth softened, making his lips appear fuller. It only lasted a second, maybe two, certainly not much longer than that. It was gone as dramatically as it had come. He went back to wearing his perfect mask with cold eyes and a face that showed no expressions or even hints that expressions were even possible.

As scary as those real smiles were, it also made me understand why Malachi was a "ladies' man." He was an attractive male with high testosterone levels and a good build. His face was timeless with only a shadow of stubble that was always well groomed. His green eyes were brilliant even when they were cold and distant, a green that was unnatural in a human being or any living thing for that matter. His dark complexion made them seem even greener. His skin was naturally a shade darker than mine, speaking of something Mediterranean in his ancestry; even in the winter he had a tan. In contrast, he had brown hair that was lighter than mine, darker than a dirty blonde, but lighter than a true brunette. He kept it cut very short, hiding the secret that it was naturally curly.

Also, Malachi was tall with a lanky, but athletic build. For everyone else on the planet, I considered lanky and athletic an impossible combination. Malachi was exactly 192 pounds, with muscle definition around his arms and legs and washboard abs. What made him seem lanky was that he was six feet, ten inches tall, with a fifty-eight inch inseam, meaning my nose was almost even with his navel. The long legs made him seem taller and thinner.

Being a woman with no interest in sex, I didn't know if high testosterone levels were important to other woman, but I had a feeling they were. Women seemed to be attracted to dominant, alpha male types fueled by testosterone. Malachi certainly fit the bill, except with me.

I was a problem for Malachi, a weakness. It was hard to see, even harder to understand. Most people believed Malachi wanted to jump my bones. This wasn't actually the case. If I ever decided to develop a sex drive, Malachi would be at the front of the line, vying for first dibs, but it wasn't really because he wanted to have sex with me. It was because he couldn't control me. I could and would and did tell him no whenever it struck my fancy. Very few people said no to Malachi and no one ever said it more than a few times. I had been telling him no for decades. No, you can't torture my roommate. No, you shouldn't abuse your position of power for your own amusement. No, you can't pick up women when I'm with you, it's weird. No, you can't kick that guy's ass just because he's a jerk.

The other problem was that since I did tell Malachi no, he had come to depend on me. Not like most people depend on their friends, but like I depended on Nyleena. In the darkest recesses of Malachi's mind, it was my voice he heard when he needed to make a moral decision. If my voice ever disappeared, bad things would happen. He knew it. I knew it. As long as I was alive and well, the voice remained present. However, I was aware that Gabriel had been responsible for keeping his leash while I'd been in a coma and it had been difficult. As a result, after I had been put into the coma, Malachi had called the hospital every day to check on me. That's how he'd managed to be there when they woke me.

Standing next to him, in the dark, with a dead body in the house behind us and serial killer on the loose, I couldn't imagine my life without him. One day, that would change.

He'd cross the line or I would and we'd be forced to put the other one down. Until then, I was fine with him standing beside me in the dark. It was better to have the devil at your hip than behind your back.

"Ok, is he going after Gertrude, Joe and August or will he let justice take care of them?" I asked.

"Beats me," Malachi stubbed out his cigarette. "If they weren't in federal custody, I think he'd go after them, but they are. He has a list of targets, but I don't know who they are. John Bryan more than likely, also in custody. Any enemies you had as a child, that list is too long for us to protect. He killed a guy because the guy shot at you in high school."

"And was trying to frame me for murder," I added. Gabriel had told me the story at the hospital the first day after Nyleena's surgery.

"Framing you for murder might have been the bigger incident," Malachi conceded.

"I also think the list would include Nyleena's enemies. He swears he did not mean to shoot her in the face. Killing her enemies would be a good way to prove it."

"Does Nyleena actually have enemies? Part of the reason I have issues with her is because she's such a goody-two-shoes."

"Nyleena is a federal prosecutor. She has enemies and she is not a goody-two-shoes, she just is not deranged like you," I thought for a moment, "or me for that matter. She's had speeding tickets and parking tickets and once, she drove after smoking part of a joint."

"Nyleena smokes pot?" Malachi looked doubtful.

"No, she smoked pot in college with other college kids. She did it like seven times. You know how many times I've smoked pot? None. She does normal 'bad' things. We are the aberration, not her, Malachi."

"Well, when you put it that way, she's still a goody-two-shoes, she's just experimented with life a little."

"How many times have you smoked pot?" I asked, suddenly curious.

"Once," Malachi looked at Rollins. Rollins was still on the phone, but he hadn't said anything for a long time. He looked defeated. "It slows down your reflexes."

"You realize we are being outsmarted by a serial killer?"

"I'd say he's a genius though and he's had a lot of experience."

"We are supposed to be geniuses, yet, he is still outsmarting us."

"He isn't really outsmarting us, we just don't have any leads."

"Do you think clues are going to fall out of the sky and magically land in our laps?"

"Nope." Malachi walked towards Rollins. He took the phone from the other agent, said a few words and hung up. "You want to know where Patterson Clachan is going to be. You're going to have to set a trap for him."

"How do we do that?" Rollins' voice was barely audible.

"Her," Malachi pointed at me.

Ten

It was just after six in the morning. We were heading to Sikeston, Missouri. We'd been awoken by Rollins telling us there was a message for us there. I didn't really like the sound of that. I liked it even less when I discovered we were going to be traveling by helicopter.

In theory, I didn't mind flying. I didn't look out the windows and we had a private jet, these helped. This helicopter seemed to be nothing but windows. We weren't as high as a plane, but it didn't matter, if we crashed, we were probably going to die. I wasn't afraid of death, but I wasn't ready for it yet. There were still things to do, like fly a kite. I had never flown a kite in my life. It seemed like a shame to die before trying it. I made a mental note to fly a kite when Nyleena got better.

The noise was awful. Even with the headset that was supposed to dampen it, the whirling blades droned in my brain. By the time we landed, an hour after takeoff, my head was starting to throb. I popped a pill when I thought no one was looking and gratefully put my feet on the ground.

For the first time, we had two crime scenes. One was a house, the other a field, my opinion hadn't been asked about which we were visiting first. I climbed into the waiting SUV clutching my overnight bag like a life-line.

Despite being a well-traveled Missourian, I had never been to Sikeston. The population sign declared 40,000 people called it home. This was roughly the same size as our capitol, but about half the size of my hometown. This also meant it wasn't exactly rural. Traffic flowed smoothly along the roads. I couldn't remember what day it was, but I figured it was a workday, given the traffic and the time of morning.

I leaned my head against the side window. I'd been shoved in the back seat, which was fine, I had no desire to engage in conversation with Rollins or the police officer driving us. The window was cold against my forehead. The cold soothed my head some, but the throbbing continued. I hadn't been allowed a soda on the helicopter, the caffeine would have helped. Without opening my eyes, I picked up my bag and rooted around until my hands clasped a lukewarm bottle. Not bothering to zip the bag back up, I pushed it gently from my lap and opened the soda. A hissing fizz sound filled the backseat as the seal was cracked for the first time.

I drank with my eyes closed, tilting my head back, chugging at the bottle hard enough to cause the sides to begin to collapse. A hand touched my shoulder, the wide palm was hot even through my jacket. I shook my head and the heat disappeared.

"We're going to see the body first," Rollins announced from the front seat. I considered giving him the finger or Tasering him for simply interrupting my solitude. The migraine medicine was starting to flood my blood stream. It was a combination medication, filled with acetaminophen, a mild muscle relaxer, caffeine, and codeine. I rarely took it, because I didn't like the effect of the narcotics, but I knew that out here, I was going to need to kick it quick. I didn't have time for a slower medication.

The noise of city life was receding. I opened my eyes. We were on a two-lane highway, slowing down as trees cropped up on either side of the road. I didn't know if Sikeston was part of the Ozarks or not, but it was pretty. We turned down a county road.

"He left the body in BFE?" I asked.

"I don't know where that is," Rollins said.

"Never mind," I sighed. "He deviated, he does not remove bodies from the crime scene."

"This is going to get strange," the officer in the front seat said. "The farmer was spooked before he woke up and found a dead teacher."

"Teacher? Spooked?" I asked. Malachi handed me a folder. I frowned at it. I couldn't read in the car, it would set off motion sickness, especially with a migraine looming. When the SUV stopped, I scanned the file quickly. The teacher had moved, often, every year actually for the last twelve years. He finished a school year and moved to a different place. Not all of them were in Missouri, Sikeston was only his third school in the state. He'd also taught in Tennessee, Kentucky, and Illinois. This information raised all kinds of red flags. Normal people didn't move every year, especially not teachers. Teachers were stable persons, who grew roots easily. Teachers who didn't, were up to no good. He'd taught kindergarten or first grade, nothing older. It explained why his victim pool wasn't filing complaints, most children molested at such a young age, didn't say anything for years. I believed it was because they didn't have the words to explain what had happened or how it had made them feel.

We stopped at a farmhouse. The front yard was well kept. A large building could be seen behind it, a good ways from the house. I studied the building quickly, as we walked to the front door. It opened before we reached it.

"Bud, this is the FBI, they're here to talk to you about what happened," the officer, who I now saw had the double bars of a captain.

"The dead guy or the mutilated cattle?" Bud asked.

"Mutilated cattle?" Malachi asked, his attention suddenly focused solely on the farmer. I groaned without realizing it. Malachi ignored me. "What mutilated cattle?"

"Well, yesterday morning, I woke up and had three dead cows in my yard. They'd been cut up pretty bad." Bud started.

"We're here about the dead teacher," I interrupted, stepping forward. "US Marshal Aislinn Cain with the SCTU. I'm guessing you raise turkeys judging by the barn set-up you have."

"That's right, which is why the cattle are weird. I don't have any cattle and neither do my neighbors. Then this morning, I found the dead guy, cut up the same way." Bud told me. I stifled another groan. This was going to be a nightmare.

"Around back," the captain said to us. I followed the captain, leaving Malachi to ogle the turkey farmer. As I rounded to the back of the house, I groaned again, much louder. The bodies of the cattle were still there, near the turkey barn and our dead body. I was hoping the death of the teacher would be more interesting, but I knew Malachi, and I was fairly certain the teacher would receive nothing more than a cursory glance.

My eyes avoided the cattle as I walked past. I'd seen pictures and video of them before. It always grossed me out; rotting human carcasses were fine, I was growing used to them as part of my job. However, I still got a squicky feeling in my stomach when I drove past road kill.

Of course, that depended on how the human had died. My stomach gave a determined flop and my throat began to burn with bile. It had been a long time since I had thrown up at a crime scene, I certainly wasn't going to do it here, but I wanted to. The victim was completely naked. It was obvious his genitals were missing, as were his eyes, and lips. That part didn't bother me. Patterson had taken some sharp implement and cored out the victim's anus. That horrified me. Entrails dangled from his behind like a giant tape worm trying to escape.

Rollins cleared his throat several times. No one was standing near the body. I completely understood, I was four feet away and wishing I was at home, under the covers. Malachi was slowly sauntering towards us, his eyes focused on the cattle.

"Hey Blake!" I shouted, suppressing the urge to vomit as I opened my mouth. "This one is right up your alley." I'd heard the stories, probably from Malachi. Cattle mutilations often involved the removal of the eyes, lips, udders, and anus. The position and extreme mutilation had been done for Malachi, like a sick Valentine's secret between lovers.

"Huh?" Malachi had stopped at the last cow. He was kneeling next to it, looking at me.

"We have a dead teacher. Teacher trumps cows." I reminded him.

"We have a dead pedophile who happened to be a teacher, there's nothing interesting or surprising about it," Malachi answered, pulling on gloves.

"I believe this one is different," I started walking towards him. "This one requires your special attention."

Annoyed, he stood up and joined us. He stared at the body for a moment, then his gaze darted back to the cattle, then back to the body.

"Think Patterson did it on purpose? How would he know?" Malachi asked.

"The local paper ran a story because we haven't had any cattle reported missing," the captain said to us.

"There's your answer. I believe the teacher was dead for some of it, but not all of it." I pointed to the missing genitals. "Too much blood flow there for it to have been post-mortem."

"I agree," a man stood up. He was one of the brave ones, not standing forty feet from the dead man. "And the eyes were also removed while he was alive. Tentatively, I'd say cause of death is blood loss."

"Fun," I ground my teeth together.

"Fun?" Rollins turned red.

"You're going to have a coronary," I told him. "Relax. Malachi has a good plan, we just need a day to implement it."

"If we don't have a day?" Rollins asked.

"We will," I assured him. Malachi had gone back to looking at the cattle. I sighed. This was a problem. Malachi was fascinated with animal mutilations. He'd seen a horse in the desert somewhere in New Mexico, it'd just been

lying by the side of the road. His obsession had
gotten worse when he joined the FBI because as
a member of the VCU, he could access files from
the Department of Forestry, Natural Resources,
Conservation, The Interior, and the FBI. "You
about done, Mulder?"

"If I'm Mulder, does that make you
Scully?" Malachi asked, mostly disinterested in
what I had to say.

"I'm not a red-head."

"I'm taller than David Duchovny."
Malachi stood. "Explains why the farmer was
spooked. I just can't imagine where the cows
came from. There's no signs they were killed
here, no signs of predation, nothing. It's like
they just appeared in this guy's backyard."

"Here we go," I crossed my arms over my
chest. "We are not going to have this discussion
again. They did not appear out of thin air and
little green men did not drop them from UFOs."

"As a rational, intelligent person, I can't
believe you don't believe in aliens."

"I do believe in aliens. I also believe that
if they have ever bothered to visit us, they ran
away, because we're the backwoods hillbilly
yokels with no teeth and dueling banjos in this
universe. They'd be better off abducting
dolphins than humans. Even our smartest
human would not be able to hold an intelligent

conversation with an alien. As such, I do not believe they are abducting humans and experimenting on them. It seems even more unlikely they would abduct cattle and kill them, unless they were just hungry and lips and assholes were a delicacy. However, if they wanted lips and assholes, they could grab a hotdog at any convenience store."

"We did have a report of a UFO the other night," someone from the rank and file offered.

"See?" Malachi looked at me.

"A UFO sighting does not mean aliens dropped dead, mutilated cows from the sky onto this man's turkey farm. A UFO sighting is exactly that, a sighting of an unidentifiable flying object, unless that object was the cattle, the two are not related." I answered, getting heated. "You are obsessed with this nonsense. Let's go see the crime scene."

"You are going to call me obsessed? This from the girl who nearly wets her pants every time there's a case of Bubonic Plague," Malachi was going to say more, but the guy next to the body stopped him.

"Excuse me, but if you two are done, there's something in his mouth." This guy had to be the medical examiner.

"It's his penis," Malachi answered. "Patterson Clachan does it for effect with pedophiles."

A few men groaned in the distance. I had the decency to not throw up. This was a new horror that I didn't want to think about. We began the trek back to the SUV. Malachi was slow, still fascinated by the cattle. I considered Tasering him again to get him moving, but figured it was a waste of a cartridge.

Eleven

Walking into the house where our teacher had been butchered was a grave mistake. Pain instantly pierced my brain, blinding me. My knees gave out and I sank to the floor with a shriek. I quit breathing and willed my heart to stop beating. Arms grabbed me roughly, yanking me up and outdoors. The cold washed over my face, freezing the tears that I hadn't felt start to fall. A voice drifted into my head, a voice that sounded concerned. I turned my head and vomited.

Hands touched my hair and I felt myself fall towards the sound of the voice. The body felt hot against my exposed flesh and warm through my coat and shirt. I felt hot, as if I had been set on fire. The throbbing that had once existed had been replaced by a pounding, every beat felt like demons stabbing my brain with pitchforks.

The voice that was talking was drowned out by my own heartbeat echoing in my ears. However, the pain was beginning to recede. I opened my eyes. The person holding me wasn't Malachi, it was the unknown captain of the Sikeston police department. After a second, I closed my eyes again.

"She's hypersensitive to smell," Malachi shouted. "If she had that kind of reaction, there is something in there that needs to be cleared with a HAZMAT team. Air freshener will give her a migraine, but that, that was something different."

"She popped a pill on the helicopter," Rollins shouted back. "Maybe she's having a bad reaction to that. I think you're getting carried away."

"Freon," I whispered to the captain, the only person close enough to hear me. "Freon is leaking."

"She's saying something about Freon," the captain repeated. The words reverberated in his chest, I could feel them.

"I need a bed and some good migraine medicine." I told him. "First, you need to find the Freon leak."

"What?" Malachi asked, he was on the ground next to me, appearing out of thin air. "What's going on, Aislinn?"

"There's a Freon leak in the house. I had a headache, so the reaction to it was much more severe than it should have been, but I've smelled it before. There is Freon in the house. As it has evaporated, the fumes have built up in the living room. I do not think it was meant for us."

"We should get you to a hospital," Malachi suggested.

"Nonsense," I huffed. "It's just Freon. I need a bed and a migraine pill. The fresh air is already making me feel better. If I abused the stuff, I'd need a hospital. Of course, I would also blow my brains out because the migraines would be non-stop and I would be miserable."

"You're already miserable," Rollins said.

"I'm nothing," I told him. "Misery requires emotion and most of the time, I feel none. Please get me to a hotel or motel with a bed." I leaned heavily against the captain. "And you should have a HAZMAT team sweep before anyone else goes back inside. If Patterson punctured a Freon line, the gas was meant to make the Sikeston first responders ill, not us. It's rarely fatal."

"It's not his MO," Malachi walked over to me and touched my hair gently. "I'm going to get you to a hotel, where you can rest. I'll bring you detailed photos of what we find."

"We can use this to our advantage," I told him. "Why kick each other's asses when I can get sick off a Freon leak and blame Patterson. He's disturbed by Nyleena's condition, imagine if he injured both of us."

"That's a pretty good idea," Malachi started ushering me to the SUV. I didn't fight him. My head didn't hurt like it had after entering the house, but it was still pounding. A nice bed and a hot shower would go a long ways toward making me feel better.

Rollins didn't feel the need to accompany us. He grumbled about a HAZMAT team. The captain drove us, Malachi packing me into the front seat, him sliding in behind me. I leaned my head against the window and watched the town roll by. It was a nice little town. It wasn't spectacularly beautiful, but it wasn't falling into ruin either. Of course, I wouldn't remember most of this trip when I woke up.

It used to scare me to have migraines at work. I'd wake up in a strange room, disoriented and panicked. A chunk of my life missing, few to no memories, except the migraine pain. It would take a few minutes for me to remember I was in a hotel room, chasing down a bad guy. Those minutes were hard to explain. Beyond the panic and disorientation was a feeling of foreboding. Sometimes, Xavier or Lucas would hang out in my room while they waited for me to wake. I could handle that. The panic dissipated with the knowledge they were there. It meant I was safe. They'd fill me in on what I missed, I'd chug a soda, and go back to work.

I wasn't sure what was going to happen when I awoke this time. Having Malachi in the room might make me feel safe or it might freak me out. Sometimes, even I found him unnerving.

The captain, whose name I still hadn't asked and wasn't going to right now, stopped in front of a real hotel. The kind where all the doors opened onto interior hallways and you needed keycards after certain hours to enter said hallways. I refused to stay in a ground floor room, so did Malachi. Shit happened on the ground floor that didn't happen on the higher ones, mainly because it was a whole lot harder to scale a building to the second or third story.

Captain Anonymous walked us into the hotel. He waved at the woman in reception. We took an elevator to the third floor of the Holiday Inn and he pulled out keycards. He held them up.

"Are the rooms together?" Malachi asked.

"Yes," he answered.

"Middle room for Aislinn," Malachi looked at the cards. For the first time, I noticed he was carrying my overnight bag. The captain raised his eyebrow at this. "People will randomly attempt to break into her room from time to time. It's easier to respond if she's wedged between law enforcement that expects it. She's a magnet for yahoos and whackos."

I leaned against the wall as Malachi swiped the card. The light turned green and he opened the door before entering. I knew he was checking all the visible area for intruders.

"I do not actually hunt serial killers, I just show up wherever there is one and they find me," I smiled at the captain.

"That isn't true," Malachi corrected. He pushed me inside, closing the door behind us. "Well, it's sort of true." He said with the captain out of hearing.

"Great, go get me pictures."

"I was going to help you change first."

"Uh, no," I told him, my face drew into a pinched sneer. "You will not use my migraine as an excuse to fondle me."

"Trust me, I have no intention of fondling you. In this condition, you'd skip the Taser and go straight for the Berettas or a knife, both of which would leave big holes in me." He opened the bag and pulled out my pajamas. "Interesting."

In one respect, I was a very normal person, almost nobody saw my pajamas. Nyleena, Lucas, Xavier and Gabriel, but the three men were exceptions to the rule. If I would stop waking them up in the wee hours of the morning, they wouldn't see my pajamas, only Nyleena would know what I slept in. This particular pair had kittens on the flannel pants. The top was long sleeve, also flannel and dead center, it had a large kitten head with a box over its head saying "Purrrfect." I never bought plain pajamas, they were purchased at an online store that specialized in flannel pajamas, possibly meant for elderly women. I'd gotten my polar bears, kittens, and Halloween themed PJs from the site. However, I was getting ready to place another order, because they had just gotten in new ones that had dancing penguins on them.

With my life, it really was about the little things; a good meal, a new pair of flannel pajamas, a trip to a bookstore, these were the things I appreciated above all else. While most women preferred silk or satin pajamas, I really did like the soft, downy feel of thick flannel.

"Do not make fun of my kittens," I said.

"Oh the jokes that come to mind," Malachi looked at me.

"If you say the 'p-word,' I will Taser you," I warned him.

"I am aware. Shower quickly, when you are out, I'll pass you your pajamas through the door, you can dress and I'll tuck you into bed, then go back to our primary crime scene."

As I walked past, I yanked my pajamas out of his hand and gave him the finger. I turned on the shower and the infrared heat lamp in the bathroom after I shut the door. I waited sitting on the countertop until the water began to steam up the mirror. Stepping inside, my skin instantly warmed. I hadn't realized I had gotten so cold. It was caused by the sudden blood pressure rise associated with the migraine. High blood pressure made you sweat, pain made you sweat, pain also made you not realize you were sweating. I stepped out, wrapped up in a towel and realized there was a problem. I hadn't grabbed underwear. I sighed and opened the door.

Malachi shoved a pair of underwear at me without being asked. I was a little unsettled that he had stood in front of the bathroom door waiting for me to request them. I was even more unnerved that he had touched my underwear. I dressed and exited the bathroom. Flopping down on one of the beds, I took a pair of socks from the bag and slipped them on. Malachi handed me a pill and a soda.

"Eat, drink, sleep," he told me.

"Will one make me taller and the other smaller?" I inquired.

"You won't be going through any keyholes or expanding through the ceiling if that's what you're asking."

"At least you got the reference." I popped the pill and realized I had no idea what I had just taken. "What was it?"

"Oxycontin," Malachi told me.

"Good grief," I groaned. "I need food and I'm going to sleep for forever. Why would you do that to me?"

"Because you need your sleep. I need you bright eyed and bushy tailed when we do find Patterson Clachan. That won't happen if you have the lingering effects of a migraine. If I'd had DHE, I would have injected you myself, but all I have is Oxycontin from being shot by some idiot a few weeks ago." He put the bottle on the nightstand and picked up the phone. He ordered food from the restaurant in the lobby and said he'd pay extra to have it delivered to the room. I picked up the pill bottle. The label said there were 60 pills inside. It seemed very full, so I opened the lid and began counting.

There were exactly 59 left. "I would have to be in some serious pain to take an Oxycontin."

"But you'll push them off on me."

"You are in serious pain right now."

"You're a jerk. How long before the food gets here?"

"Most people would give body parts for an Oxycontin, but you treat it like it's the most evil thing on the planet."

"Food? Here? When?" I asked slowly.

"About fifteen minutes."

"I need milk," I told Malachi. "My stomach will be upset before the food arrives."

Malachi sighed and stood up. He crossed the space between the beds and door in only a few steps. He said something to the officer outside. He left the door open and came back into the room. I moved to the small table.

Someone who was not the captain arrived a few minutes later with a to-go cup and a Styrofoam box. The cup had milk in it. The box had a chicken sandwich in it. The sandwich had ranch on it, I would have preferred mayo, but didn't complain. I ate the food and drank the milk as quickly as possible. After finishing, I climbed into bed, just in time for the Oxycontin to kick in. I felt like vertigo was sweeping over me accompanied by an urge to sleep. I closed my eyes.

Twelve

A tangy scent filled my nose; sweet tomatoes, minty cilantro, a hint of lemon, and the bite of onion. In other words, someone had fresh Pico de Gallo in my room. This could mean only one thing, someone had Mexican food in my room. My eyelids didn't want to come apart. My head felt foggy. My body felt tired.

However, there was hot Mexican food in my room. More smells were starting to filter through the tang of the Pico; chicken, lightly seasoned, grilled corn, green peppers, rice, sour cream, beef, and flour tortillas, to name a few. I pried my eyelids open. A box sat inches from my face, the lid open. It contained all sorts of goodies; a grilled chicken taco still wrapped in foil sat in the lid, Mexican rice, a cheese enchilada smothered in enchilada sauce, and a quesadilla stuffed with mushrooms and onions were in the bottom part. Also in the bottom, on top of everything was sour cream, Pico, lettuce and cheese dip. I felt like crap, but at least I had something good to wake up to.

I shrugged off the covers and forced myself to sit up. Malachi came into view. He picked up the box and moved it to the table.

"How do you feel?"

"You're a jerk," I answered. "But at least you brought me Mexican."

"It's Tex-Mex, technically, from a Chevy's across the street. I figured if it couldn't wake you up, nothing could."

"How long did I sleep?" I stood up, my legs feeling wobbly.

"Twenty-seven hours, thirty-five minutes, and approximately, forty-seven seconds, give or take a few seconds," he answered. "The good news is that Patterson hasn't killed anyone in that twenty-seven hours. He's called you six times, but he hangs up every time I answer."

"That's because he knows you're a jerk too." I bit into the food, savoring the flavors and smells. Malachi stared at me, his food untouched. He kept fiddling with a paperclip. I knew something was on his mind, but whatever it was, I didn't want to discuss it. I wanted to eat and then, I wanted to track down Patterson Clachan.

"Are we going to talk about the elephant in the room?"

"What elephant?" I asked, annoyed that I was only half way through my meal.

"August is my uncle and your cousin."

"So?" I looked at him blankly. "You and I are not related. You would have to be related to Gertrude or me to Tennyson for there to be a familial connection between the two of us. It's a fluke. Think about all the people in Columbia that we have turned out to be related to over the years. Remember that girl in junior high that you dated for a week before finding out she was your second cousin on your father's side, twice removed or some such nonsense? Our families have deep roots in a town of 100,000 people. It really is not that surprising that we share a relative."

"It doesn't bother you that Tennyson fathered August?"

"Nope, Gertrude and Tennyson would have made a perfect couple. They should have married. They could have spit out dozens of miniature serial killers, all of them sadistic cannibals. Then maybe they all would have been arrested long before now. Why does it bother you?"

"I don't know," Malachi answered, putting the paperclip down, but not picking up his fork. I stared at my friend of more than twenty years and found concern in his face.

"You are not Tennyson, Malachi. You share one trait with the man, a genetic mutation, nothing more. Do not get me wrong, you can be an amazing jerk, but you are not your grandfather. Every time you need to be reminded, look at me. You've never physically tortured me, attempted to rape me, or just beat me up because you could and you've had twenty plus years to do it. We'll ignore the psychological mind games you play just to watch people squirm, I realize that everyone needs a hobby and that happens to be yours. I do not take it personally when you do it to me." I thought for a moment, "and when you get too out of control, there's always a Taser handy."

Malachi smiled at me; a genuine smile. I had, in fact, Tasered Malachi more times than either of us cared to remember. Most of them had not been because he was physically out of control, it was almost always a mental thing with him. Like all good psychopaths, he could be charming, devious, and manipulative. I hated the "charming" Malachi more than I hated the "manipulative" Malachi, but it was the manipulative Malachi that sometimes needed to be Tasered. It was a reminder that real people had feelings and pressing their buttons could cause them emotional pain and turmoil. When you didn't feel emotion, and Malachi felt less than I did, physical pain was the only thing that penetrated the darkness.

"We have a reprieve from Patterson, but I believe it is a short reprieve. How do we use it to our advantage?" Malachi asked after a few minutes.

"Beats me, you know more about him than I do. I get that I'm a weakness, but I do not believe it is the same type of weakness as yours. If it was you, I would set a trap at the hospital, because you would come see me. However, Patterson has never attempted to visit me in the hospital. Did you get the crime scene photos for me? Did you figure out the Freon leak?"

"Yes and yes," Malachi pulled out a folder from under the table. "The Freon leak was coming from the basement. It would appear that our pedophile was a little paranoid. All the windows were taped. Not just the bottom sill, but the entire window frame. And I know you're going to give me what for about it, but there's another interesting aspect. Our victim claimed to see a UFO a few nights ago. He reported it to the police."

"Did the paper run the story?" I asked, not yet opening the folder. I could eat and look at crime scene photos, I'd even adjusted to eating around dead bodies. However, when I had a choice, I didn't mix the two.

"They did. It was the headliner for four days. It appears several people in the area spotted a UFO and then the cattle mutilations turned up, then Patterson turned up."

"Well, I do not believe Patterson is connected to the UFO sightings or the cattle mutilations. That would require him to be an alien and my DNA is on file. If part of the DNA was extraterrestrial, I think someone would have said something. However, that could be how Patterson found the victim."

"You think he's scanning newspapers for headlines of UFO sightings?"

"No, but I think he's well-read and I believe he keeps up on current events. Also, he probably does internet searches for the names on his hit list. The real question then becomes, why did he suspect our victim was a pedophile?" I asked.

Despite having vocalized the question, I knew the answer. Either Patterson had a personal connection to the pedophile or he had one with a victim. Even in a world where philanthropists were just as likely to be serial killers as crack addicts, people never really suspected their neighbor of being capable of such atrocities. When they did get suspicious, they still didn't voice it for fear of being wrong. You didn't tell people you thought your pastor was a serial killer unless he was captured, then you said things like "I always thought there was something off about him" or "he's such a nice guy, I can't believe he could be responsible." Either were acceptable answers that eliminated any responsibility on the person with the suspicion. I'd heard both statements so often, they irritated me. If I had a quarter for every time I'd heard that, I'd have been a billionaire.

Finding out whether Patterson had known the teacher or a victim was the key. With this in mind, I opened the folder with the crime scene photos. I had to give kudos to Patterson, all his crime scenes were bloody, gory, and gruesome. The ceiling was the only thing without spatters of blood. The restraint system on the recliner was very similar to the restraints that had been on the bed of James Okafor. The last picture was of the basement where several window air conditioner units were sitting on the floor. Fluid had pooled around a few of them. I held up the picture.

"Perhaps he hallucinated the UFO and Freon poisoning can lead to paranoia." I suggested.

"The fact that there's still liquid on the floor rules that out. If it had been punctured several days earlier, it would have evaporated. It seems that the victim was in the process of working on them the day before and then Patterson came into his life sometime during the night."

I shrugged and went back to the pictures. Crime scene photos can only give up so much information. There was nothing frenzied about the attack, the lack of blood on the ceiling proved that. Castrating a person is a bloody affair. In most cases, there would be arterial spray. Arterial spray is high velocity spurting that can go ten or fifteen feet into the air or across a room. With the victim in a reclining position, it seemed almost impossible for the spray not to hit the ceiling, unless Patterson had done something to ensure it didn't.

The missing arterial spray bothered me. We knew the victim was alive when he was castrated, so how had Patterson not gotten spray on the ceiling? And why had he bothered? The answer dawned on me slowly, as I stared at the photo of the ceiling. The spray would have landed on him.

It was one thing to get spray from the neck or the thigh on yourself. It was messy, but it was just blood. The same could not be said if the spray came from the penis. If I was Patterson, I wouldn't want that on me.

Thirteen

Another day passed with no corpses turning up. The press was all over the story that I was in dire straits at the hospital from Freon poisoning. It still seemed to be working. Patterson kept calling my cell phone and Malachi kept answering it, at which point Patterson would hang up.

Rollins was still debating our next move. With Patterson not killing, he didn't know where to go. Malachi and I were no help there. I was of the opinion that he would be home, most likely in Kansas City, waiting to find out if I was out of the hospital and out of danger. Malachi believed he was holed up wherever his next victim was located.

Without knowing what alias Patterson was using as his full time identity, it was impossible for either of us to really know. We couldn't track his movements and we didn't know whether Patterson was dirt poor or ungodly wealthy. Our best lead was the crappy identi-kit sketch that made him look like Howdy Doody.

For the first time, I considered that. There were no photos of Patterson. They'd found none in the belongings of his sisters or any of our other family members. His military photo was missing from the records. Even his driver's license photo from before the time he'd killed his wife was gone. Changing your name was easy in comparison to erasing every photo ever taken of you. I wasn't sure how a person could do that.

My book had lost its appeal. I'd been reading a book about Russia in the Middle Ages. It was a good book, but my mind kept interrupting with thoughts of Patterson. Malachi sat across from me at the little table in my room. He was also reading a book. Both of us had jumped on the eBook revolution. Like me, Malachi could read twenty books a week, even with a busy schedule. It was impossible to lug that many books around from chase to chase. Currently, Malachi read on a tablet.

"What are you reading?" I asked, giving up on Russia.

"A book," he replied curtly.

"My mom, Elle and the kids need to go into protective custody," I informed him.

He looked up from his tablet and stared at me blankly for a few moments. I could see his mind running over what I had just said, attempting to figure out the reason why. He put the tablet on the table, face up. He was reading a book about UFOs. This didn't really surprise me.

When we were children, Malachi and his family went on vacation in Arizona. He swore he saw a UFO one night from his hotel room. The next morning, the news was buzzing with stories about a massive disease outbreak on a ranch that had killed almost all the cattle. To Malachi, the two became a single event. In his mind, the UFO had caused the cattle deaths and if they could do that to cattle, they could do that to humans. In our teens, he had tried to convince me that extraterrestrials were responsible for most human plagues throughout history. Becoming an FBI agent had only given him more fodder to support his theory.

This was the real reason I watched shows like Ancient Aliens and UFO Hunters. It gave me a foundation to work from when Malachi started talking about ancient aliens and UFOs. I didn't disbelieve him, but I didn't agree with him. I believed he did see a UFO in Arizona all those years ago. I didn't buy the theory that they were mutilating cattle or spreading plague.

However, it wasn't entirely out of the realm of possibility either. There were lots of things humans just didn't understand yet. One of my medieval history professors had thought the same as Malachi, the Black Death could be explained, but only partially.

"I give up, why does your family need to go into protective custody?" Malachi finally asked.

"If Patterson finds out I'm fine and this was all a ruse, he is going to be pissed. Pissed off serial killers are far more dangerous than just serial killers having a good time." This was true, pissed off serial killers tended to go on sprees. Technically, Patterson was on a spree, but it was a controlled spree. He was finishing his list before he got caught, died or whatever was going to happen when this ended.

"Point taken." Malachi began to type furiously into his phone. "Done. The VCU is moving them now."

"Great," I frowned at him.

"Don't comment on my reading material."

"You're a big boy, you can read whatever you want, Spooky. That is not what I'm thinking about. How did Patterson erase his driver's license photo and his military ID photo?"

"It's been fifty years, they don't check those things very often. Any good hacker could have done it."

"You think my eighty-six year old grandfather is a hacker?"

"No, I think he paid someone to do it."

"Oh," I sighed. "I'm tired of sitting here. We should be doing something, busting down doors and making an arrest."

"You tell me where to go and we'll do exactly that."

"Bah, details." I got up and began to pace the room. "Hasn't our crack forensics team learned anything yet?"

"There was some dirt on the floor, but it could have come from anywhere. Someone showered and left black hairs in the drain, but we expected that. Fingerprints match some cold cases that were already attributed to Patterson. We don't know where he lives or where he gets his money."

"But we know that Joe, Gertrude and August are probably on his hit list."

"So?"

"So, Gertrude and August are in federal custody in Kansas City, but my Uncle Joe is in the Boone County Jail."

"You think Joe is next on his list?" Malachi asked.

"Could be," I shrugged.

"Let me get this straight, he drives to St. Charles, kills three men there. Drives down here to Sikeston, kills the teacher. Now he's making his way back to Columbia? And he started in Kansas City. Why not kill a closer target?"

"Does he have a closer target?"

"I don't know, I don't know who he intends to kill. The list could be six names or it could be six hundred names. We don't know enough about him to make that call. No one does."

"I believe there is one person who does," I replied.

"You want to interrogate Gertrude?" Malachi frowned.

"No. I want you to interrogate her, with your new FBI buddy. I'm just going to watch from a different room."

"Why me?"

"Because you can be scary as hell." I answered. "It's either you or Brent Timmons, but I think letting the Tallahassee Terror interrogate my great-aunt is illegal."

"Why him?" Malachi asked.

"Because, at the moment, I cannot think of any other psychopath who wouldn't mind roughing the old lady up."

"I'm not going to rough up your great-aunt. She might be evil, but we need information, not speculation."

"She is evil." I agreed with another, longer, heavier sigh. "Someone should rough her up."

"I should put my family in protective custody," Malachi suddenly grabbed his phone and started typing furiously again.

"You didn't think of it when I did?" I asked.

"No," Malachi admitted.

I let that drop. Malachi's family was rarely his first thought. They were rarely his second or third thought either. He attended holiday and birthday celebrations with them, called every week to talk to his mother, but it was mostly a courtesy call to let them know he was alive and doing fine. If they spent more than fifteen minutes on the phone together, it was unusual.

"I need air," I announced.

"You may enter the hallway, it's been secured, but you can't leave the floor," Malachi informed me, picking his tablet back up.

Grumbling and rolling my eyes, I entered the hallway. Hotel rooms aren't the worst places on the planet, hotel hallways are. They were always depressing. The lighting was bad, there were peculiar odors, ones even I couldn't identify, but attributed to the mass of people that traversed them and hide behind the locked doors. The carpets were dirty with tracks where the maids ran carts through them every day. Even the walls were dreary, covered in a drab paint that was supposed to be a neutral color.

I leaned against one of these horrid walls, trying to clear my mind. My normal logical mind seemed to have deserted me. I hoped it was temporary.

A short older man walked out of his room, pulling his door shut behind him. The man had dark hair, a touch of gray at the temples, but nothing more. He turned and began walking away from me, a silver handled cane in his hand. Surely it wasn't that easy.

"US Marshal, stop," I ordered. The man kept walking. I shouted the order again, this time louder. The man continued towards the elevator. I had my doubts about him being Patterson, but it wouldn't be the first time I had been stalked up close and personal. I began moving down the hall at a fast walk to catch up with him. He looked over his shoulder just a little and took off.

For an older man, he was quick. I had to push myself into a run, shouting for him to stop. My options were tackle him or Taser him.

Because of his age, I wasn't really sure about Tasering him. The electric shot could trigger heart attacks and nerve damage, with the way mine was set, it would probably cause his heart to explode.

I tackled him, putting my weight into it, we both tumbled to the ground. He kicked and made strange noises. I frowned as I got him flipped over. He did resemble the identi-kit sketch, but I doubted he was Patterson Clachan. The strange noises were him trying to vocalize, probably telling me to get the hell off of him.

Doors were opening and Malachi appeared next to us. I stood up, held out my hand to the poor man I had tackled. He gave me the finger, which I admitted I deserved, and struggled to get up on his own. Malachi reached down and gave the old timer a hand, practically pulling him to his feet.

He gestured wildly at me. I hung my head. Malachi signed back. He'd run because he'd thought I was crazy. He hadn't heard me shouting for him to stop. I had assaulted a deaf man. Now, I was really glad I hadn't Tasered him.

Missing

Patterson sat in his hotel room, pissed at Malachi. He knew he shouldn't be mad at Malachi, it wasn't his fault that the FBI was lying to everyone. He was following orders. It was required for him to keep his job, but he was still angry. Something told him that Aislinn was fine, grandfather's intuition maybe, but Malachi kept answering her phone. If he wanted to talk to Malachi, he'd call Malachi.

As if to confirm his suspicion, a few hours earlier, a van had pulled up in front of Malachi's family's house and ushered the entire group inside. It didn't take a genius to figure out that this was a protective move and that the men and women in masks were part of a federal extraction team.

He cruised the streets, not really looking for anyone. Joe had a scheduled court appearance tomorrow. He would be in attendance, at least for the transport. Last night, he'd readied his spot near the sheriff's department which housed the jail.

Sadly, he wasn't sure what to do with himself in the meantime. He'd considered carrying out another revenge, but that would alert the police to his presence. He'd made an art out of not being discovered. A serial killer couldn't kill for fifty years without learning the art of concealment and moderation.

But as he cruised the streets, he wanted to kill. No, needed to kill. The urges he'd been fighting for over half his life were all he had left. Some people enjoyed weddings and the birth of their grandchildren and if he was being honest with himself, he had enjoyed these events. Without Lila though, they had seemed hollow, like something was missing. Unless someone kidnapped Aislinn Cain and forced her into marriage, those events were also over. She would never willingly marry. She would never have children. If Nyleena lived, she might, but Nyleena was forty. Whatever biological urges she had to reproduce were being overwhelmed by the passage of time.

He stopped at an all-night diner near Broadway. Inside was a varied crowd; drunken college students, old people who couldn't or didn't sleep anymore, and other people that looked tired but unwilling to give into the callings of the Sandman. He ordered a hearty breakfast. Age might have been trying to suck him into the abyss, but he kept himself fit, very fit, meaning he could still indulge in a hearty breakfast once in a while without adding to his waist line.

Another group of drunken students entered the diner. Patterson checked his watch. The bars were just starting to close. He wasn't sure what day it was, he had never been very good at keeping track of them, but he guessed it was a weekend from the number of people in the diner.

Behind the drunken students, a group of younger kids came in from the cold to partake of the after-hours ritual. Patterson watched them all as they found booths and tables. They were loud, annoying. He didn't like young people. They frittered their life away on trivial things; fights about boyfriends and/or girlfriends, partying, trying to be popular. In his eighty-six years, he had discovered none of these things were important. Family was important. Being yourself was important. Being happy was important. Drunken people felt happy, but a chemically induced happiness wasn't the same as real happiness. Popular people often hid who they really were so that everyone would like them, especially girls. And most college students were more interested in their parents' money than their well-being. This last one, could be changed, most grew out of it, but it required them to graduate college and begin their own families for them to appreciate their parents.

He watched all this with annoyance, as he chewed his food, not tasting it or enjoying it. Their presence had ruined it for him. Another girl walked in. This one caught his attention and kept it. Unlike the others, she wasn't boisterous. She wasn't obnoxious. She was demure, moving with hesitating steps as she wound her way to the table of younger kids.

In his mind, he imagined Aislinn and Nyleena had been like that. Hesitant, quiet, unsure of whether socializing was a good thing or not. This last was probably more of an Aislinn trait. She had never been one to socialize. Patterson had been glad when she found Malachi. He wasn't the most stable fellow on the planet, far from it, but he loved her as only a psychopath can love. Patterson had seen all the signs. Malachi had been in love with her from the day she gave him that baseball. Of course, Malachi didn't understand it as love and Aislinn, while she did love him, it wasn't the same sort of love. Sometimes, it irritated Patterson, for as long as Aislinn was alive,

Malachi would never settle down, have a family, know the pleasures that could be gleaned from a stable life. He wasn't mad at Aislinn for this, he was mad at himself. If he hadn't lost control, Aislinn might have been different and then Malachi might have had his happily ever after. Aislinn might have as well.

Unfortunately, he couldn't take it back. Aislinn was who she was. Malachi was who he was.

An argument arose at the table the young girl had just sat down at. It escalated quickly. Another girl grabbed the younger's hair and jerked her head back before punching her in the face. Patterson just reacted, not thinking and came to the defense of the younger lady who reminded him of his precious Aislinn. He grabbed the arm of the aggressive girl and stared at her. She let go and stared back. For a moment, she acted like she might attack Patterson, but something stopped her. She attempted to jerk away, but Patterson was still strong and held her wrist tightly.

"Whatever offense she's committed that you think is worthy of beating her up, is imaginary. In ten years, when you've become an adult, you'll regret this moment. If in ten years, you don't, you haven't really grown up. Picking on weak doesn't make you strong, it makes you weaker than they are," Patterson informed the aggressor.

"Go away, Grandpa," the girl sneered at him.

"Bullies always find someone who is bigger than they are, someone who won't take their nonsense. Are you a bully?" Patterson asked, ignoring her order, and refusing to let her go. The diner staff had now crowded around to watch. It was worth a gaping stare or open mouth. An old man restraining a young woman to keep her from beating up another young woman.

"Old man, let her go," one of the drunkards stood from his table.

"I don't believe this involves you, young man, go back to your food." Patterson shot him a warning glare that the idiot was too drunk to notice. He stepped towards Patterson, sucking in air, flexing muscles to make himself appear bigger. Patterson rapped him smartly on the shoulder with the head of the cane. He stopped, immediately grabbing the injured spot. His wails were loud, his drunken bravado quelled. Patterson rolled his eyes at this display. He was far outdoing it. The love tap wouldn't have done more than leave a small bruise.

Sirens sounded outside. Patterson frowned. He'd just made a huge mistake. If they ran his fingerprints, he was sunk before he got to finish his work. He shouldn't have intervened. He should have let someone else handle it. He let go of the girl's wrist as the first officer came through the door. A man in a cook's uniform began gesturing wildly and pointing. But he didn't point at Patterson, he pointed at the girl Patterson had been holding.

"And the boy?" The cop asked.

"The old man was defending himself and rapped him on the shoulder with his cane," Patterson's waitress told the officer. "I think he's being overly dramatic. He didn't hit him that hard."

"Sir?" Another officer had come in as the waitress had started to speak. He now walked over to Patterson. "Can you tell me what happened?"

"Yes, sir," Patterson smiled and gave a small nod. "This girl," he pointed to the older looking of the two, "grabbed the other by her hair and began hitting her. It seemed unnecessary, so I stepped in. I grabbed her arm to stop her and held it, while the cook called you. As I did, this boy here," Patterson pointed to the still howling college student, "stood up, told me to mind my own business and began advancing on me. He'd puffed up his chest and clenched his fists. I took that to be threatening.

When he got within a foot or so of me, I hit him with the handle of my cane. Not too hard, just enough to make sure he didn't come any closer. I might be able to restrain the wrist of a teenaged girl, but I can't imagine I would fair too well with an older male. I'm too old for that fight."

"I see," the officer looked at him. "Do you have any ID?"

"Of course," Patterson pulled out his wallet and handed a driver's license to the officer. The officer frowned as he read it.

"Mr. Clachan, why are you in town?" This turned some heads in the dinner.

"Please, call me Virgil. I was called by my great-nephew and told about what had happened with our family. So, I drove up from Florida to see if there was anything that needed to be done. I've been hiding from my sister and my brother for years. With both of them now in custody, I figured it was safe to return."

"He's listed as a missing persons," the other officer confirmed. Patterson gave a small chuckle.

"I was never missing, my sister Nina knew where I was, as did one of my brothers, who has sadly passed away. My father sent me to live with relatives, out of the state, in 1935. This is my first time back in the state of Missouri."

"We're still going to have to take you to the station and clear all this up," the second officer handed him back his license.

"Of course," Patterson led the way out the door. As long as they didn't fingerprint him, it would all be ok. "Please make sure the girl who was assaulted gets home safely."

Fourteen

I put my phone down and stared at Malachi in disbelief. He stared back, wanting to ask questions, but waiting for me to offer up the answers he sought. However, I didn't know where to begin. My great-uncle, who had to be older than dirt, had miraculously arrived in Columbia, Missouri and one of my cousins had gone to collect the old man.

The impression had always been that Virgil Clachan was dead. To find him alive and kicking, was a shock. It was even more shocking that someone in the family knew Virgil Clachan wasn't dead.

The story, as I had heard it, was that Virgil had been killed when he was fifteen years old. The manner of death had never been discussed and I had assumed he was killed by someone in the family. To learn that he had been shipped to relatives out of the state because Gertrude, at six years old, had accused him of molesting her was a shock. An even greater shock was that no one believed Gertrude, even then. For the first time, I wished I was closer to someone in my father's family so that I could call them and find out the details. So, I called my mom instead.

"What do you mean Virgil Clachan is alive and in Columbia?" My mother asked after I had told her. Malachi danced in his seat across from me. It was another layer in the sordid Clachan family that he was curious about.

"I mean he was picked up at the Broadway Diner after helping stop a fight and Chub's son, Carl, went to the station and collected him."

"That's not possible." My mother scoffed.

"He told the police that he was sent away because Gertrude made his life miserable, despite being only six years old."

"That I believe. She accused all the boys of molesting her, even Fritz."

"Who's Fritz?" I asked.

"Uncle Chub," my mother answered. So, he did have a first name. That was good to know. "Fritz was the most well-adjusted of the bunch."

"So, why is it impossible?"

"Because Virgil wasn't killed for messing with his sister," my mother stopped. "Trust me, he's dead."

"What do you know?" I asked.

"It's just gossip, honey, but that isn't Virgil. I don't know who he is, but he isn't Virgil."

"Mom."

My mother gave a long, heavy sigh and hung up on me. I stared at my phone. It was always surprising to be hung up by my mother. She was strong, determined, and willing to protect me, but she was also very kind, very easy going and very, well, mom-ish.

"Well?" Malachi asked.

"Mom says it cannot be Virgil."

"The police checked out his story, it all checks out."

"I cannot help that. Mom says Virgil is definitely deceased. I do not know why or how, but she was fairly adamant about it."

Records indicated that Virgil Clachan had started a construction company in 1946 in Las Vegas, Nevada. He'd retired to Florida in the late 1980's. He was worth millions. He'd never married, never had children and my cousin had vouched that he was indeed Virgil Clachan. Malachi pulled something up on his tablet. He turned and showed it to me.

The driver's license picture was of an older man with dark hair, blue eyes and smile lines. His ears were normal sized, his nose was normal sized and while he didn't appear to be 94 years old, that was common in my family. Gertrude looked old because she was frumpy, but even with liver cancer, Nina hadn't looked more than sixty, despite being in her eighties. Dark hair and blue eyes also ran in the family. I stared at the picture for few more minutes and sighed, there was a problem.

"It's not Patterson," I told Malachi.

"Why?"

"I have brown eyes," I answered. "My mom has blue, which means my dad had to have brown. If you look at pictures of my grandmother, she also had blue eyes. That means that Patterson Clachan has brown eyes. However, Uncle Chub, Aunt Nina and Gertrude all had blue eyes, so it does run in the family. The man posing as Virgil has blue eyes, he cannot be Patterson. But if he is not Patterson and he is not Virgil, I do not know who he is."

"Could you have another great uncle you don't know about?"

"No." I answered. "Nina and Gertrude were the youngest. Sometime in the early 1940's, someone walked into my great grandparents' house and shot both of them.

They then took a knife and stabbed my great grandfather seventy-two times. Nina was suspected, she still lived at home, but no one could prove she'd done it. Or find a motive for the killing. Everyone else was married by then. I suspect it was Patterson."

"But are you positive that Nina and Gertrude were the youngest?"

"As positive as I can be."

"Why would he resurface now?" Malachi stretched out his long legs.

"Because Gertrude's in custody. It could bring out lots of whack jobs. Virgil was never found, he was officially listed as a missing person for the last eighty years. The Clachans have money, lots of it, squirreled away in a trust to be used by one generation at a time. With Gertrude in custody, the money would pass to the next generation, but if Virgil is alive, he gets to draw on it. But why would he if he's worth millions?" I thought about that. "And how did the trust get as large as it has gotten? The family was dirt poor during The Depression, they were eating people to get by."

"You want to follow the money?" Malachi asked.

"Yeah, I think I do." I answered. "It seems illogical for there to be money after The Depression, but not before."

Malachi began working on his tablet. He wasn't as good as Michael had been, but he was better than me at using government databases. His fingers swiped the screen, making no noise, just moving quickly. There was something to be said for that, it wasn't nearly as annoying as the clacking of keys on a keyboard.

"Interesting," Malachi leaned back in his chair. "The trust was started in 1942, by a Bernard Clachan."

"He was a great uncle, dead now."

"He started it with nearly $500,000."

"That is a whole lot of money for a soldier. Especially in the '40's."

"It is, but he seems to have used his wages well, investing in the recovering stock market, mostly in munition companies. Then in 1946, regular deposits start getting made by none other than Virgil Clachan. At first, the amounts are small, a thousand here, two thousand there, but after 1957, the amounts start getting much larger, $200,000 or so at a time. Then Fritz begins making deposits during the 1970's after investing in a start-up department store. It seems he got in on the ground floor. The conditions of the trust are as such, money is doled out to people over fifty-five, anyone disabled, or a one-time withdraw can be made with two approved signatures for anyone in the family. So, if you needed money, let's say $300,000 you could get it, if you got two of your cousins to sign off on it." Malachi shook his head. "Virgil is well off, but there's about a hundred million dollars in this family trust. And other people have been making donations as well, including Nyleena, most of your cousins, and your mother. It actually looks like a tithing. Everyone seems to be donating ten percent of their yearly income."

"Wow," I settled into a chair and thought about that. "Does Patterson have access?"

"No."

"So, that's not how he's getting his money."

"I think we should pay your Great Uncle Virgil a visit. We'll get you released from the hospital and head to Columbia. Maybe he can shed some light on Patterson."

"In 1935, Patterson was nine years old."

"And Nina said he was already a killer."

"Huh," I hadn't considered that. "There's the motive for the murder of my great grandparents, although it kind of eliminates Patterson as a suspect."

"Yes, and it makes Nina the prime suspect again."

"All things considered, maybe patricide was not such a bad thing in this case. If he was using Patterson to kill the farm hands, it would sort of justify someone killing him."

"Why not kill him at the time?"

"Because they were all too young. Virgil was the oldest and he was born in 1920. Chub and Bernard were next, then a girl I don't know, then Patterson, then the twins; Gertrude and Nina."

"What unknown girl?" Malachi asked.

"She died when she was only a year or so old," I told Malachi. "I do not even know her name."

"That's a lot of kids in eight years."

"There are a few with less than a year between them. Bernard and Chub were ten months apart. The girl and Patterson were only eleven months apart. I think there was sixteen months between Bernard and the girl."

"Why'd they stop after the twins?" Malachi asked.

"Female problems arose," I shrugged having no idea what that meant, but that's what I had been told.

"Well, Virgil would be in his nineties. We should go before he keels over."

"Bernard was in his nineties," I frowned. "The ages do not line up. Virgil cannot be the oldest, Chub was in his eighties when he died and I was a teen then. Bernard died of complications from surgery a few years ago. What the hell?"

"A case of misdirection? Who told you how old everyone was?"

"Nina," I sighed. "Ok, so Bernard was in his nineties when he died. Chub was in his eighties. They would have to be the oldest boys and at least one would have had to have been born before 1920."

"Your family is an enigma."

"My family is the epitome of dysfunction. They hide everything, reveal only a few tantalizing clues, and leave the rest to the imagination. See if someone can find birth records on them."

"I'm not your flunky."

"Fine, see if Rollins can find birth records on them. We should probably fly to Columbia, we've already wasted a lot of time here."

Fifteen

It seemed unfair that my great uncle Chub had named his child Carl Christopher Clachan. However, he had. Carl was older, like a lot older. It had never dawned on me how much older Carl seemed to be than my father. I'd say there was a good ten years between them, if not more.

He was in his seventies, frail with a slight build. Short with almost no hair, but what was left, hadn't lost its color. My dad's family didn't seem to age. Very few went bald, even fewer had grey hair, their faces had lines, but not wrinkles, few became stooped and bent with time, even terminal liver cancer hadn't aged Nina more than a few years.

Next to him sat an even older man. This was theoretically, my great uncle Virgil. He had dark hair, not black, but a deep, rich brown that could pass for black in the right lighting. His eyes were a shocking blue, almost like a husky's eyes, but this was a genetic trait carried in my family, several people had blue eyes or very light blue eyes. The family seemed attracted to others with blue eye as well, people like my mother and my grandmother. His face and hands had a few liver spots on them, but that was to be expected. My mind was trying to impose what we knew about Patterson and draw conclusions of his looks based on Virgil's bone structure and facial features.

"You look like him," Virgil said to me.

"Like who?" I asked.

"Patterson," Virgil answered. "More than I thought you would." Rollins was standing near us. Malachi and I had taken seats, Rollins had insisted on standing.

"I don't suppose you have a picture of Patterson?" Malachi asked.

"No one has a picture of Patterson," Virgil answered. "The boy was camera shy, the man was camera phobic. If they hadn't needed soldiers as bad as they did, he wouldn't have been able to enlist. As I understand it, when they went to take his picture, he had a meltdown. Eventually, they gave up on getting his picture and just shipped him overseas to die with the rest of the foot soldiers."

"But he did not die," I pointed out.

"No, like his brothers, he turned out to be a survivor. They all came back from the war a little off, but I understand that was common. Patterson and Bernard both served in companies that liberated a few concentration camps. The horrors they saw. Patterson wouldn't talk about it, Bernard eventually did though."

"You've been in contact with all your brothers?" I asked.

"Until their deaths, yes. For a time, I even stayed in contact with Patterson, but after the incident with Lila, the communications stopped. I figured he had gone off into the woods and killed himself. I was surprised to find out he didn't. I think my brothers knew this though."

"You think your brothers knew?" Rollins asked.

"Fine, I know they did. Patterson may be a killer, but he isn't the only one. I'm not excusing what he's done, I just know that under the circumstances, it's more surprising the rest of us weren't serial killers."

"Are you talking about Nina?" I asked.

"No, Bernard killed our parents." Virgil sighed and took a drink of a glass of tea. His hands shook just a little. "He came home on leave for some reason, probably mental health and realized our parents were Nazi sympathizers. That didn't sit well with him.

They argued and Bernard discovered that our father was also a member of the Ku Klux Klan. He lost it. After what he had seen in Europe, he couldn't believe his parents were like that. So, he killed them. You can call it a mercy killing if you want. It saved Nina. It might have saved Patterson if it had been done a few years earlier. If Bernard hadn't killed them, someone would have eventually. Our father was a brutal son of a bitch. During The Depression, Fritz had something to say about our diet and our father took him out to the barn and nearly beat him to death. After that, we never spoke about our food source again. We had a sister named Abigail. She got sick when she was a year old, the doctors were slow to make a diagnosis, so he threw her off the second floor landing. She died. He said it was to keep the rest of us from getting it. There was also another brother, one before Chub was born, that he killed because the boy was slow. Since our mother gave birth at home, with the help of relatives, most of us weren't even registered as being born until we were a few years old. Back in those days, before the government decided to track us, less records were kept."

"Who was the oldest?" I asked.

"Of those that survived or everyone?" Virgil asked.

"Everyone," I frowned.

"Bernard, the slow boy, Chub, another boy, me, Abigail, Abigail's twin who died at birth, Patterson, Gertrude and Nina, also twins, and another baby, but that baby died in the womb and mom had to have a hysterectomy afterwards."

"When was Bernard really born?" I asked.

"During The Spanish Flu outbreak. However, his birth certificate was switched with the boy our father killed, so it looked like he was born in 1920. He was 20 when he enlisted, but his birth certificate said he was 18. Chub was born in 1921. I was born in 1923. Patterson in 1926. The twins in 1929."

"I thought Patterson was eighty-six." Rollins stated.

"That depends on who you ask," Virgil answered. "He was born in 1926, but his birth certificate says 1928. Our father couldn't keep track of time and didn't register us until it was time for us to start school. He got the months, days and years wrong on all of us. You have to remember, Columbia might have been a city, but Hoop-Up was twelve miles from it. We didn't own a car until after The Depression, the only one that did was one of my dad's brothers. He took care of the stuff that had to be done in town. My father didn't even like coming to Columbia. Hoop-Up didn't have a registrar, occasionally someone came out to do the census, but that was it. It was still rural in the 1920's and 1930's."

"So Patterson is really eighty-eight." I shook my head.

"Yes," Virgil answered. "My brother Fritz started using Chub when World War II broke out, because Fritz was a Germanic name. You know, there was another reason for Bernard to kill our parents. During The Depression, dad made Patterson do a lot of the killings. Bernard didn't like that. He ignored the fact that we were eating people, but he didn't like our father using Patterson as the killer. Bernard and he went at it, each landing blows. Our mother stepped in and Bernard accidentally hit her. She pulled a gun on him, actually shot him in the arm, and then dug the bullet out herself. Dad stuck a wooden stake through it, making sure it hurt as much as possible and told Bernard if he ever lashed out against either of them again, he'd kill him."

"If your father was a killer why use Patterson?" Malachi asked.

"Because if they'd been caught, they wouldn't have given Patterson the death penalty because he was so young." Virgil answered.

"Why stay gone so long?" I asked.

"Gertrude was a horrible child and grew up to be a horrible woman. She may not be directly responsible for anyone's death, but she contributed to more than a few murders. She's manipulative in ways you'd never understand." Virgil answered. "That woman is about the most vile, evil bitch on the planet. Satan himself is more merciful."

I stared at the man proclaiming to be my uncle for a long time without saying a word. He didn't look a day over sixty. He was physically fit with a slight limp. If he wasn't a Clachan, I'd eat my hat. Exactly what Clachan was the part I couldn't figure out. He wasn't Patterson. Patterson didn't have a limp or liver spots or the scar that I could see on this man's face. My mother swore he wasn't Virgil, but did she really know? Virgil had disappeared long before my mother married into the family. I'd gone to the funerals of Bernard and Chub, while I wasn't close with Bernard, I did know him well enough to know that it had been his corpse in his coffin. He had a slight accent that reminded me of the west coast.

"Ok, I think we're done," I stood up. "It was a pleasure to meet you Virgil. Good to see you again, Carl."

We walked out with something nagging at me. Something that gave me pause because I still couldn't figure out what it was. I turned back and looked at Carl one last time before getting in the SUV. He looked like Chub, slimmer, but definitely a resemblance. As I climbed into the backseat, I took a moment to look at myself in the mirror. He'd said I looked like Patterson.

"Malachi?" I asked.

"What?" He turned in the seat.

"Do I look like my mom or my dad?"

"Mostly like your dad. Your sister looked like your mom. Eric and you though look like Clachans."

"What about Nyleena?"

"Nyleena looks like your mom."

"What would happen if we replaced Patterson's nose and ears with ears more like mine?"

"It would look odd. Maybe if we used your dad's features or Eric's, but not yours."

"Why not mine? Virgil said I looked like Patterson."

"And you might, to some degree, but your features are more feminine. Your ears are smaller, your nose has been broken a lot, and you've developed a small droop in your left eye from nerve damage. The nose is the only thing

~ 183 ~

noticeable," Malachi added quickly. "The eye thing is only perceptible when you've known you as long as I have."

"My memories of my dad are fuzzy. I remember Uncle Chub better, but all I can say is that he sort of looks like Virgil in my memory."

"Bernard, Chub, Virgil, they all looked similar, except the eyes. Bernard had hazel eyes," Malachi informed me.

"Huh," I sat back and stared out the window. I wanted to call my mom again, but I was pretty sure that without torturing her, she wasn't going to give me the information I wanted. I couldn't torture my mother. Even I had lines that couldn't be crossed.

Sixteen

Rollins was tucked into his bed, tired from the day. His snoring penetrated the flimsy walls of my motel room. Malachi was watching TV. It had taken twenty minutes for me to find the show on my own TV, *Monsters and Mysteries in America*. I'd turned it off when I discovered the episode was covering the Dogmen of Michigan, the Beast of Bray Road and the wendigo. Normally, I would be curious by exactly this sort of thing, but after hearing Gabriel's story, it bothered me.

Besides, I had other things on my mind. Something about my Great Uncle Virgil had just been off. I had yet to figure out exactly what it was. I'd tried distraction, thinking if I took my mind off of it, it would come to me, but it hadn't. So, now I stared at the ceiling, tucked under my own covers, snug in a pair of pajamas, with my house shoes still on and my hair still pulled up from the day. Despite being in bed, I wasn't ready to sleep. My mind was still struggling over Virgil's sudden reappearance.

My phone told me the time. It was after midnight. I dialed my mother anyway. She answered.

"Are you in trouble?"

"I need to know why this cannot be Virgil Clachan."

"Aislinn," my mother sighed. "Because Nina told me that Virgil had been killed by his father."

"That's what Virgil told me too." I sighed. "After Gertrude accused him of molesting her."

"Gertrude supposedly made those claims against all the boys. Nina said it was because Virgil was still trying to practice cannibalism after The Depression ended."

"Thanks mom, go back to bed."

I hung up. Virgil had still been practicing cannibalism. What the hell was wrong with my family? Serial killing cannibals seemed to be a common event, with the exception of Patterson. Patterson was so scarred from the experience that he couldn't butcher an animal, let alone eat one. How that fit in with him being a serial killer was still in limbo, the two seemed contradictory. Malachi was right, my family was the poster child for monsters in the making.

Was that it? Was it that simple? Was Virgil a psychopath and that was why he set off alarm bells? It definitely was part of it. However, I'd spent most of my life in the company of a psychopath. That shouldn't have been enough.

I kept trying to convince my overactive imagination that it was because he'd just reappeared after all this bad stuff had happened in the family. That was the most logical part of the entire thing though. I had rushed to Nyleena's side. With Gertrude in custody, Nina dead, and Patterson a wanted man, he was the only one of his generation left. Also, he'd been donating money to the trust fund for years.

It was one more thing that ruled out Patterson. Patterson hadn't been in California in the 1940's. He hadn't gone on the run until a decade later.

My memory replayed the meeting. Carl and Virgil's faces were both gone, my memory unable or unwilling to remember them. They were faceless shadows of men in my mind.

There it was, just a little thing. He hadn't offered to shake hands with Malachi or myself, yet he had shaken hands with Rollins. Malachi and I rarely shook hands. I was a bit of a germophobe and Malachi was certain anyone who wanted to shake his hand was just looking for excuse to have him extend his arm so they could insert a knife between his ribs. To anyone else, this might seem paranoid, to me, it made perfect sense. However, in our society, a handshake had significance. To ignore the handshake was not just impolite, it was downright unacceptable.

Malachi's TV went off. Footsteps moved across his room. Obviously, being on the FBI's budget wasn't as good as being on the US Marshals' budget. The motel was a dump. It wouldn't surprise me to find out it rented by the hour. I'd heard rumors about it during my childhood.

There was a knock on my door. I pulled my gun and went to the door. Opening the door with gusto was a specialty of mine. My mind conjured up horror images when I considered looking through the peephole; like someone stabbing me in the eye or firing a bullet into my brain. Neither of these were acceptable scenarios in my opinion, so I never looked through them.

Malachi stood in front of it. His body obscuring the view behind him. I ushered him into the room.

"You should be sleeping," he told me.

"So should you. What's up?" I asked.

"Tomorrow, we're moving to a different hotel. This place is horrid. I can't imagine what a forensics team would find if they came in with luminal and a black light."

"I have some Lysol with me. It stinks, but I do have some."

"Not everyone's nose is as a good as yours."

"Is that why you don't enjoy food like I do?" I asked.

"Yes."

"Hey, one last question," I began moving around, grabbing my bag and digging out the Lysol. "What do you see when you look in the mirror?"

"What do you see when you look in the mirror?"

"I'm serious."

"I know." Malachi frowned. "I see a reflection. I know it's me, but I don't feel connected to it."

"Me either. Sometimes I look at it, confused for a few moments, thinking that maybe it's not a reflection, but someone looking back at me from inside the mirror. Do you have trouble with dates?"

"Like romantic dates or time?"

"Time," I clarified.

"Yes. I have alarms set to remind me of important things like holidays and birthdays. I can't even tell you what today is."

"Virgil or the man pretending to be Virgil, I have not made up my mind about that yet, said that my great-grandfather had trouble with dates."

"From that you think he's a psychopath?"

"No, it's just another piece of the puzzle. He obviously had rage issues. The inability to keep track of time adds strength to the theory. How many mentally deranged humans do you think my family could create?"

"Dozens. Patterson, Virgil, and Gertrude were probably more nurture than nature, but Ian wasn't. Your dad wasn't. You were, to some degree. Some of your cousins have the hallmarks of having anti-social personality disorder. Is that what's keeping you awake?"

"No, Motel Hell is keeping me awake. I do not feel secure here."

"Do you want to bunk with me or vice-versa?"

"Nope," I answered. "I think I feel safer alone."

"Suit yourself," Malachi looked at me. "How many sets of pajamas do you actually have?"

"I do not know, they take up three drawers in my dresser." I answered, closing the door on him. Malachi's interest in my pajamas wasn't all that unsettling. He slept nude, I imagined he didn't understand sleeping in pajamas.

With my room empty, I went back to thinking about Virgil. This was going to be a stumbling block for me. I needed to know what he knew about Patterson. If Virgil could give us some insight, it might help us find my grandfather. Just thinking about the word "grandfather" made me feel weird. Here I was, knee deep in blood and all because of my own grandfather. A grandfather who had become a stalker in order to be close to me. In some ways, his humanity was showing through that. I believed him about Nyleena, I believed he had not meant to shoot her in the face. This didn't mean I wasn't going to rough him up when putting him in a car, but it did mean I wouldn't kill him. Besides, Malachi wouldn't let me kill him anyway.

Of course, I could use the super-Taser to put him out of commission for a few moments. It wouldn't take but a few moments. After I thought that, I had to reconsider it. Patterson was strong. He'd taken out a sniper. He'd literally beat the man to death. It might take both Malachi and me to subdue him, and that would be nightmarish.

There was only one thing I could do; take a nice hot shower. Few things could beat a hot shower and it was a great place to solve riddles. The noises from Malachi's room had stopped. Like Lucas, he could instantly fall asleep and instantly become awake. I envied that ability. It was rare that I spent less than two hours falling asleep. Showers occasionally helped, but normally if I was going to fall asleep fast, it required an injury. I hadn't been seriously injured in months. As a result, I hadn't been sleeping well. For the last unknown number of days, I wasn't sure I was sleeping at all.

The shower might have lasted five minutes. The water never got hot. I wrapped up in a towel and flipped on the hair dryer. The blast of hot air felt good on my chilled skin. I was prone to cold-induced pain. Something about all the injuries creating nerve damage, not in my skin, but in my brain. As a result, it liked to think cold sensations were actually physical pain. Sticking my hand in a cooler was a form of torture.

Flipping my hair forward, I dried the underside first. Cold induced pain could even be triggered by cold droplets of water. I didn't know whether to classify my hair as long or short. It went below my shoulders but didn't touch the small of my back. It did hold a lot of water and it would cascade in rivulets before beginning to drip down my flesh. It was these that I hoped to prevent with the hair dryer.

With my hair mostly dry and my pajamas back on my body, I exited the bathroom. Instantly, I knew something was wrong. I hadn't turned off the lights, but someone had. I reached for a gun and realized I'd left them on the table. I opened my mouth to scream and felt a jolt of pain run through me. My body went rigid. My muscles seized up. Maybe I didn't like my new Taser all that much after all.

Seventeen

How many serial killers could exist in a town of 100,000 people? I was beginning to think it was a lot more than anyone had ever expected. Less than two weeks ago, we had taken one off the grid, putting him in federal custody. Patterson Clachan had claimed a second. Now, I was positive I was in the grasp of a third.

There were several clues. I awoke in a basement, chained to an antique dental chair. There were copious amounts of dried blood on the cement floor. There were several jars of fingers in various states of decay. The place had a strong smell of death and I was guessing the floor was covered in more than just blood. I didn't think about what was in the chair, I'd throw up. This killer wasn't huge on hygiene. However, the final clue was the guy sitting in front of me in a folding chair. He clapped when he saw that I was awake.

Even with serial killers, a good glare from me is enough to stifle some of their enthusiasm. This was not the case with this guy. He smiled wider.

The chains holding me weren't that well wrapped. I had some room for movement. However, they went around my waist, wrapping several times, fastening me to the chair. This meant that unless he was going to decapitate me or killing me quickly some other way, there was a good chance the chains were coming off.

My would-be killer's clothes were filthy. He smelled of body odor and rotting food. His pupils were dilated far too wide. His teeth were a mess. There was a chemical scent to the body odor. If this guy wasn't on meth, I would have to reevaluate my intelligence level.

He wasn't my first meth head serial killer, just the first that had managed to capture me. I'm guessing the motel was a normal hunting grounds for the guy. I would definitely be speaking with Rollins when I got out of this place.

"What's with the fingers?" I asked, attempting to engage the guy. He wasn't going to be intimidated by me, especially while he had me chained up. Most drug addled killers couldn't be intimidated like normal serial killers.

"Fingers, fingers, fingers," he giggled. "I like fingers. Crunchy. Crunchy. Crunchy. Like pretzel sticks. Fingers. Crunchy."

"Oh boy," I said.

This was going to be interesting. I got the impression that he didn't enjoy eating the fingers. If he did, they wouldn't be decaying in jars. For some reason, this guy just liked to keep the fingers. It was about more than trophies. The decay indicated that he had taken them in and out of the jars. Or that the jars contained nothing more than water. Even the most unstable serial killers knew better than to store their trophies in water for preservation purposes.

If I was going to go up against a meth addict, I was going to need to rethink my game plan. I had no weapons and the basement didn't seem to hold much except the jars of fingers and the shelves they sat on. Unfortunately, the shelves were obviously a meth induced DIY project. They were made of cheap pressed wood, cannibalized from other things. The shelves weren't the same sizes and some of them were so unlevel that the jars had slid to one side.

Decaying fingers in jars weren't exactly a great weapon either. The jars might be useful, but I wasn't all that interested in shredding my hands wielding pieces of broken glass against this guy. I didn't know if he was in the high stage or moving to the tweaking stage. One was a lot more problematic than the other. If he was high, he'd be easier to overpower. His lack of actual, coherent sentences though, lead me to believe he was moving out of this stage.

The tweak comes before the crash. It's the period during which a meth addict is the most dangerous. They have hallucinations and their aggression level rises. This is also the stage when they enter a full psychotic break with reality. One of the side effects for a non-psychopath in a psychotic break, was the inability to register pain. I'd be dealing with a rage-fueled version of Malachi. Despite the fact that I occasionally baited him into exactly those sorts of situations, they were situations I could control, because I had created them. That was not the same as this guy.

My assessment of the basement had taken only a few seconds. But they were precious seconds. The idiot in front of me began to massage my hand. He didn't have a weapon in his hands and while the chains weren't exactly tight, they weren't loose enough for me to punch him either.

"What's your name?" I asked.

"Name? Name. Names. Many names. So many names. To go with the fingers. Names. What's your name?"

I frowned at him. He was bending down, leaning his face close to me. His breath moved across my hand. His mouth opened and he sucked two of my fingers into his mouth. He stopped, releasing the tainted digits and grinned. His hands attempted to undo the chain that held my arm to the chair. As it released, I understood exactly how he removed the fingers and exactly how to get out of my current predicament.

He sucked both fingers back into his mouth again. I had no idea what sort of germs this guy might be carrying. I would need antibiotics when I escaped. I would need a tetanus shot and maybe an update on several other vaccines.

Most people's instinct would be to try and pull their fingers straight out of the offensive orifice. As his teeth scraped my skin, this was not my instinct. I flexed my fingers, curling them at the middle knuckles. Pressure increased on the skin, but it was more because of my own movements. My short fingernails scraped his tongue and he moved them more out of reflex than pain. However, it made room for my fingers against the back of his front teeth and the bottom of his mouth.

The bottom of the mouth is an interesting spot. It's sensitive to touch, because aside from chewed foods and liquids almost nothing ever touched it. Unchewed food tended not to slip below the tongue. There is also very few layers of skin between the outside and the jaw bone. As a result, no one liked to have it touched.

My fingers pressed down against it and the pressure from his upper teeth lessened. It increased on the bottom. I felt both of them break against my finger bones. I was definitely going to need some serious medications. I pressed harder, forcing his head down. He fell out of the chair, struggling to get away from me. In his intoxicated state, this was easier said than done. I struggled against the chains while digging my nails into the thin skin of his front jaw.

He jerked away. My fingers still had his teeth in them. I balled my hand into a fist and punched him regardless, feeling the teeth bury themselves deeper into my skin. He stood and I punched him again. The blows were strong, landing squarely on his jaw and then his cheekbone. Something in my hand crunched. Pain shot up my hand, but I could ignore the broken bones.

My struggling and aggressive movements were freeing me from the chains. My bottom moved easier in the chair. Without thinking, I began moving my legs, loosening the chain even more. I now realized that it was a single, large chain. Using my broken hand, I grabbed the chain and punched the meth head in the face again. This time I was rewarded by the sound of his bone breaking.

He fell to the ground and rolled for a few moments. He was more stunned than hurt and I knew this. There was only a few moments to completely remove my restraints. As I worked to release my legs, he got back up. He grabbed my other free hand, this time putting three of my fingers in his mouth. This guy had a real thing about fingers. I couldn't punch him with my hand in his mouth. The force would have been devastating to me. I repeated my earlier movements, curling my fingers and pressing down. The broken hand finally freed my legs. I stood, keeping hold of his lower jaw. Now though, I had leverage. I put my thumb on the underside of his jaw and began to pull outwards as well as pressing down.

His jaw dislocated with a satisfying pop. His hands flailed wildly around us, not connecting with anything. Noises emanated from his throat, but without his jaw working, they weren't articulated.

There was a wet sucking noise. Warm liquid rushed over my hand, filling his mouth with blood. My gaze found his smile unnaturally widened. I removed my fingers.

Removing his jaw seemed to have an effect on him. He lay on the floor, his hands clawing at his face. I kicked him in the face, feeling his jaw shatter beneath my boot. All the facial damage and bleeding was taking its toll on him. I found the stairs and began climbing them. He attempted to follow, but the stairs were a hindrance. It was like he couldn't figure out how to go up them. I made it to the top, closed the door behind me, and shoved a large dresser in front of it. Where this guy had gotten a dresser or why he had decided to put it in the hall was beyond me. Not that it mattered at the moment.

There was a phone in the kitchen. I grabbed it and called Malachi.

"Special Agent Blake," his voice sounded strained.

"You let me get kidnapped by a serial killer. What the hell is wrong with you?" I shouted into the phone.

"Oh my god, are you ok?" Malachi asked.

"No! The bastard is a meth head and tried to bite off my fingers."

"Where are you?"

"That is a great question. I'm in the kitchen of a meth head who likes to bite off fingers. That's where I am."

"Go outside and see if you see any street signs."

"I know what to do. How could I be twenty feet from you and still get kidnapped by a serial killer? An unorganized tweaking serial killer on top of that!" There was a loud bang at the door.

"What was that? Aislinn, get out of the house!" Malachi shouted.

"Un-fucking-fathomable," I said as the dresser toppled over and the door opened enough for the killer to begin squeezing through.

"Aislinn!"

"Track the damn call." I set the phone down on the counter, leaving it off the hook. The killer was now in the hallway, attempting to get over the overturned dresser. I shook my head. The guy was more zombie than human at this point. I walked over and kicked him in the forehead. He went down. His chest rose and fell, his hand twitched, his leg jerked. He was alive, but his time was limited if he didn't get to a hospital. I picked the phone back up. "Send an ambulance."

"Are you ok?" I heard Malachi ask. I ignored him. My rage was still up. The darkness still engulfed me. I hadn't even realized it was there until now. Realizing it didn't make it go away. I stood in the kitchen, watching the killer bleed, and waiting for the cavalry.

Eighteen

Rollins came through the door first. Paramedics were close behind him. One tended to me, three others dealt with the drug addict I'd beaten up. Malachi came in last, very last, even after the uniformed officers.

"My Taser?" I asked. "Is it here?"

"No, it's in your luggage. I got part of a license plate." Malachi told me.

"Great, it did me no good, but I appreciate the effort." I snipped at him.

The moment we were alone, I was going to kick his ass too. There was a good chance Rollins was going to feel a little bit of my wrath as well. Malachi hadn't been the only one twenty feet away. If it had been the SCTU, I wouldn't have had to try to rip the jaw off the killer.

"You have teeth in your fingers," the paramedic told me. "And I'm positive the hand is broken."

I looked at my hand. It was swollen and turning colors. My fingers looked deformed and crooked. The hand itself was also misshapen, looking clubbed.

"The reconstructive surgeon can remove the teeth." I told him. "Can I get a tetanus booster and do you guys give hepatitis boosters? What other things might I need? Antivirals? Antibiotics? He's a speed freak. What sort of diseases are common in speed freaks?"

"Uh, you'll be treated, he'll be tested. If you've had your hepatitis shots, you don't need boosters. When was your last tetanus booster?"

"I do not know, probably in July."

"Then you don't need one."

"Can I have one just in case?"

"No." The paramedic told me.

"Are you sure?"

"Tetanus is the least of your worries. Methamphetamine users are more likely to carry hepatitis, HIV, AIDS, and a whole list of bacterial infections. You'll be given antibiotics quickly, both a large dose and an IV drip. The teeth give you a secondary pathway for infection. Since you crushed your hand, it could be a difficult recovery. They are going to have to do surgery to repair it, thereby increasing your risk for infection that much more."

"Great. Killed by gangrene and hepatitis."

"Are you a hypochondriac?" The paramedic asked.

"No." I answered.

"No, she's a germophobe." Malachi gave a twisted grin.

"When my hand heals, I'm going to break your nose." I told him.

"I look forward to it," Malachi wiggled his eyebrows at me. I sighed. Sometimes, dealing with Malachi was a losing battle. I was still pissed at him and Rollins. However, I was beginning to think Rollins deserved the brunt of my anger. It had been him that put us in that crappy motel and made me a vulnerable target.

They put the killer on a gurney and began to wheel him out. I looked around the house for the first time. It was amazingly well kept for a meth head. There was furniture. Usually, most drug addicts sold their furniture to buy drugs.

"What's the deal with this place?" I asked.

"We're checking on it," Rollins finally spoke to me.

"Hmmm," I looked at him. It was probably a good thing my Taser was in my luggage.

"What?" Rollins asked.

"I'm Tasering you in my head because I do not actually have one. When I get out of the hospital, I expect to be put in a real hotel, one with security measures." I told him.

"Noted," Rollins looked away and decided to go busy himself somewhere away from me.

"Ready?" The paramedic asked.

"I suppose."

"There are reporters outside already." Malachi looked at me. "And they're asking why the SCTU didn't realize there was a second serial killer at work when they were here last week."

"Good lord, it has only been a week?" I heaved an even heavier sigh. I wanted to sleep. Being anesthetized wasn't ideal, one day I'd go under and not wake up, but I slept well when I was under. There were no dreams on anesthesia. "Unwrap my hand."

"I can't do that. It shouldn't be exposed to air."

"It will give the reporters a good story and give us an edge." I looked pointedly at Malachi.

"I'd do as she says." He nodded.

The paramedic unwrapped the hand he'd just bandaged. He wasn't happy about it and his slow movements ensured I knew it. When the hand was unwrapped, I looked at Malachi.

Blood no longer dripped from the wounded fingers. This was a problem. The press liked blood. Patterson would freak out when he saw it. Scabs had formed over the teeth. To the horror of the paramedic, I picked them off. The blood began to flow again.

"What are you doing?" The paramedic began searching through his supplies.

"Don't worry, you can do all that in the ambulance. Although, I'll probably scab over again by the time you get around to wrapping it again. I clot fast."

"Ready?" Malachi asked. I nodded. Our superiors were not going to be very happy with us. I was about to give an impromptu press conference to bait Patterson Clachan.

"Marshal Cain!" "Special Agent Blake!" Voices overlapped as a group of about six reporters stood outside on the sidewalk, shouting at us. My dealings with the press had not always been good, as a matter of fact, I'd say they had all gone terribly awry. I hoped this one didn't spiral into another press-related nightmare.

"I'll give a short statement, no questions," Malachi took control. I stood beside him, letting the blood drip from my fingers onto the ground. Reporters were having a hard time looking at me. "In the early morning hours, someone broke into Marshal Cain's motel room and Tasered her. He then abducted her and brought her here. She managed to fight him off and escape to a telephone at which time she contacted the FBI. We arrived on scene and Agent Rollins took control. This is his investigation. The VCU and SCTU are consulting on another case at this time, it was a coincidence that Marshal Cain was abducted. I want to repeat that. In no way is this case related to our current case. The SCTU and VCU did not miss a second serial killer working in Columbia as is being reported. There is no evidence that this man is a serial killer. There is evidence that he is a drug user and that Marshal Cain was abducted because of the suspect's drug addiction. More information will be released in the coming days, as we learn it."

"Marshal Cain!" A woman yelled at me, thrusting a microphone towards me. "Did you rip the suspect's jaw off?"

"It is impossible to rip off a person's jaw," I lied. It could be done. I had almost done it. The tearing sound of his flesh had stopped me.

"How did you escape?" A man yelled at me.

"I fought him off."

"No, how did you escape?" The man repeated the question. I couldn't tell the press

I'd nearly ripped his lower jaw off and beaten him with a chain.

"I just told you."

"What was he going to do to you?" A different man asked. I sighed and glared at him. He moved away from the front.

"I said no questions," Malachi bellowed. "We will give you information as it becomes available. Now, Marshal Cain needs to go to the hospital. We ask you to respect her privacy during this time. Agent Rollins will be giving a statement after we have learned more."

Malachi touched me. His hand on the small of my back. It was a gesture for the press. We both knew how to stage a good story. They'd be confused about whether to write about the possibility of a romantic entanglement between the SCTU and the VCU or the possible serial killer. It would be harder since instinct told me that the victims were probably the "disposable" part of humanity; prostitutes, drug users, and the homeless. The press didn't cover these stories very often, they had more salacious stories on the burners.

I entered the ambulance. The paramedic immediately went to work on my hand. The bleeding had indeed stopped.

They ran the sirens all the way to the hospital. We ended up at Boone Hospital. I was rushed in and given immediate attention. A doctor came in only minutes after my arrival. He frowned at me.

"What did you do?" He asked.

"I beat a killer with a large chain wrapped around my fist. Although, I'm fairly certain I broke the hand before I wrapped it in the chain. When you X-ray it, you're going to find teeth embedded in my fingers. I'm a heavy clotter and scabs have formed over the wounds. I'd like to get those out as soon as possible as well as starting on antibiotics. I do not know what sort of bacteria grow in the mouths of drug addicts."

"I'll give you a local and peel off the scabs," the doctor told me.

"No need," I answered. My hand was having difficulty unclenching on its own. Malachi took hold of my wrist, as I used my other hand to uncurl the fingers. It hurt, but I'd endured worse. Once my hand was open, I peeled the scabs off for a second time. The nurse left the room. I think it was the noises involved in opening my hand. The doctor frowned even harder at me, but said nothing. Malachi let go of my wrist. "Thanks."

"You'd do the same for me." He said.

"No, I would actually open your hand for you." I told him.

"I had considered that." Malachi admitted.

The doctor brought our attention back to him by clearing his throat. A new nurse came into the room. She had a tray with different torture devices that I recognized as medical tools.

"We really should give you a local." The doctor told me.

"It will take ten minutes for full effect. I want these out now. Like three hours ago now. I can take the pain, I cannot take having the teeth in my fingers. I feel like they are burying themselves deeper into my flesh as we speak. They're like parasites, boring into me. We do not have time for a local and I do not care about scars. Just get them out, please."

"Ok," the doctor sighed and took hold of my hand. "You know, I could be doing more damage to your hand, right?"

"It will be fine."

"What if they aren't teeth, what if they're bones?" The doctor asked.

"Then they are not my bones. The teeth broke off and lodged in my hand before I began beating the suspect with a chain."

"Oh," the doctor got a weird look on his face. "The hospital is buzzing with info that a law enforcement officer nearly ripped the jaw off someone."

"How? He went to University Hospital." Malachi said.

"Doctors talk, especially about things like this."

"Yes, it was me, he tried to bite off my fingers, so I dug them into his mouth, breaking off his teeth into my flesh and then I forced him to let go by nearly ripping off his jaw. Now take the teeth out of my fucking hand!"

"Calm down," the doctor told me. "Do you want a sedative? You've been through quite the ordeal."

"No, I want you to remove the teeth from my hand. Then I want you to X-ray my hand, figure out how many bones are broken and if it can be fixed, then I want someone to fix it to the best of their ability and then I want to go back to work and catch the serial killer I'm actually after and not some speed freak who likes to bite off people's fingers!"

The doctor let go of my hand and backed away from me. Malachi touched my shoulder. His face was hard.

"You are going into a full psychotic episode. You need to take a breath." Malachi told me.

"I am not." I answered.

"Yes you are. The rage is consuming you, making you paranoid and angry. This goes beyond the calm, Aislinn. This is not a road you need to go down. I need for you to remain sane. Do you want a sedative?"

"I do not want a sedative," I said, feeling myself start to calm down. "You're right, I'm having an episode. I need a moment." I was going to say more, but my phone rang. The number was listed as "Private." Only one private number called me.

"Well?" Malachi asked.

"Hello?" I answered the phone, ignoring him.

"Are you alright?" Patterson asked me.

"I nearly ripped the jaw off a serial killer this morning. I beat him with a chain afterwards. I think I broke every bone in my hand and I have the killer's teeth embedded in my fingers. Now, Malachi thinks I'm having a psychotic episode because I've moved from the dark calm to a place of complete rage. Based on that information, what do you think?"

"How were you kidnapped?" Patterson asked.

"I was Tasered with my own Taser by a meth head. Somehow, he got into my motel room while I was showering."

"You lived. I'd say that's a good day. How long will you be in the hospital?"

"A day or so."

"I know how much you hate hospitals," Patterson answered. His voice suddenly sounded tired. "I'd help if I could."

"I'm sure you would, which is why our suspected serial killer is under lock and key. If you kill cops to get to him, I will take it as a personal affront."

"Understood," Patterson answered. "However, considering what you did to him, I think he got what he deserved. I have other matters to attend to anyway."

"Tell me about Virgil," I sprung the question on him.

"There's nothing to tell. He's my brother."

"He's supposed to be dead."

"So am I." Patterson answered.

"No, you're supposed to be in federal custody, like your sister."

"I am nothing like my sister." Patterson became angry, his voice becoming strained.

"I believe you." I soothed his ego.

"I look forward to meeting you, in person, granddaughter. Now, I need to go." Patterson hung up.

I looked at the doctor. "Let's get this over with. I promise not to have a meltdown. I need to think and I cannot do it with these injuries." As an afterthought, I looked at Malachi, "Patterson said he had to go. I'm guessing he is about to kill someone."

Transporter

Patterson didn't notice the cold or the freezing rain that was starting to fall. He sat in his car, thinking. Aislinn kidnapped by a serial killer. He'd let her down. In the years that followed Callow, he'd always been there to prevent such things. When Gerard Hawkins had broken into her apartment, Patterson had been outside, waiting, watching through the window. If Hawkins had gotten the upper hand, he would have moved heaven and earth to keep her from getting hurt. Yet, his vendetta had taken him elsewhere in recent days and she'd been abducted, again.

First Nyleena and now Aislinn, he was losing his touch. He was getting old. Patterson knew that his mind was going. A doctor would confirm it, eventually, probably when he landed on a slab. He wondered if Xavier would do the autopsy, since it wasn't an SCTU case.

The blame for this most recent incident wasn't entirely his fault though. Malachi had been there. That other agent had been there. And she'd been put up in some seedy motel that was not secure.

It bothered him, because he liked Malachi. Malachi was good for Aislinn, he helped keep her sane. Maybe he wouldn't kill him, just remind him of his duty. It didn't matter at the moment though. He'd come back to them, later. Right now, he had someone else to deal with.

He took aim as the van transporting his son, Joseph, exited the parking lot of the sheriff's department. Patterson didn't have the sniper training that he felt he needed for this job. He'd never been a hunter. During the war, he'd been infantry, a foot soldier, marching towards the enemy on the ground.

The first shot hit the side window near Joseph. The window didn't shatter and the bullet didn't penetrate the glass. He didn't stick around for a second shot. He loaded his gear into his car and left. No one would suspect the old man behind the wheel of a Lincoln, driving the speed limit.

They didn't. He slipped through the net and drove into town. He was back at his hotel in less than ten minutes. Despite his calm demeanor as he entered the hotel, he was seething inside. How could he have not realized that they would have bullet proof glass on the transport van? It was a stupid mistake. A rookie mistake made by a rookie killer, but he wasn't a rookie. He was a good at this, it was what he did best.

He rethought his current situation. Perhaps this whole thing with his granddaughters had him off balance.

The urge to kill, and it was an urge, a physical need no different than eating or sleeping, surged through his body. It made his hands tremble, like a man needing a stiff drink to start the morning. The heart in his chest beat too slowly. His mind could think of nothing else.

The urge would have to be slaked. He couldn't get to Joseph, but there were others and these others would suffice. It wouldn't be as satisfying. The urge might need two or three victims, sacrificed to quiet it. He'd been here before, after killing Lyla, he'd run away, because his bloodlust wasn't satisfied and he hadn't wanted to harm his children. She hadn't been a satisfying substitute for his sister, Gertrude.

Leaving the hotel, he disposed of the rifle after wiping it down and removing the other bullet from the chamber. He pocketed it without much thought. The list in Columbia was short, primarily consisting of Joseph. However, there were others in neighboring areas. Now, he headed south on 63, headed to the capitol, Jefferson City. There was an old friend there that he hadn't seen in a while. It was about time he did.

It was a half-hour drive to the city and another ten to the friend's house. Patterson parked in the drive, not worried about neighbors. If they wrote down a license plate number, they'd find it belonged to someone named Gertrude Clachan. Since the news had already announced that Patterson Clachan was the elusive, yet brutal serial killer still on the loose, it didn't matter.

He got out and walked slowly to the house, using his cane for support, despite not needing it. Once in front of the door, he used the head of the cane to rap sharply twice upon the wood. It left a slight indentation that made Patterson smile.

"Go away," the voice inside shouted.

"And if I refuse?" Patterson answered back. He heard movement inside. The door opened. The older man sighed at the sight of Patterson.

"Do I know you?" The man asked. He was in his fifties, with a large beer belly and a bald head. Patterson instantly disliked him.

"Patterson Clachan," Patterson answered.

"You're wanted for murder," the man said.

"I know," Patterson walked past him, into the house. "How have you been, Roger?"

"How do you know my name?"

"I know a lot about you." Patterson took a seat.

"I should call the police."

"You should, but you won't."

"Why won't I?" Roger narrowed his eyes at Patterson.

"Skeletons," Patterson answered. "Lots of skeletons."

"Not as many as you," Roger didn't call the police. He took a seat in a chair across from Patterson.

"True, few people have as many skeletons as I do." Patterson thought for a moment.

"Are you here to kill me?" Roger asked.

"Yes," Patterson shrugged.

"Who are you to play judge, jury, and executioner against me?"

"Just the man who knows your sins," Patterson answered. "I may not be in a position to judge you, but to play executioner, well, that's what I was born to do."

"And what sins do you think I've committed?" Roger asked.

"Twenty years ago, my granddaughter was kidnapped by a man named Callow. He enjoyed sexually torturing the children and killing them."

"He acted alone." Roger sneered.

"Oh, I know that, but he had a video recorder set up in his torture chamber and a camera on a tripod. He videotaped all of his exploits. The problem is, they didn't find the tapes. I spent eighteen years trying to figure out exactly what happened to them. They weren't catalogued by the police. Then I found one of them. It was in a box at a garage sale, imagine my surprise. I very nicely asked the garage sale person where the tape had come from and after some time, he told me he'd bought it from you, for $200. I tried to turn it over to the authorities, but they wouldn't listen. He was an old man, senile, possibly suffering from dementia or some other brain eating disease. Unfortunately for you, I'm not. Here's what's going to happen, I'm going to torture and kill you and leave the tape next to your mutilated body. My granddaughter and her friend are going to find it and put two and two together. Consider

~ 222 ~

yourself lucky that you'll be dead. You don't want to face the two of them, they are psychotic and feed off each other's negative psychotic energy. When they find the tape, you cannot imagine how much rage they are going to experience. At least if I torture you, it will end quickly."

"Why would I sit here and agree to let you torture me to death?"

"Oh, I'm sorry I gave you the wrong impression, you don't have a choice," Patterson moved like a jaguar going for the kill. He rapped the cane against the cheekbone of Roger, the peddler of child porn. Roger's face crunched with a satisfying thud.

Patterson pounced, he didn't have any rigging with him, but he had duct tape and rope. He bound the man's hands together first, tying the knots so tight the fingers instantly began to swell and the hands change color. He did the same at the ankles, then pushed him into the chair. He waited to gag him. There was some information that he wanted. He positioned his cane over Roger's hand. Roger was blubbering.

"Roger, I just have a few questions, which you are going to answer or it gets worse." Patterson stood over the other man. "When police searched Callow's house, they didn't find any tapes, not even one of Aislinn Clachan.

How is that possible? How did you get there and take the tape after she escaped?"

"Go to hell!" Roger spit on Patterson. Patterson wiped away the offensive liquid with a gloved hand. The gloves were plush black leather. Being spit on was nothing new to Patterson, he'd been spit on several times before. It always annoyed him.

"Now, now, Roger," Patterson looked at him. "We'll have none of that. It goes much easier for you if you just tell me what I want to know. I'll give you one more chance, what happened to the tape of Aislinn Clachan?"

"You're going to kill me anyway." Roger protested.

"That's true, I am going to kill you. It can be slow or fast, your choice. For example, I can remove your eyes while you're still alive if you prefer."

"My eyes?" Roger looked skeptical.

"My mother used to use them to make soup stock. I'd open the ice box door and there would be a jar of eyes in the fridge. It was creepy. So, now I do it, I'll take out your eyes and put them in the fridge. It's up to you whether I do it while you're alive or dead. And Roger, it really hurts to have the optic nerve cut while you're alive. Also, one minute you can see, but there's a horrible pain and the next, you're blind and it hurts even worse."

"You'll have to give me more information, I don't know the kids by their names."

"She was the one that escaped, Roger. She's the one that killed Callow and escaped."

"Oh, yeah," Roger looked solemn for a moment. "Mark didn't tape her, at all. Most of the girls had tapes made the first or second day he had them, but not that last one. He called me the second day and told me there wouldn't be a tape. He wasn't sure what it was, but he couldn't go near her once he had her in his possession. That little bitty girl frightened him. I guess in hindsight, it was justified. When he did finally get up the nerve to kill her, she ended up killing him, with a plastic spoon of all things."

"Another question, Roger. How many tapes were there?"

"Total?" Roger looked at him. "Hundreds. Mark would tape a session or two, then pass the tape along to me. Since he kept the girls for as long as possible, they each had multiple tapes. You found one at a garage sale?"

"The children were moving their father into a nursing home. They didn't realize what it was, they thought it was a movie recorded off

TV, but I recognized the name of the 'actress' in it as being one of the girls killed by Callow. One more question, Roger, and this is very important, did you participate?"

"Hell no. I haven't even seen what's on the tapes. I just knew Mark and Mark wanted to move the tapes, I helped him do that."

"Good," Patterson brought his cane up and brought the handle down on Roger's hand. Roger screamed, Patterson shoved a sock into his mouth and put duct tape over it. "You know, Roger, you shouldn't lie. It breaks the bonds of trust. Since you told me about Aislinn, I'll still honor our agreement and take your eyes after you're dead. But the rest of it, you're going to be very much alive for. The video I have has your voice in the background, telling Mark Callow that you have a buyer for the girl if he wants to sell her instead of kill her. Did you guys sell any of the girls?"

Roger shook his head emphatically. Patterson brought out a knife, showing him the blade. Roger shook his head "no" again.

"Let's hope not Roger, because if I find out you lied to me, I'm going after your children and grandchildren after I'm done here. And I will find out. I always do. So, do you want to change your answer?"

Roger shook his head "no" again. Patterson nodded once. The blade plunged into the skin between two ribs. He turned it sideways, pulled a large set of needle nose pliers from his trusty bag and inserted them into the wound. Carefully, he opened them, feeling the weakened bones break. With the ribs broken, he goes back to the knife, making the wound larger, cutting a large slit over the rib bones. Patterson smiled at Roger.

"This is going to hurt, but you should die quickly," Patterson inserted his gloved hand into the wound, the bones ripping at his gloves. His fingers touched Roger's beating heart. Patterson closed his eyes, clamping his hand around the pumping organ. It was racing. He pulled until the heart was out of Roger's body. Roger looked shocked for a moment, then his eyes glazed and all signs of life were extinguished. Patterson put the heart on the kitchen table, before returning to the body. He removed the eyes and put them in the fridge. Roger wasn't worth much more than that.

For the final touch he placed the video tape, now covered in bloody glove prints, on the table. The spine read "Touched by an Angel" and had the old man's name next to it, like a property stamp. The top label said "Guest starring K. Lassiter." Kari Lassiter had been kidnapped two weeks before Aislinn. If only Aislinn had been kidnapped first, the entire thing could have been avoided. Now, they'd connect the two murders, if they hadn't already. Patterson was glad. He wanted everyone to know why he had killed both of them.

Nineteen

Some people were annoying. Some situations were annoying. My current situation was annoying and my current nurse was annoying. It wasn't anything she could control; she seemed to be one of those naturally happy, bubbly women with bright blond hair, beautiful hazel eyes, perfectly straight and white teeth, and a smile that made her head look like it was going to split open. I didn't envy her looks, she was attractive for a woman in her 20's and I could appreciate her beauty. I couldn't stand her exuberant and overwhelmingly happy disposition.

I kept trying to convince myself she wasn't that bad. She was nice. She was courteous. She was willing to get me anything I wanted, within reason. I didn't begrudge people happiness, I thought most people deserved some happiness in their life. It was just that her happiness was leaking all over me and I wasn't a happy person. I was a contented person. There was a huge difference between the two.

Happiness required a person to look at the world and see the good. I looked at the world and wondered which city I'd be chasing a serial killer in next. If I hadn't been working for the SCTU, I would be living in a city, waiting for the next serial killer to show up at my door or slip in through my window.

Besides true happiness and joy were a little beyond my scope of feelings. I could feel contented, happiness required life altering events. When Nyleena woke up from her coma, I'd be happy. It wouldn't last more than a few hours, but for a few hours, that life altering event would make me happy.

I was alone. The nurse, Kelsey the Bubbly, had refused to go grab me Arby's while she was on duty. Considering that was exactly how she had worded it, I wondered if that meant she would not be as opposed if she was off duty. That had created a conflict, the Jiminy Cricket voice in my brain told me I could not impose on her that way, I didn't know the woman and she wasn't my personal assistant, even if she volunteered. The side that was me, and not Jiminy "Nyleena" Cricket, told me it might be interesting to see if she would actually do it and I'd get Arby's out of it.

The fact that her voice was back was comforting. It wasn't prophetic and it wasn't a sign. I didn't believe in them either. I had listened to a saved voicemail this morning and it had restarted her voice in my head. This was a good thing, since I felt I was becoming a little too much like Malachi without her.

"You have a visitor," Kelsey bounced into the room. I was in a secure area of the hospital. This meant a private room and a security guard at the door. I was positive the security guard was probably bored out of his brains.

"Is it someone I know?" I asked Kelsey.

"He says he's a relative."

"Did he give a name?" For a moment, I wondered if it was Virgil. Although, why Virgil would visit me was a mystery. We had no real family ties except for a last name I had changed years ago and a blood-line that I didn't claim.

"Aiden Clachan," Kelsey frowned for the first time since I had been moved into the room.

"Hm," I frowned with her. "I suppose he can come in. You might have the security guard on alert in case I decide to kill him or vice-versa."

"Um," she looked at me. "Are you related to the Clachans' that were recently arrested?"

"Yes, but I did the arresting. My family bonds are not that strong." I winked at her and immediately wondered why. Winking was an odd gesture. It indicated flirtation and like. I didn't flirt and I certainly didn't like her. So why had I winked? It must have been the Demerol.

"Ok, I'll let him know," the smile was back on her face. Maybe the wink had been a good touch.

"Aislinn," Aiden walked into the room.

"Aiden, what can I do for you?" I didn't smile at him and I certainly didn't wink.

"Can't this be a social call?" He asked.

"We've never had a social call. As a matter of fact, the last time we spoke, I held a butcher knife to your throat and you stabbed me with a meat fork." My family has more issues than Reader's Digest.

"True, but I deserved the butcher knife to the throat, I shouldn't have stabbed you with the meat fork."

"This conversation is getting tedious, Aiden."

"Always so bored by family," Aiden smiled and sat down. I tried not to sigh, but it escaped anyway. "How's the hand?"

"It's broken, they put stuff in it to hold the bones together. I give it three weeks and I'll need surgery again. How's the wife? How many children do you have now with other women?" I asked, needling him to get him to move along. Aiden was my dad's first cousin, making him my second cousin. He was one of Bernard's children or grandchildren, I didn't know, I couldn't keep them all straight. He had fidelity issues and I had made an announcement at a family reunion once that he had knocked up one of my classmates. That had led to the whole stabbing/butcher knife incident. In his defense, the classmate was of legal age. It didn't excuse his infidelity though. If you were going to bother getting married, you shouldn't cheat every time you turned around and saw a hot girl.

"Ouch," Aiden grabbed his heart, pretending that I had wounded him. "I guess I deserve that, but I've changed my ways."

"Yeah, so has Patterson." I scoffed.

"That's actually why I'm here."

"You want forgiveness?" I frowned harder.

"No, I came to talk to you about Patterson. Is catching him really that important? Hasn't the family been through enough in the last week and a half?"

"How can I put this? Patterson is a killer and not just your average killer, he literally butchers people. He rips or cuts out organs. I just saw his handiwork with a knife where he castrated a pedophile." I pursed my lips. "Of course, the pedophile deserved it, but that does not mean it's legal. We cannot have crazy people running around castrating people and nailing their internal organs to furniture just because it's fun."

"He's not any crazier than you."

"That is neither here nor there," I commented quickly. "He cannot keep dodging justice."

"Putting an eighty-six year old man in jail is justice?"

"He's eighty-eight according to Virgil and yes, it is. He slaughtered my grandmother. God only knows how many others he's killed. It is not like he's going to Sing-Sing or some other notoriously horrid place. He will go to the Fortress and it's nice in there, just ask my brother." I said. For the first time, Aiden showed real emotion. I read it as distress and concern. His brow furrowed, creases formed at the corner of his eyes and mouth, and his cheeks just sort of deflated.

"How is Eric?"

"Good, they treat him well inside and he seems fairly happy with his life there."

"How are Ella and the kids?"

"Also good, still crusading for his release. The kids have adjusted well."

"If you're going to go ahead and continue to chase Patterson, there's something you should know," Aiden stood. "He's had years to settle his own scores, he's settling someone else's now."

"Yeah, mine by the looks of it."

"That's what I was getting at," Aiden looked at his feet. "You killed Callow, but your dad thought there was another guy involved. If anyone can find this guy, it's Patterson. He's," Aiden paused, searching for the word. "He's crafty and he's a very good planner."

"And you know this because?" I asked.

"Granddad told me a lot about him when I was young. He hasn't really gone after anyone that was directly related to you until he killed that guy a week ago here in town. Now, he has."

"You know this to be fact?"

"No, but he didn't do it while my granddad was alive, he would have mentioned it. Granddad kept a scrapbook of kills he thought might be Patterson's. I brought it with me." Aiden produced a large album from a bag. I hadn't noticed the bag, the Demerol must be making me sloppy. "I had a hard time getting this in here. I was searched twice and it was nearly confiscated. I told them if you didn't see me, I'd give it to them to pass along to you. But you did, so I'll give it to you personally."

"Thanks Aiden, that is very thoughtful."

"It's fucking weird, Aislinn, let's be honest. I have no idea why my granddad kept the scrapbook and I never saw it until he willed it to me after he died. Which is also weird, because if he wanted you to have it and he did, he shouldn't have passed it along to me. I was pretty sure you'd be waiting to kill me when I walked in the door."

"I considered it, but makeshift weapons are scarce in this room and my Demerol drip is controlled to keep patients from an accidental overdose." I shrugged.

Aiden sat the scrapbook on the table in front of me. He waved and walked out. I wasn't exactly sure what to do with it. Did I open it? Did I want to know how many kills Bernard thought Patterson had? Did I wait for Malachi and Rollins? Where the hell were Malachi and Rollins? I hadn't seen them all morning. As Aiden had put it, it was fucking weird. Malachi had a tendency to hover when I was in the hospital. I dialed his cell.

"I'm busy," Malachi growled.

"I want Arby's and how are you busy? Wait, did Patterson kill someone? Are you bringing me pictures? Who was the victim?"

"I'll bring you Arby's and tell you all about it later," Malachi hung up. I immediately redialed.

"Why can't I tell you I'm busy and you just leave me be?"

"You did not give me a chance to tell you that my cousin, Aiden, dropped off a scrapbook that his grandfather Bernard had been keeping of suspected Patterson kills."

"I'll look at it when I bring you Arby's and tell you what I'm busy with. Until then, don't you look at it." He hung up again.

Well, that was just unrealistic. Telling me not to look through it, just made me want to look through it more. I began reaching for the cover.

"How was your visit?" Kelsey the Bubbly came back into the room.

"Do you like your family?"

"I like most of my family," Kelsey the Bubbly responded.

"I dislike most of my family, including Aiden who just left. They're a weird lot, full of cannibals and serial killers; men who cheat on their wives and men who think the sanctimony of marriage is more sacred than the Holy Grail. Spending time with my family is like being trapped in a psychiatric ward, unsure if you're the patient or everyone else is and you're free to leave whenever you want."

"I know how you feel, families are weird." Kelsey the Bubbly grabbed an extra pillow and began adjusting my bed. "My family was touched by a tragedy a long time ago and most of them never got over it, but I don't see it like they do. It was a tragedy, but Kari wouldn't want us to mourn her loss for the rest of her life. She'd want us to move on, live and love, again." Kelsey shrugged. "My mom thinks it's offensive that I can be happy all the time."

"I find it offensive." I told her.

"Yes, but I've been warned that you are grumpy and difficult. The charge nurse actually got a call from someone named Gabriel Henders telling them to find the nicest nurse with the patience of a saint to tend to you. So, they handed me the job. I have no other patients right now because of you. I don't know if that's a good thing or a bad, but I'm getting paid overtime for it. And you have been keeping me busy with your call button."

"My own nurse and I cannot have Arby's?" I raised an eyebrow at her.

"No, you can have Arby's, I just can't go get it for you. What if you need to wipe your butt and can't because you broke your hand or something weird?" Kelsey the Bubbly giggled at me.

"You are not wiping my butt."

"I'm just saying, that's the sort of thing I'm supposed to do, not go get Arby's. You can have something delivered though. I know, hospital food is so controlled and rigid, it isn't great. Your diet has no restrictions, so you're free to eat anything."

"Someone's bringing me Arby's later," I admitted.

"Awesome!" Kelsey the Bubbly smiled wider. "Anything else I can get you at the moment?" Somehow, she had fluffed my pillows and added an extra one while talking to me without me noticing or complaining. She was good.

"What's your last name?" I asked.

"Why?" Her smile never faltered, but she did raise her own eyebrow.

"I'm a US Marshal, I like to know things."

"Lassiter," she told me. "I'll be back in about twenty minutes to check on you again. Call if you need me earlier."

I stared as she exited, my mouth open. Few names penetrated my memory, Lassiter was one of them. Actually, all of Callow's known victims were seared into my brain. Not just their names, but their faces. Occasionally, I wished

I'd been his first choice, it would have saved some young girls from being tortured, raped, and murdered. I guessed Kelsey was in her early twenties and that her big sister had been one of Callow's victims. His last victim to be exact. His next choice had been poor and I'd killed him. This was why I avoided being in Columbia. There were all sorts of ghosts.

Twenty

I didn't have my Kindle. My iPhone was about dead. There weren't any books or puzzle books in my room. It was a dicey situation. I was being left to my own devices and with my own thoughts. We were entering dangerous territory for a sociopath.

However, with nothing to do but think, it was hard to not have a few introspective moments. I'd come to the conclusion last time that I was a boring human being. I chased serial killers. I did puzzles. I played out-of-date video games. I read books. I watched TV using a hard drive and computer, so it wasn't like I was catching the latest episode of whatever sitcom was currently popular and I probably wouldn't have gotten the jokes anyway. That was the extent of my life. Occasionally, Nyleena dragged me out of my house to do something, but it usually ended badly. My family stopped by more frequently when I was home and I still wasn't sure I enjoyed that. My co-workers, my cousin and the psychopath that lived down the street from me when we were kids, were the extent of my friends. To make it even more depressing, the same psychopath now lived two streets over from me in my federally protected neighborhood for bad-ass police officers and anyone else in the criminal justice department that worked with serial killers and mass murderers.

Since I was already aware that I was boring, my mind decided to latch onto another aspect of me. I had nearly ripped the jaw off of a serial killer. That said all sorts of things about me, none of them good. It indicated that I did have some physical strength associated with the psychopathology. I also didn't care that I had done it. It was more interesting, than horrifying. It didn't take a genius to figure out that unlike most psychopaths, I did care for other people, even if I didn't understand them. In theory, sociopaths weren't supposed to care about others, but I had met many sociopaths that cared about a small core group of people in their lives. These were the people they tried not to use or abuse. Psychopaths tended not to have that core group, they tended to have a single individual. This only applied to the mentality of people with anti-social personality disorder. Borderline personality disorder was a much less controlled form of sociopathology and psychopathology. They weren't usually functional in society.

The best I could say was that I was not a Borderline Personality. I wondered what it was like to sympathize with other people or to empathize with other people. Nyleena could do that. She could hold someone's hand and tell them she understood and they believed her. She cared. She could empathize and sympathize. I was only capable of spouting the dictionary definition of the two emotions. A part of my life was lacking because of this, it was part of the reason I didn't feel human at times.

My gaze fell on the scrapbook. I could stop thinking about myself. This was vitally important, as I was starting to feel irritated by thoughts of my screwed up life.

A little voice in my head, not Nyleena's, told me to put on gloves. I growled at that voice. I didn't need Xavier up there too. There was only room for one, maybe two, if you included my mother, but every girl has their mother's voice trapped in their heads. Those that didn't could torture the life-giving woman who carried her for nine agonizing months with a swollen belly and cravings for strange foods like ice cream and onions or peanut butter sandwiches with dirt between the layers of sticky goo and bread.

I closed my eyes as a memory came to me. My faceless father, sitting at a table, eating ice cream with a plate of tomatoes next to it. It wasn't onions, but I remembered my father always eating tomatoes with his ice cream. I wasn't sure if he ever actually cut the tomatoes up and put them on the ice cream, but I felt he did. I had no idea what to do with this memory, so I pushed it back down and stared at the scrapbook. I couldn't open it without gloves. I didn't want to page Kelsey the Bubbly, I was sure she needed a break from me. As my dedicated nurse, I wondered what her hours were. The desire to press the button and find out was consuming. Eventually, I stifled it.

I flipped on the TV and found nothing on. My phone was at 8% battery life. This meant I had just enough for one phone call. However, I didn't know who to call. My family was in Kansas City. I had family here, but I wasn't close to any of them, I didn't even have phone numbers for the majority of them. Malachi's mom would have helped me out, but she was in protective custody. Nyleena's mom and dad were both deceased. That left me with one phone number. The digits danced through my mind. Was I really bored enough to make this call? The answer was "yes."

"Hello?" The woman on the other end answered.

"Hey, it's Aislinn Cain."

"Aislinn, it's been years. What are you doing?" She asked.

"Well, I'm calling because I'm in town, more accurately, I'm at Boone Hospital, I broke my hand and it needed surgery."

"I saw the news yesterday," her voice grew cold, distant.

"Yeah, so I'm at the hospital, my phone is dying, I have nothing to do, no books, no puzzles, nothing, nada, zip. I was wondering if you could bring me an iPhone charger and stop by the gift shop and buy one of each of the puzzle books. I will compensate you for your time and the purchases."

"What type of iPhone?"

"Um, I do not know. It's got a screen and a case on it."

"Is it an iPhone 4 or 5?"

"How do I find out?"

"What size is the hole for the charger?" She sighed.

"Small," I answered.

"I'll do this, but it's going to cost you."

"Great, I have money here," I told her. She hung up on me and I wondered if I really did have money here. I pressed the "call button" on my bed. Kelsey the Bubbly responded very quickly, within seconds. I'd never had a dedicated nurse. I wondered what this was costing someone. I knew the hospital wasn't paying for it out of the kindness of their hearts.

"What do you need?" She asked, smiling. She practically radiated positive energy and sunshine.

"I need my wallet." I told her. My phone beeped and died on the bed next to me. "I have someone bringing me a charger for my phone and some puzzle books so I do not go insane thinking about myself."

"Why would thinking about yourself make you go insane?"

"I do not do well when I have downtime. I tend to do a lot of soul searching and it is not pretty."

"You don't seem so bad to me," Kelsey said.

"I nearly ripped a guy's jaw off and broke my hand beating him with a chain."

"Yeah, but he deserved it and he was really high, I doubt he even noticed."

"Nothing gets to you, does it?"

"Not really," Kelsey pulled out a plastic bag from somewhere mystical. Inside were my clothes, including my wallet. "You know, we sell phone chargers and puzzle books in the gift shop."

"I know, but my wallboard says I cannot leave the room."

"True, but if you had called me, we could have called the gift shop and charged the items and I could have gone down, gotten them and brought them back up to you."

"Well hell," I groaned. "Instead, I'm getting another visitor."

"Who'd you call?" Kelsey handed me the bag and I dug through it getting my wallet. I did have cash.

"My aunt. She is not real happy about coming to see me."

"Why would your aunt not be happy to see you?"

"Her husband shot me a week or so ago and was arrested as a result. He was an evil minion of my great aunt who was arrested for helping her son cover up the fact that he was a serial killer who had faked his own death."

"I know, I read the papers." Kelsey looked at me strangely for a moment. "And watch the news. I'm guessing she doesn't like you enough to bring you Arby's."

"If she brought me Arby's, she'd make sure it had arsenic in it first, but it's the only phone number I can remember." I didn't tell her why I could remember it.

"Hey, Ms. Cain," Kelsey gave me that strange look again.

"It's Aislinn or Ace," I responded then looked at my Demerol drip again. How much of this shit were they pumping into me? I never told anyone to call me Ace.

"Ok, Aislinn," Kelsey averted her eyes. "I want to thank you. Because of you, I'm a happy person."

"That's strange," I told her, raising my eyebrow and frowning.

"My family knew Mark Callow. He worked with my dad. He abducted my sister, Kari, after a workplace, family oriented picnic thing. I didn't know it then, I had to look it up later, but he did have a type. You and my sister both fit it. But, if you hadn't killed him, it would have been me. It would have been my other sister, too. He could have killed for years without detection and my parents would have been devastated by the loss of all three daughters. I was only a year younger than Kari. My sister Karen is two years younger than me. So, thank you for getting justice for Kari and saving my sister Karen and me from a similar fate."

"Um, you are welcome," I said hesitantly. Callow had come before the serial killer laws were enacted and before the concept for The Fortress was even thought about. He would have ended up in a plain old prison, which would have served him right. Although, while The Fortress was good for holding serial killers and channeling their intelligent behaviors, it suffered the same problem as other prisons, the inmates did not like pedophiles. Most pedophiliac serial killers were being sent to a converted facility while they built a second prison like The Fortress, to house those sorts of killers. Their life expectancy, even within the confines of The Fortress, wasn't long. August would end up in the new one, eventually, if he lived that long.

Twenty-One

My wallet contained a $20 and two $100 bills. My aunt laid claim to both of the hundreds as she dropped off two puzzle books, a package of ink pens and a cheap iPhone charger that was definitely not a genuine Apple product. I didn't complain, she had never liked me. For some reason, it was one of the few phone numbers I had memorized.

Malachi's visit was just as short. He handed me a bag from Sonic, not Arby's and a manila folder that was stuffed with materials. He promised to return after they got done with whatever they were doing.

I didn't press him for information. Theoretically, I was getting out tomorrow. He'd have to catch me up on everything at that time.

The Sonic wasn't Arby's. It was good, but I had my heart set on an Arby's Philly cheesesteak. Kelsey came in while I ate and made small talk. I wasn't really sure what to say to her at this point. It amazed me that she could have this sunny disposition after losing a sister to the brutality of Callow.

She left, taking my trash with her and replacing my empty soda with a fresh can. My agitation had lessened. I couldn't be mean to her knowing that Callow had touched her life as well. When I left Columbia this time, I hoped not to return for a while. Shakespeare's would ship frozen cheese pizzas all over the country, I'd have to make do with those.

My attention went to the folder. I didn't know what goodies were inside of it yet. However, a stamp on the back side told me it was from our forensics team. I opened the file.

When opening a file folder, the first thing you should see is a piece of paper with typing and hand scribbled notes. In this case, it was a vivid photo of James Okafor's body on his bed, beaten to a bloody pulp. The next forty items were more photos. I moved past these quickly, deciding I didn't really want to look at them again.

After some searching, I found the report summary on James Okafor's murder. Cause of death was multiple blows from a small, blunt, heavy object, in other words, blunt force trauma. The forensics team had even gone so far as to draw an interpretation of what had caused the blunt force trauma. It was a small rectangle, roughly two inches long, tapering towards the top. There was a second piece of vital information. While the majority of the blows had been landed this rectangular object, some had been created by a second object and it had left a different impression in the skull. They had cast the impression and taken a photo of it. It was a face, the face of a Green Man.

The Green Men are basically a nature symbol. It is the face of a man, sometimes made out of leaves, sometimes with leaves surrounding it. There are depictions of Green Men growing branches or vines from different parts of their face or from behind their head.

Green Men are found in many cultures. However, most modern depictions are based on the Celtic symbol. My house was filled with them, Trevor had carved them into my bed and into my table and chair set. I found the Green Man unsettling. My personal fascination with Green Men had begun when I was a kid. There had been a book on Celtic myths in my house. The fairies had been interesting. The dragons had been dragons. But the Green Men had piqued my interest and captured my attention. I still didn't understand why.

The idea that Patterson had a Green Man on something heavy enough to leave an impression on bone, gave me pause. Did he know of my fascination? If so, why did he have such a thing in his possession? Did he have an obsession with Green Men as well? What did that say about me? The next line of the report summary captured me. It stated that the scientists were fairly certain that the flat end was the rear of the cane handle and the Green Man was on the front of the handle. I had imagined the cane to have the standard rounded handle, not the bar-style handle that could be decorated at the front and back to show off to people.

Traces of carbon steel and titanium had been found in the wounds. That explained the weight and durability of the cane head, but it didn't explain why the cane itself hadn't broken. They found no other particulates within the wounds that could not be explained away as dust.

They also hadn't found a rifle. Not finding a rifle was problematic. If he was indeed our sniper, why didn't he have the rifle? They found bullets for the rifle. I decided to come back to the missing firearm.

Someone had interviewed Nick the Bomber. Nick knew James Okafor. Nick had worked with a guy named George, who was in fact, our third victim. George had been friends with James. They had both been in his house on multiple occasions. This strengthened the idea that James Okafor was the sniper, but the missing gun was a problem.

The final piece of information was that James was here on an asylum visa. His friend, George was as well. There was no information about why they were being granted asylum, but their home country was listed as Zaire. Only Zaire had failed to exist as a country in 1997 and had officially been renamed to The Democratic Republic of Congo. We already suspected that James and George had been involved with the Congolese death squads, but why they had been granted asylum was an interesting question. It was also way above my pay grade. I could bug every official on the planet and never get an answer. There were two options, I could obsess about this missing information that was likely to be completely pointless, or I could get hung up on it and miss the important things. I filed it away for later contemplation.

The next report summary was about George. George hadn't been beaten to death. He'd been gutted, in more common Patterson fashion. There was no information regarding why George had been a target, unless he had just picked the wrong people to be friends with. However, in this day and age, it was hard to know who was normal and who was a serial killer. Holding that against a person would result in a whole lot of dead people.

George's death had been much faster. He'd died after only a few minutes, the report stated that he had been slit from stem to sternum and that his liver was the first thing to have been removed. While a person could live for a while without a liver, the shock of having it ripped from your body while you bled profusely from being cutting open would lead to a quick death.

He'd died only an hour after James Okafor. It had been bloody. They'd found biological material in the shower and a set of men's clothing that didn't belong to George in his bathroom. That sounded like Patterson. It was also the end of the report. Part of me wondered how many sets of clothes Patterson went through in a year, since he seemed to like to discard of them at crime scenes.

The third summary was about the FBI agent. They'd found traces of blood and vaginal fluid on his body. Considering his wife was two-hundred miles away, I was guessing neither was hers. That raised questions for me. My impression was that Patterson had been intent on killing at least one of the agents and this guy had made himself the primary target. Blood, vaginal fluid, and no wife screamed prostitute. Going with my gut, I was willing to bet he was beating up a prostitute and Patterson walked in to save the day.

This gave me an idea. I texted Malachi asking to put out a request for information from prostitutes in St. Charles that might have encountered our FBI agent. If I was right, she might be able to give a better description of Patterson or she may be totally useless, but I had found prostitutes to be fairly good at remembering physical details of a person. I chalked it up to being part of their job.

This might seem like a strange assumption, but when a person really started thinking about it, it made sense. Prostitutes were really good at knowing there was a serial killer at work long before anyone else, if they were targeting prostitutes. They shared information about abusive clients and clients that were just too weird to be trusted. They had to be able to provide descriptions of the client, their normal mode of transportation and on more than one occasion, the SCTU had discovered they could also remember license plate numbers.

Like George, the FBI agent had been cut up. His hands were removed, lending more credence to my abuse theory. His thighs had been shredded with a blade. Some cuts had been made to the chest deep enough to show his ribs through them. Cause of death was blood loss. This seemed about right, given his injuries. The real evidence that it was a Patterson kill were the missing eyes and there were clothes on the bathroom floor that didn't belong to the dead agent.

The final report was on the mugger. He was killed by two blows to the head. Both bore the emblem of the Green Man, imprinted on the bone. His death had been the quickest yet. He had no other damage except the removal of his eyes and the stab wound going through his chin.

Closing the folder, I leaned back against the bed. I still didn't know what Malachi and Rollins were doing. I had a feeling they were dealing with a dead body. The curiosity of whose dead body was almost overwhelming.

Normally an unknown dead body killed by The Butcher would be rather consuming. At the moment though, another thought was worming its way into my brain. The cane. How many old men walked around with decorative canes? I tried to recall the last time I had been to a grocery store and how many people there had used canes. There were a few, to be sure, but they hadn't been ornate, they had been functional. Standard metal shaft with rubber on the head and foot. Some even had four feet. None of them had wooden shafts or metal grips.

Yet, my great uncle Virgil had been using a cane with a wooden shaft and metal handle. His hands had covered the front of it, even while he walked, but I had noticed grooves etched into the metal.

My mind latched onto the movie *The Usual Suspects*. It replayed the scene of Verbal Kint, walking out of the police station, unfolding his crippled hand and leg, changing the way he stood, the way he walked, even the way he held his cigarette. In those few seconds, he'd gone from being Verbal Kint to Keyser Söze.

The details were still fuzzy, but like Verbal Kint's transformation into Keyser Söze, Virgil Clachan and Patterson Clachan were one in the same. My gut told me that Virgil had died, probably before Patterson grew into adulthood and Patterson, returning from war, and worried about his urges, had created a new Virgil. A Virgil that could commit murder and disappear, like mist on a lake. However, things had gone awry when Patterson had killed his wife and he'd become Virgil Clachan full time.

Now, I had two tasks. The first was easy, find out everything I could about Virgil Clachan. The second was not, remember what the old man had looked like and start removing the bits of him that were a disguise. Patterson wasn't bald and he didn't have blue eyes. If these features were fake, I was sure there were more.

Twenty-Two

"Patterson is Keyser Söze," I told Malachi and Rollins as they arrived to pick me up from the hospital. Kelsey the Bubbly bounced around the room, collecting my things and telling everyone what a good patient I was. Since I was many things, good patient not among them, I figured it was because she was one of the few truly good people that always saw the silver lining and believed in fairies. Of course, believing in fairies wasn't actually a bad thing, if a few more people believed in fairies, we would probably have fewer serial killers. It was a great example of chaos theory in action.

"What?" Rollins asked.

"Keyser," I started.

"For those that don't speak Aislinn Cain," Malachi interrupted, "it's from the movie *The Usual Suspects*. Kevin Spacey plays a criminal named Roger 'Verbal' Kint and tells this huge story about how a group of criminals were lured to LA to do some dirty work for a madman named Keyser Söze. The entire time, everyone is trying to convince him the madman is a myth, then when Spacey leaves the police station, you discover that he is actually Söze. So, who is Patterson 'Verbal Kint'?" Malachi asked.

"Virgil Clachan," I answered. "I have not worked out all the details, but it makes sense."

"The descriptions are similar, but they aren't a match," Rollins reminded me.

"That's because the best disguises are not particularly elaborate, especially when assuming a whole new identity. Remove the wig and the colored contacts and you have a man with lush black hair and brown eyes. Stop limping and you have a man that carries a cane for effect, not need. It is pretty ingenious. He could easily pass as one of the brothers. Only one went bald, but several of them have the light blue eyes and having a limp or stoop at his age is not going to be questioned, just accepted. If it was not for that damn cane, I would not have figured it out." I told Rollins.

"The cane?" Rollins frowned.

"We've established that Patterson Clachan carries one for effect, not need. If you're going to carry a cane, but not need it, you do not want one of those modern metallic doohickeys. You want something that is ornate, beautiful, and attractive. Virgil Clachan theoretically needs the cane, but he does not carry one of those metal ones, he carries one that is beautiful and ornate, something to be admired. A hundred years ago, it would not have been given a second look, but now, you do not see many ornate, functional canes. They have the metal body and rubber no-slip grips." I said excitedly, leaving the room and waving good-bye to Kelsey the Bubbly. She waved back.

"Did you two bond?" Malachi asked.

"Her sister was a victim of Callow. She's fairly normal, a little too happy and optimistic, but I cannot help feeling something for her. I do not know that I would call it bonding, but we had a common foe that I vanquished, and it means something to both of us." I shrugged.

"So, you bonded," Malachi replied.

"Sure," I sounded less confident in his assessment of the situation. Any time I met someone touched by Callow, I had a feeling I couldn't explain, but it made me determined to like the person, regardless of how much their personality was in direct conflict with my own.

"You two have issues with staying focused. If what you say is true, what does that mean?" Rollins asked.

"We visit Carl," I answered. "He's probably dead, but there is nothing I can do about that now. If he's not, it will be good. Unfortunately, to get an accurate description of Patterson, we are going to have to peel back the disguise. I'm not sure how much is fake. The eyes. The hair. The limp. Who died yesterday?" I asked.

"No one and the sheriff's department is being a pain in the ass," Rollins said. "Since no one died and we can't prove it was Patterson, they won't let us view the crime scene."

"If no one died, how do you have a crime scene?"

"We have a bus," Malachi jumped in. "A bus with a bullet lodged in a window. The bullet was two seats behind Joe and all the sheriff's office would tell us was that it was a .22. I think it was James Okafor's rifle."

"Proof that you can't cannot be good at everything," I pointed out.

"True," Malachi started to say more, but was interrupted by Rollins.

"This guy is a million years old, how can he always be ahead of us? How'd he know about Joe Clachan being on that transport?" Rollins whined. I hated whining, unless I was doing it, then it was fine.

"First, he is not a million; he is not even a hundred. Yes, he is old, but I would bet he is in better physical shape than you. Second, a quick search of Casenet will give you a court date, it is not hard to figure out when transports come and go." I answered.

"The Curse of the Clachans strikes again," Malachi gave me a wry smile.

"There is no such thing," I told him.

"That's what you think, but you're still alive and so is Patterson. All evidence points to the fact that both of you should be dead. Obviously, you haven't met the gruesomest thing possible yet." Malachi's smile disappeared. "Although, you came close."

I shuddered at the very thought of the Brazen Bull. If it hadn't been for Lucas, I'd be cooked, literally, along with my niece, Cassie. They would have been scraping our flesh off the bronze while someone tried to pry apart my shriveled up internal organs. Death by fire was bad, but death by heat was worse

"I keep hearing whispers about this stupid curse, what is it?" Rollins asked.

"From who?" I turned on him, hoping he felt very small.

"Police officers at CPD, deputies at the sheriff's department, Malachi, FBI agents, people that have history with the Clachans," Rollins paused.

"There is no such thing as curses." I walked indignantly to the SUV.

"If there is, the Clachans' have a seriously bad dose of it," Malachi told Rollins. "Almost no one dies of old age. Some die really old, but not of old age. One of them even spontaneously combusted at the age of 102."

"They did not," I huffed. "They set themselves on fire, deliberately."

"But did they die?" Malachi asked.

"Well, no," I admitted.

"How did they die?" Rollins looked horrified.

"Trampled by a runaway team of horses," I answered. "It happens."

"It does happen, but not in the 1940's." Malachi answered.

"It's still not a curse, haven't you ever heard the phrase 'live by the sword, die by the sword?' We are a violent lot, it seems only right that we would die violent deaths. Karma is entertained by our suffering." I said.

"You believe in karma but not curses?" Rollins asked.

"Maybe," I shrugged. "There are a lot of things I might believe in."

"Aislinn is a skeptic, not a non-believer. There's a difference," Malachi said. "What are the chances that Carl's alive?"

"I do not know, I guess that depends on what happened after we left. What do you remember about Virgil's cane?" I asked.

"Dark wood, not sure what kind, not something I've seen before. Silver handle, but now that you mention it, he used it weird, keeping his fingers over the front of it when he walked."

"To hide the Green Man on it," I offered.

"To hide something," Malachi agreed.

Malachi drove. I sat in the backseat and contemplated his words. He was right, I was a skeptic and not a non-believer. I couldn't rule out the possibility that demons, wendigos, and Bigfoot were all real. Just as I couldn't rule out the possibility that curses did indeed exist, just like coincidences.

Malachi was a believer. He believed that cattle mutilations were the work of aliens. That demons did possess some people and make them do evil things. Even the notion of curses were easy for him to find reason and logic behind. This made him both an optimist and a pessimist. Believers always seemed to have more answers than non-believers. Even skeptics like myself couldn't fill in the blanks like he did. It was strange to think of a chess grand-master and scholarly author of papers on quantum mechanics who had come to work for the FBI chasing serial killers and secretly investigating UFO reports, cattle mutilations, and stories of abductions.

Long ago, I'd learned not to argue with him about these beliefs. Not because they were irrational ramblings that he stuck with contrary to all evidence, but because he could make them sound rational. If I argued too long, he'd convince me and then I'd be stuck as a believer too.

The drive was quiet, all of us waiting to find out. It struck me as odd that Patterson had not only been here, masquerading as his dead brother, but that many in the family seemed to know that Virgil was alive and well. My research had taught me that Vigil Clachan had made a killing in Las Vegas as a general contractor. The man was worth hundreds of millions. I couldn't imagine having that much money. I could imagine Patterson using it to fund his murderous exploits.

Being a serial killer automatically created certain obstacles for law enforcement. Being a serial killer with means complicated those obstacles. To be a serial killer, one was expected to live in a flop house, sullied by blood and gore, along with a plethora of cats and notebooks full of ramblings. This was not the case. I had actually never seen a serial killer living in squalor. I'd heard about them, sure, killers like Robert Berdella from Kansas City had lived the life of a hoarder. Experience told me those stereotypes were dangerous, it was more likely for them to live in single story ranch houses in quiet suburbs.

However, with Patterson's money, he could be renting hotel suites and having champagne parties. His wallet was fat enough to bribe delivery men into hand-delivering unlabeled packages containing body parts. I thought of the *From Hell* letter thought to be the only true Jack the Ripper letter. Hand-delivered packages always spelled gloom and doom.

Malachi turned into Carl's driveway. To my surprise, Carl stepped out onto the porch. He had a large cigar in one hand, clippers and lighter in the other.

Seeing Carl alive meant that either I was wrong or Patterson had no reason to kill him. It would be hard to convince me that I was wrong. Carl was a harmless old man to Patterson. Even if he knew Patterson was Virgil, he was unlikely to comment or question it.

"Hi Carl," I waved with my broken hand.

"Girl, you always was a trouble magnet. What'd you do now?" Carl lit his cigar. I didn't know him well. I had known his father though and had liked him immensely, so I ignored the hostile tone in his voice.

"Kidnapped by a junkie, broke my hand beating him up. It could have been worse, I could have lost," I told the older man as I stepped onto his porch. He offered me a cigar, which I took. I clipped the end. Rollins glared at me as I lit it up. Things were changing with Gertrude out of the picture. My entire family seemed to be breathing a sigh of relief. My presence was no longer a thing to be feared, just dealt with, like an annoying fly that refuses to leave you alone.

"That would have been worse. Now, what did I do to warrant a second visit from the cousin I haven't seen in years?"

"It's about Virgil. I think he's Patterson Clachan."

"Could be," Carl seemed to think about it. "But if it is, do you want to mess with it? I know, it's your job and Patterson is unlikely to kill you directly, but he can make you miserable with that blade of his. Wields it better than a surgeon with a scalpel, he does."

"Do you think he's Patterson?"

"Dad always told me it was his brother Virgil. I've never asked any questions. It isn't just me either. He's visited several of us, none of us ask questions."

"Because you might not like the answers," I took a long tug on the cigar. It was rare for me to smoke one, but for the sake of getting information I could manage. Also, it was a good cigar, nothing cheap.

"Aye," Carl nodded. "Remember, Patterson does a good job of keeping himself under control, but he isn't perfect. Asking the wrong question will give you the chance to examine your own internal organs before you die. Or worse."

"He does things that are worse?" I asked.

"Depends on who you ask. Gertrude believes he's capable of anything. Nina never did, she always thought he was tempered. I don't know what that means in relation to Patterson, but I'm not sure which to believe. I imagine the truth lies somewhere between the two stories."

"Why would you let Patterson in your house?"

"Because if you're wrong, I've turned away an uncle. If you're right, it's better to stay on Patterson's good side."

"Thanks Carl," I left him on the porch.

"You're not smoking that in the SUV." Rollins informed me. I raised an eyebrow.

"You don't waste a good Cuban, no matter who it offends," Malachi told him.

"Cuban cigars are illegal," Rollins turned on him.

"So they are," Malachi nodded. "I dare you to try and arrest her for smoking it. Better yet, go arrest that old man for having one. Considering the life he's led, he's allowed a good cigar and a good glass of brandy when he wants."

"What makes him so special?" Rollins asked.

"He's been killed six times," I told Rollins. "At least six times. He has the scars to prove it. Carl's a survivor."

"Why has he been killed at least six times?" Rollins asked as I climbed into the SUV with my cigar still lit.

"Just has," I shrugged. I wasn't going to get into the details of Carl's life. He didn't need to know that Carl was a former prisoner of war. "So, he thinks it's possible that Patterson and Virgil are the same person. He just does not ask questions."

"Well, the wrong one could result in him being slit from stem to sternum." Malachi said. "When that's a possibility, it's hard to convince yourself to ask the right questions."

Twenty-Three

Despite the time I spent in morgues, with Xavier cutting corpses up, dead people still bothered me. Patterson was managing to fill my monthly quota of bodies. Also, he rarely just killed a person, he liked to mutilate them.

This one had a tiny difference that made me stare at it. Patterson had cut a hole in the chest, split the ribcage with something and pulled out the heart. My imagination had it still beating in the elderly man's hands as he nailed it to the table. I wasn't positive how long a heart beat outside the body, I doubted it was long enough for Patterson to nail it to a table, but that's what my imagination thought it should do. It was evident that the victim had been alive when Patterson literally ripped the man's heart from his chest.

Next to the heart was a video tape with a haunting last name and first initial. My imagination didn't have to do anything except

look at the tape. I knew what was on it. I had
seen the camera hidden behind the wall while
I'd been Callow's captive. Either she was being
raped and tortured or she was being killed.
Neither seemed very pleasant.

However, what the video tape had to do
with the man in the chair, missing his heart, was
a mystery. A geeky looking person was doing
something on the man's computer. Another was
doing complicated looking things with his home
entertainment system. My presence was
completely pointless. The only thing I knew was
that Patterson Clachan had been here.

It wasn't just the restrained dead body
with its heart on the table nor was it the cryptic
message contained on the horrifying videotape.
He had actually written it on the walls, in blood.
It didn't say "Patterson Clachan Was Here."
That would have made me suspicious. It said
"A Gift For My Granddaughter." Whether the
gift was the body or the videotape, I hadn't
figured out yet. I was betting it was both.

Malachi thought the guy in the chair was
a trafficker of child porn. I didn't know much
about child porn or trafficking in said materials.
It seemed unlikely that this loner, in his run
down house, in a not so great neighborhood of
Jefferson City, was trafficking in the illegal
material. However, that didn't mean he didn't,

it just meant that I expected people who peddled porn of any type, lived in houses like Hugh Hefner's. Sometimes I thought I needed to get out more.

Another geeky-type, this one female, came into the room. She carried a strange looking device. Malachi's face lit up, as much as it ever could. Whatever this woman was carrying, pleased him. I was positive this was a bad thing.

She found a clean-ish spot on the kitchen table and began doing things with wires and the magical machine she carried. A screen appeared from thin air. Someone in gloves and a complete vinyl suit, including mask, handed her the VHS tape.

I turned away. I'd seen Callow. He hadn't done anything to me, except feed me crappy food, but I was the exception.

Screams suddenly muffled the shuffling noises in the house. Screams from a little girl. My body turned even though my brain told it not to. On the screen was a girl, roughly eight years old, with blond hair and big brown eyes. Her skin was fair, where it was visible. Blood pooled on her stomach and her chest heaved and fell too fast.

My brain finally regained control and I turned from the scene. I didn't need to watch a snuff film. I didn't need to know what would have happened if I hadn't killed Callow and gotten away.

"Aislinn," Malachi's voice was soft, but demanding. I turned back around. The guy from the chair, minus twenty years of age, was in front of the camera. Kari was dead, blood escaped from her mouth in a tiny trickle that looked like red drool. Her eyes were glazed over, filled with a vacant, lifeless stare. Callow also appeared on the tape. He was spattered with her blood, wiping at it with a handkerchief. At that moment, if I could have resurrected him and killed him again, I would have. The hate raged inside me. If I was a monster, Callow was something worse. Unfortunately, I couldn't think of anything worse at the moment.

"Turn it off," I told Malachi. Malachi went to hit the button and the scene changed. A different girl sat in front of the camera. Her hair wasn't blond, but a light brown. Her skin was darker, her eyes were the color of roasted coffee. I stared at the eight year old version of myself. Beside me was a plate of meatloaf. In my hand was a spoon. My little fingers were wrapped around it, not tight, but like I was securing the weakened spot where the spoon met the handle.

My memory didn't remember me doing that. Callow stuck his head in the alcove. His hand came into view of the camera and for the first time, I saw that he held a knife. It had been hidden by his body. This snuff film was about to get much worse.

The video suddenly turned off. The look on my face had been serene. It wasn't just calm, it was collected. I had known exactly what I was about to do and it showed on my face. I had always imagined it had been screwed up into a scowl or a frown of determination. To see that it wasn't, made me pause.

"Where's the rest of the tape?" Rollins asked.

"Not made," I told him, looking at the dead man in the chair. I hadn't seen him at the house that night. Obviously, he'd been there though. Obviously, he had been preparing the tape for my death or worse and when I killed Callow instead of the other way around, he'd panicked. It explained why the video camera was empty when they found it. It also explained the heart on the table. Patterson had ripped out his heart for me. There was something to be said for that.

"Did you know?" Malachi asked.

"I never saw a second person," I told him. "I swear, I never saw a second person. I would have remembered."

"You looked young," Rollins' voice dropped an octave, sympathy creeping in with the realization that I was the eight year old on the tape. His mind was now imagining all the bad things he thought Callow had done to me.

"I was eight," I admitted. "I never saw the knife either. If I had seen it, I probably would have used it on him after stabbing him in the eye with the spoon."

"You stabbed him in the eye with the spoon?" Rollins asked.

"This is an old story. Yes, I was abducted by a pedophilic serial killer at the tender age of eight. The night he brought me meatloaf, I used the spoon handle to stab him. It went into his eye, breaking off when it reached the back of the orbital socket. While he flailed around, I grabbed his head and began beating it against the floor of the room he held me in. I did that until he stopped moving, then I ran outside the house, screaming my head off until the neighbors all came running." I told him.

"Wow," Rollins looked unsure of what else to say.

"I lived four houses down from the killer. Aislinn lived two streets over. He was a nice guy, always supporting the school fundraisers of the neighborhood kids, right up until Aislinn killed him and escaped. He even helped search for her." Malachi said the last with disgust. "Now we know why this guy was killed, but how did Patterson get ahold of the tape in the first place?"

"I think I know," I looked at the wall. In smaller letters, it said "Garage Sale, Orlando, Florida, 1342 Woodgarden Rd."

"Well?" Rollins asked with more patience than he had shown toward me before. I hated sympathy.

"When you have to put your favorite old person in a home, you do what with their stuff?" I asked.

"You have a garage sale," Malachi said, looking with me. "We can find out who bought the tape originally. He gave you multiple gifts. Think he might have erased the end of the tape, so that it didn't show you killing Callow?"

"No," I told Malachi. I frowned. I could remember the sound of the video recorder clicking off. However, I had said I didn't remember. It was easier that way. Malachi knew that I remembered more than I admitted. What did one do when haunted by ghosts? "Let's go have a drink."

"You don't drink." Malachi told me.

"I am aware, let's go have one anyway." I walked out of the crime scene into fresher air. It was cold as hell, January in Missouri was like that, sometimes. Sometimes, you could play baseball in the front yard while wearing a T-shirt. This was definitely not one of those winters.

Cleansing the palate and olfactory system was the only good thing about cold weather. Summer made the smells and tastes worst. Depending on what part of spring and autumn, the same thing happened. Winter though, winter had its own, unique smell. There was a musty quality that helped cover up other smells. The fragrant evergreens released more of their unique scents, tainting the air with their musk. If snow was on the way, it was that much better, because snow also has a smell, like sunshine, it couldn't be described, but you knew it when you smelled it.

Malachi and I ignored the fact that Rollins was still inside the house. Malachi pulled out the keys to the SUV and we headed to the nearest bar. I wasn't a drinker. There were too many potential threats for me to drink. The fiasco with the meth head a few days earlier were proof of that.

We parked on one of the main streets in downtown and entered a sport's bar called Spectators. Because we had just come from a crime scene, we headed to the basement instead of sitting with the regular patrons. A Kansas

City Chiefs game played on all the screens. Clusters of people sat around the TVs, cheering their team on to victory.

There was another sight too. Nine men and one woman were clustered at tables next to three dart boards. I watched with interest. I had never thrown a dart, but the concept and principles were not unknown to me. They looked happy. While most emotions were outside my scope, envy wasn't among them. The green-eyed monster reared its ugly head and shoved itself down my throat. I wanted to be happy like they were. I wanted to smile easily and have a good time out with friends and not worry about serial killers or rapists or muggers. For the first time, I realized I missed my team.

Aside from the man currently trying to figure out what sort of cocktail to order me and my cousin who was lying in a coma in a hospital room with a gunshot to the face, they were my only friends. My mother sort of counted. She was my mother, but she was also my friend, if I would let her. My life could be summed up by a bunch of scars and a handful of people that mattered. The envy devil roared inside me again.

Malachi returned with a bartender. The bartender carried a tray with several cups and glasses on it. The bartender sat them on the table and Malachi began arranging them. I grabbed the first glass. It was partially filled with an amber liquid that smelled spicy. It burned as it entered my mouth, despite being ice cold. The burn didn't abate at my mouth though, it continued as I swallowed, travelling down my throat and warming my stomach.

The next cup was more of the spicy amber liquid. I tossed it back as quick as the first, determined to chase away the ghosts that were currently haunting me. Malachi gaped at me. I pointed to another cup.

"I ordered us food and I think you should slow down," Malachi said.

"It's good, tastes like cinnamon."

"It's Fireball whiskey and you're doing shots of it like there's no tomorrow."

"Shots?" I frowned at the word. I'd never done a "shot" before. I'd heard other people talk about them though. "Are there more?"

Malachi frowned at me. Not his usual frown, but a concerned frown. He pulled all the cups to his side of the table. His arm wrapping around them, protecting them from my grasp.

"What's going on?" He asked.

"I intend to get blind drunk. You might have to carry me out of here." I looked at him.

"Did you say you ordered food? What did you order me? Am I going to like it?"

"Oh my," Malachi sighed and pushed another cup towards me. "That one tastes like black licorice."

Watching

After two days of no one finding his newest body, he'd phoned in an anonymous tip. He now sat in a bar, watching his granddaughter. She was acting odd, even for her. He watched her gag down a cup of Jägermeister then go back to drinking shots of Fireball. She'd had six in less than twenty minutes. Patterson wondered what she was drowning.

He nursed his own drink, a whiskey mix of Jack Daniels' and Coca-Cola. Thinking ahead, he'd left the cane in the car. No doubt they were starting to put together the pieces and were watching for it. He'd also donned a Chiefs cap to cover his dark hair and darker colored contacts to hide his eyes. It always amazed him how different a person looked when you changed the color of their eyes.

Food arrived at Aislinn and Malachi's table. Aislinn ate slowly, savoring the food. The sandwich was something meaty with a few vegetables and a heaping plate of homemade potato chips. As he watched, he realized that it was his fault she was drinking heavily. They hadn't just seen the video tape lying on the table and sent it to be analyzed, they had watched it. She had watched her eight year-old self-preparing to murder her captive.

While the killing was justified, Patterson knew all too well what death did to a child that age, even a sociopathic or psychopathic child. He hadn't intended for her to watch it. Since the night in the woods, outside August's makeshift animal house of horrors, Patterson had been making a lot of mistakes. It had started when he didn't walk in and kill August. Then there'd been Nyleena, followed by his failure to kill Joe and now, he'd unnecessarily caused Aislinn to relive the moment of her first kill.

Patterson understood that lots of killers loved that first kill. He hadn't. He believed Aislinn hadn't either. For the first time, he realized that he and Aislinn were a lot alike. They might have been born with the ability to kill, but if their hands hadn't been forced that first time, they probably wouldn't have grown up to be killers. Well, he might have, war had done more damage than his father. But not Aislinn, she would have grown up an emotionless shell of a human being, getting by with whatever life she chose to excel at.

He hadn't thought about his own first kill in decades. He had no desire to relive it now either. He drained his glass, shoving the memory down and walked to the bar. He couldn't atone for the hurt that Aislinn was currently feeling, all of it his fault, but he could continue his mission and free her from her own demons. Of course, she'd find more demons without much trouble, they would flock to her like eagles looking for prey.

"See the table with the attractive young woman and the very tall gentleman?" He asked the bartender.

"They're hard to miss," the bartender answered.

"I know. I'm going to pay their tab," Patterson pulled out a card and handed it to the bartender. The name was written as Virgil Clachan. "When they've finished their night of binge drinking, run this card and give it to the young lady."

The bartender frowned at him.

"She's my great-niece," Patterson said. "We had a falling out when her father died. We've had another death in the family and at the funeral a few days ago, we had another fight. I want her to realize that I take full responsibility for the fight. If she has my card, she has to come see me to return it. However, I'm not going to interrupt her evening and make a scene here."

"Sure thing," the bartender obviously relaxed. One thing about Patterson, he made people feel at ease. Malachi could do it too, it was part of their charm, a piece of the personality that was entirely fictional, but effective camouflage. It was not a skill Aislinn had learned.

Patterson left through the bottom entrance, into the back parking lot. He got into his car and sat for a moment. He'd gone to Spectator's because of the homemade potato chips. He didn't know what had brought Aislinn and Malachi there too. Perhaps just an instinctual pull that neither would have been able to explain. Or maybe it was the homemade potato chips, few places did them as well and almost no place did them better.

The thirty minute drive back to Columbia was uneventful. Patterson drove it on autopilot, thinking of his next challenge. He'd failed to kill Joseph, he wanted to blame it on his poor skills with an unfamiliar rifle, but the truth was, he'd just never been good at long distance kills. Of course, a close up and personal kill was out of the question. He'd be arrested or killed on site and that just wouldn't do.

As much as he hated to, he had to let
Joseph go. He stopped at his hotel, picked up
the possessions he had left there and began his
move west. There was another stop along the
way, in Boonville, but the detour would only
take a few hours. Afterwards, he could stop at
the A&W, he liked their burgers and root beer.
It would be like a reward for a job well done.

It was another half hour drive to
Boonville. His body ached with fatigue. The
A&W was closed for the night. He'd get a room,
stay in Boonville, and maybe spend a few hours
gambling. He parked in the casino parking lot
and wandered inside the building. Noise
washed over him, trying to sweep him into a sea
of gamblers with poor lighting and watery
drinks. Sure, he'd considered gambling, but he
really had no intention of spending time in the
casino. It would be busy, despite being a
Monday night.

Patterson skirted this area, found the
lobby's front desk and checked in for the night,
not under Virgil or Patterson, but another
identity. He was sure they, meaning Aislinn and
Malachi, were onto to Virgil. Rollins probably
couldn't figure out how to turn on a flashlight
with a manual and picture book.

So far, he was still one step ahead of
them. Make that three or four, but that was only

because no one knew his agenda. He was pretty sure they'd figured out the end game and dismissed it as impossible, but nothing was impossible if you were willing to go the distance. Patterson was willing to go that distance, it changed a lot of factors.

His room was tasteful, not tacky like the rest of the casino. Casino hotels were usually nice places to stay and they loved old people. Separating the elderly from their social security checks was a specialty for casinos and con men.

He'd never gambled, but he'd built several of the gambling establishments in Vegas. None of the big ones, he'd always tried to avoid the Mob and back when Vegas was still the original boom town, most of the big ones were mob connected. No, he'd built smaller ones, with fewer tourists and smaller adjoining hotels. It still boggled his mind that he'd been doing it for a decade before the second identity had been necessary. His work as a salesman had necessitated trips out of town or so he had told Lila. She had believed him, why wouldn't she?

Then his evil sister had stepped in. Lila had accused him of cheating on her, swearing that he wasn't going on business trips and she knew, because Gertrude had told her. And why had the vindictive bitch told his loving wife?

Because Patterson refused to raise her damaged, deranged son.

They were right, hell had nothing on a scorned woman and Patterson had a whole lot against them. They had ruined his life. First Gertrude, then she had turned Lila against him, making her a scorned woman as well.

He still regretted killing her. It was one of the few things in life he did regret. Lila had been his world, their children had expanded it. He missed not seeing them grow up. He'd missed the opportunity to watch his grandchildren grow up, until Donnelly had allowed him to see Aislinn one day.

The memory was as fresh as if it were repeating itself in time. It had been November. Snow had already fallen. It had been cold. Winter has its own smell, something unique that made him giddy. Or maybe it was just the opportunity to see Aislinn that made him giddy. He didn't know anymore. The two events, winter and Aislinn, were entwined in his memory, the smell of winter always made him think of her.

She had been wearing a bright red jacket, blue jeans, black sneakers, and a little silver necklace. Donnelly had agreed to let Chub take her to a fast food joint with an indoor playground. She'd gotten chicken nuggets.

She'd snuck in a small carton of milk and a bunch of orange wedges. He could even remember the way her oranges had smelled.

Chub had introduced Patterson as a "poker buddy." They'd stayed for an hour. During that time, Patterson had memorized every detail he could about the little girl. She had been shy, but once her tongue loosened, it moved at the speed of light. Even then, she'd been brilliant, explaining to him about how the Civil War had not had a single thing to do about abolition until the Union began losing the war.

Under the smell of oranges, she had smelled of rosemary and baking soda. He didn't know why she smelled of either, just that she did. At the end of the visit, Patterson had taken off his own silver necklace and removed the silver cross that hung from it. He had given it to the little girl. She had been hesitant to take it, but Chub took it and slid it on her own barren chain.

She'd worn it for years, her memory failing to grasp that it had been given to her by a stranger. In her mind, Chub had given her the cross and she wore it to help her remember him.

Patterson sometimes wondered if she didn't also have a vague memory of that meeting. Donnelly had said she didn't, but

Donnelly had said she didn't remember killing Callow either and that was a lie.

Over the years, he'd watched her from afar. Ensuring her safety, even when she didn't need it. He'd done the same for Nyleena, but Nyleena wasn't exactly Aislinn. She didn't attract the same sort of boogeymen. Although, there had been an incident while she was in college. Some creep trying to sneak into her apartment when her roommates were gone for a weekend. Patterson had dealt with him, never waking the sleeping Nyleena.

Nyleena consumed his thoughts now. She was sleeping again, but this time it was his fault. He could blame her or anything else he wanted, but it didn't change the internal knowledge that he had done that to her.

The room was starting to spin. He closed his eyes and drained the bottle of whiskey. Like Aislinn, he'd wake up feeling terrible, but hangovers didn't last long with Patterson and he wanted one more good night's sleep. One that didn't include dreams about his beautiful granddaughters writhing in pain and his hands covered in their blood.

Twenty-Four

For several moments, I wondered if I was awake or in Hell. Either was an option. I didn't remember much from the night before. I was still in my clothes and they smelled; body odor, decay, blood, vomit, grease, and alcohol all mingled. It was official, I had found something that smelled worse than a morgue and it was me.

Malachi lay on the bed next to me. He also looked and smelled terrible. His clothes were rumpled, his hair disheveled. If I hadn't looked at him for several seconds before deciding to stare at the ceiling to avoid his morning breath, I would have thought it was Xavier.

He moved. The movement caused both of us to groan. His hands rubbed at his face, as if that would cure what ailed him. It didn't, I had already tried.

"Next time you decide to get drunk, take some other sap with you. I'm never doing it again. You have no limit. I kept waiting for you to start table dancing and taking off your clothes." Malachi swung his legs out of the bed.

"I've never been drunk before." I thought for a moment. "I've also never had a hangover before. This is awful, why do people do this to themselves? It's like having a migraine, vertigo, cottonmouth, and being resurrected by a witch doctor all rolled into one."

"We got drunk, because you wanted to feel normal?" Malachi asked.

"No, I got drunk because I did not want to remember those days with Callow. My nurse was Kari's sister. I have no idea why you got drunk."

"You're my only friend, I couldn't let you get drunk alone."

There was something sad in that statement. It was something I knew, but never vocalized. Malachi didn't have friends, he had acquaintances. Sometimes, those acquaintances were very close, but he always managed to keep part of himself closed off. Instead of searching for an appropriate response, I went to the bathroom to grab a shower. Showers were cure-alls, a miracle recuperative force that could turn even the worst days into passable.

Malachi's depressing admission wasn't the only thing bothering me. This was the first time I'd ever been drunk. I was twenty-eight years old and felt like my days were limited. There were a lot of things I had never done. For the first time, I wondered if I could feel regret and if that was what I was feeling now.

It was a strange emotion to say the least, sadness tinged with a little bit of anger. Kelsey the Bubbly had thanked me for killing Callow. I wasn't thankful though. The act had created a hole in me. He should have suffered. He should have gone to jail and found out what hardened criminals did to pedophiles. And if he had lived in prison long enough for the creation of The Fortress, he should have gone there and suffered the hellish tortures that only serial killers could create.

That was the reason the tape had bothered me. I had killed him and it had been quick and rather merciful. It didn't even compare to what he had done to his victims. I'd felt the desire for revenge before, I had wanted to kill James Okafor for taking away Michael. This wasn't revenge though, revenge implied a rebalancing of the scales, at least in the mind of the avenger. This was something darker, something more primal. There wasn't a name for it. It wouldn't have healed the hole. It wouldn't have made me feel better. The dead little girls wouldn't have risen from their graves and reunited with loved ones. In the eyes of Karma, the wheel had been spun and balance had been restored. But in my soul, I felt like he'd avoided justice. Even if I believed in the concept of Hell and believed that he was serving eternity as one of Satan's favorite play things, it wasn't enough to satisfy me. I wanted more.

So, I'd gotten drunk to avoid that feeling. It had worked for a few hours. Now, I was sober and felt like Karma had kicked me in the teeth with steel-toed boots lined with spikes and the feeling had resurfaced.

The water was still running hot when I got out of the shower, but it usually did at hotels. It was hard to run out of hot water at a hotel. I'd done it, but only once.

Steam had clouded the bathroom mirror, for this, I was thankful. I didn't want to see myself now. I didn't want to look at the scars that covered my body, marking me as one of the death dealers of the serial killer world. I didn't want to stare at my reflection and wonder who was staring back.

Slowly, I wrapped my hair in one towel and my body in another. The towels weren't big enough to hide the brutality my body had seen. My memory, intent on driving me mad, flashed a quick replay of a group of people playing darts. They had been happy. They had been among friends. My mind had latched onto that image before the intoxication had sat in and decided that while I wallowed in self-loathing and pity, it would remind me of it.

I shook my head. These days one in five people would deal with a serial killer in some capacity. There was a better than average chance that at least one person in the bar last night had actually been a serial killer. My body wasn't the only one that bore the scars of this newest menace. Hundreds of thousands of people had fallen prey to serial killers since the 1960's. And that was just an estimate, possibly a very low estimate. You couldn't have a dramatic rise in serial killers without a dramatic rise in victims. Lucas liked to remind me that I wasn't alone, everyone in the SCTU had experienced a serial killer on a personal level.

Hell, the man outside my bathroom door had survived several. He'd been attacked twice by the monsters who didn't recognize him as lethal because of his suave manners and charming personality. I was positive there were a few others, others that no one knew about. Ones that Malachi had unleashed all his rage upon. Their bodies would be in worse condition than anything Patterson had created.

I stuck my head out the door, "do hangovers make you feel self-pity?"

"I'm not sure, why?"

"Just curious," I closed the door again. He was undressing, getting ready to take my place in the shower. I opened the door again. "When you look in the mirror, what do you see?"

"I see a face," Malachi answered, he was down to just a pair of jockey shorts. They were black with blue pinstripes. His body was as battered and beaten as my own. "I'm not sure it's my face though. Usually, it's the mask, the face I wear to appear mostly normal. I don't think I've ever seen my real face, I don't think we're supposed to. When we do, it causes us to have a meltdown, like you did last night. What do you see?"

"A stranger, a woman who looks like me and copies my movements, but does not feel like me."

"You see the mask too then," Malachi walked closer to the bathroom. If I wasn't me and he wasn't him, it might have been sexy. Instead, I felt like I was looking into a mirror. The face wasn't mine, the thoughts weren't exactly the same as mine, but it felt more like the real me than my reflection ever felt. "I'm sorry you saw that Aislinn, the real you, the one without the mask."

"Have you ever seen the real you?" I asked.

"No," Malachi frowned and his eyes locked on mine. "The closest I come is when I look into your eyes and they stare back at me with that cold blank stare that makes me wonder if you have a question or are wondering where to stick the knife first."

"I do not mean to look at you like that," I defended myself.

"Maybe not, but around me, you drop the mask more often, probably because I'm more monster than you."

"Good to know."

"I'm your comfort zone. You have friends and family and they mean a lot to you. But you still hide part of what you are when they are around. You don't bother to hide it when it's just us. Like now, you are staring at me and it could be that you want to ask more questions or it could be that you are admiring the scars, but it feels like your sizing me up, waiting to pounce and slit my throat. And before you ask, no, I don't know what sort of person that makes you. I think it makes you, you. Since finding out Patterson was The Butcher, you've been in this quasi-identity crisis that makes you question yourself. It's terribly annoying, I understand it though. You've often compared yourself to me, now you have Patterson to compare yourself to and the answers you're finding aren't what you want. You understand him, because his killings make sense to you. He isn't just wandering around the state, killing anyone with blond hair or wearing a purple shirt. And to make it worse, the one person that can answer your questions, is in the hospital, in a coma, unable to speak to you about your identity."

"Why am I comparing myself to Patterson? I get comparing myself to you. We've been locked in a silent battle for years, using mind games and logical tactics to put chinks in each other's armor. It's a way to connect and understand each other. But why Patterson? Why do I feel like I'm too much like him?"

"Because despite the name change and the not turning into a serial killer, you are his granddaughter. What better killer to compare yourself to than the one that donated your DNA? If Donnelly was still alive, he'd be asking himself similar questions and finding he didn't like the answers either."

"What would you know of my father's thoughts?"

"I know you've met Patterson before, live and in person. It wouldn't have happened if your father hadn't agreed." Malachi pulled me out of the bathroom. He entered closing the door behind him.

I sat down on the bed, unwilling or unable to change out of my towel. It had been a long time since anyone had said my father's name aloud to me. It was sacred, using it felt blasphemous. But Malachi was right. I pulled the small cross out of the pocket on my duffle bag full of clothes. I had met Patterson before. Like my father, his face was a blur, but he had given me the tiny cross. Chub had introduced him as a "friend" of his, but something had told me they were more than just friends. My eight year old mind had immediately made the connection between the brothers. Chub had taken me to meet Patterson Clachan and my father, Donnelly Clachan had agreed to let me go with Chub that day. Even I didn't buy the idea that my father hadn't known Patterson would be there.

Malachi exited the bathroom. He was in different jockey shorts, these were red with polka dots. I couldn't imagine Malachi wearing polka dots of any sort, let alone multicolored polka dots on his underwear.

"I do not remember his face," I told Malachi. "Patterson's I mean. I remember the way he talked though. His voice was smooth as silk and while he was introduced to me as a family friend, I could tell that the interactions between Uncle Chub and him were all wrong for friends. It did not take much for me to figure out they were brothers. That morning, my dad went out and bought me a silver necklace. He gave it to me, wrapped in a box with pink ribbon, only a few minutes before Chub come over. I asked why there was not a pendant and my dad told me there would be one soon enough, but it had to be the perfect pendant. At lunch, Patterson gave me a silver cross to put on it. My dad never asked about it, despite wearing it every day. He told everyone that Chub gave it to me and after a while, so did I."

"How does that make you feel about your father?"

"I do not remember him very well, strange since he did not die until I was in my teens. For some reason, I have blocked him out of my memories. His face is a complete mystery."

"I remember that you used to worship him. You swore you would follow in his footsteps and become a cop. Then you met Callow. Callow didn't change your father much, but he changed you, a lot. I know you don't believe that, but it's true. Donnelly became more protective of you, monitored your movements more, but he did that because he loved you. He saw that you would be like him, like Patterson, a magnet for people intent on doing evil deeds and he didn't want that life for you." Malachi sighed. "I know you say Callow didn't touch you, but he did. Maybe not physically, but psychologically, he touched you and you changed. You'd been a little bit of a trouble magnet before Callow, but after him, it was almost as if you went looking for it and it always found you."

"Malachi," I lit a cigarette. "Callow did not molest me, he did not touch me at all. His hand was shaking when he crawled into that hollow where he kept me. Callow did not molest me, because Callow was afraid of me. I have always known that. That is why I did not scream when the police arrived at his house. It would have gotten me out of there sooner, but I was enjoying the fact that he had kidnapped the wrong girl and was afraid of her. It was my chance to turn the tables on him. I planned to kill him from the moment I woke up in that hiding spot. Somehow, Callow knew."

"You've never told me that."

"I have never told anyone that. For years, I would not even admit it to myself. It was not the kill that I liked, it was the anticipation of it. Does that make me a serial killer?"

"No, that makes you Aislinn Cain, scourge of serial killers all over these crazy United States. Do you know why? Because you didn't act upon the urge again until you were forced into a similar situation. You aren't a cold blooded killer. You're a survivor, liking it doesn't make you evil."

"I did not like killing Callow. I felt dirty afterwards. I showered six or seven times during my first day home. I still dream of him. And now, I do not want him dead, I want him languishing in The Fortress, being tortured by other serial killers."

"That sounds rather normal to me." Malachi said. "If I had been in your position, it would be different. I would have enjoyed the kill and I wouldn't have just defended myself and run away, screeching like a banshee to attract attention. I would have tortured him and I would have loved every scream that came from his lips. And that is rather normal too. Not because he was a pedophile or a serial killer, but because you were a victim. I know you never think of yourself as such, but you were. Perhaps for the only time in your life, you were a victim and victims have feelings that they can't express because it makes them feel bad."

The word was foreign in my ears. I couldn't imagine myself as a victim, but listening to Malachi, I realized that the word did apply to me. It was why I had feelings for people impacted by Callow. We were all victims of Callow.

Twenty-Five

Rollins met us in the lobby. He held two bottles of water and two small packets of something. As we drew even with him, he handed each of us a bottle and a packet. I stared at them blankly.

"Well, come on then, plop, plop, fizz, fizz," Rollins grinned.

"Why is he saying the Alka-Seltzer commercial tag line?" I asked Malachi.

"You have a hangover," Rollins said.

"I do have a hangover." I agreed, staring at the bottle and packet. "So, is this a powder or a pill?"

"You've never had Alka-Seltzer?" Rollins' grin faded.

"She's never had a hangover. She's never been drunk either. I also don't think she's ever vomited on herself, gotten into an argument with a mirror, or crawled under a table to avoid being seen by goblins. The last twenty-four hours have been full of firsts for her."

"Wow. You've never been drunk?" Rollins was taking the bottle and packet back. He opened the packet and snapped two large tablets into four pieces. Then he opened the bottle of water and dropped the tablets into them. They immediately began to hiss and fizz.

My water was turning bubbly and pink. Malachi had already up ended his bottle and chugged it. If I chugged it, I was going to toss my cookies again. I took a drink, not liking the taste or the feeling. There was a hint of cherry to the tablets.

"There is no relief in this." I told him.

"It gets worse," Malachi said.

"It cannot get worse," I took another drink. Alcohol was off my list again, this time it was a permanent situation.

"Not the Alka-Seltzer, this," Malachi handed a credit card to me. The name on it read Virgil Clachan.

"Where did you get this?" I asked, flipping it over. It wasn't signed, but the stripe was wearing off from heavy use.

"He paid your bar tab last night," Rollins told me. "What's weirder is that there is a card to that account in your name too, but there isn't a signature on file. Now, we have a dead body in Boonville and we need to get some dinner into the both of you. Which do you want to do first?"

"Arby's, as we leave town," I told him. In the backseat, I ate my dinner. The sun was already starting to set. Rays of sunlight stabbed through the windows. My sandwich was great though and I could use Malachi to avoid the setting sun daggers. He was busy looking at a file folder. I couldn't read in the car, it made me sick. Staring down at my food threatened to do the same thing. It was all about the feeling of motion without being able to see the motion.

"Hey, Ace," Malachi turned enough to look at me. "The victim's name is Jeremy Cole."

"Nyleena's Jeremy Cole?" I raised an eyebrow.

"Yep."

"Of course it is, what was I thinking," I went back to eating my sandwich. Nyleena was quite a bit older than me, but she was my best friend. I knew all her secrets and some of them were less secret than others. Jeremy Cole was less secret because he was a jackass. I had threatened to kill him years ago, but he'd been arrested first. The man had served six years for assault and battery as well as sexual assault.

Nyleena had been in her last year of high school. Jeremy Cole was a "cool dude" that was a few years older than she was. They started dating. One night, he beat the shit out of her and raped her. I hoped Patterson had done something particularly nasty to him.

This newest kill earned Patterson some points with me. I was still pissed that he had shot Nyleena in the face and put her in the coma, but it waned just a little bit as I saw the crime scene tape wrapped around the house.

There are a lot of ways that you can describe death and a dead person. Except in this case, the only thing that described this guy was hacked to death. From head to toe, Patterson had taken an axe or other sharp object and disarticulated the joints. He didn't bother with the fingers or the toes, but the rest of them had been hacked through. Patterson had a sense of humor, the head had been removed and placed on a silver platter. By the looks of things, I was guessing he'd brought the silver platter with him.

The primary decor was made up of empty beer cans, moldy plates, and marijuana seeds. Just standing in the place made me wonder about the types of fungus that could become airborne and make a person sick. I was positive they were growing in the place. There was probably E.coli and Anthrax reproducing in the dirty carpet.

"We have a survivor!" Someone shouted from another room. This surprised me. Survivors were a rare thing with serial killers. I had to see, so I followed the voice down a dirty hallway to a bedroom.

Tucked inside the closet was a young woman. She was roughly my age. Her eye was black, her lip busted open, and there were needle marks on her arm.

Rollins came in and started trying to talk to her. This was an exercise in futility. She rambled about waking up to find the devil had come to visit. There was some truth to this, but I was guessing that she'd been stoned out of her gourd when Patterson came by. Since she wasn't a threat, he hadn't killed her. It was nice to know there were limits.

An EMT pulled her out of the closet. There was a note pinned to her back. I smiled. The note said "needs rehab and a bath. didn't shower here, too dirty. check casino hotel."

"Great, he's taunting us," Rollins groaned.

"He's been taunting us, you just hadn't figured it out yet. He killed the guy in Jeff City two days ago, but he still showed up at the bar where Aislinn and I went for dinner in that town, even though I'd bet he was staying in

Columbia, and he stuck a victim in a field with mutilated cattle." Malachi snorted.

"But, we have the upper hand now," I looked at Malachi. "His next stop is going to be Kansas City. He has a head start, but that's not going to matter a whole lot. We know his targets there. I would rejoice about finding the video footage from the casino, but aside from the cane, I bet he's wearing a disguise."

"Who is his next target?" Rollins asked.

"Gertrude," I answered. Somehow, Patterson had a plan to get to his sister. It would be his last kill. This was all getting tiring for him. It showed in his writing, which had a minute wiggle in the letters, indicating his hand was shaking. And his victim choice, there were other people in Columbia that he could have killed, but he didn't. He'd moved on. This one was important; for Nyleena, the head on the silver platter was a peace offering. An "I'm sorry I shot you in the face" gift. The affect wasn't lost on me. I'd tell her about it when she woke up.

I walked outside and lit a cigarette. Reporters were gathering outside the house, they invaded the lawns of the neighbors. Of course, the neighbors were invading their own lawns as well. A few peeked from around their curtains, but most were brazenly standing in their yard. How many of them had known about the drug user and abusive asshole in the house next door? I didn't know, but I felt a touch of contempt for each of them.

Smoking in the cold ranked higher than standing in rooms with dead bodies on my list of things to do, so I lit a cigarette and moved outside the protection of the tape, into the street. If I was smoking, the press wouldn't film or talk to me. It was a trick I'd learned a while ago.

As expected, none of them approached me. None of them turned their nosy, unforgiving cameras my direction. Some even moved away, back towards filming the house. Malachi stepped out and for a moment, it looked like they might mob him. But he'd learned the trick as well and lit his own cigarette. The reporters went back to standing on the dead lawns of the neighbors. Malachi moved to stand in front of me, his back to the reporters, like we were sharing important information. The protective gesture was kind of sweet. Except more than one reporter had speculated over the years that Malachi and I were an item, even before I'd become a member of the SCTU. The fact that we worked for different federal agencies only fanned the flames and fueled the imaginations of those that liked to dig up dirt on law enforcement officials. If they knew the truth, they would be shocked and horrified.

Malachi blew his smoke over my head, but didn't speak to me. I blew mine to the side, trying to avoid blowing it into his face. His body radiated warmth but smelled like blood. My eyes searched his clothing to see what he had touched to cause the smell. We hadn't been in there long enough to smell like death and blood; unless you had it on you, didn't leave trace scents.

A speck of crimson caught my attention. It soaked into Malachi's cigarette, just past the filter. I pointed at it.

Malachi looked down at his blood stained smoke and tossed it on the ground. He examined his finger, found the wound, just deep enough to create droplets. Pulling something out of his pocket, he wrapped it around his finger. It was an Arby's napkin with grease stains that smelled of roast beef and French fries. The napkin wasn't the most sterile thing he could have wrapped it in, but whatever he'd cut himself on was probably worse.

Finger wrapped, he lit another cigarette. Fascinated, I watched the napkin as it changed from white to pale pink. Malachi was less interested in this phenomenon than I was. He'd gone back to staring at the house.

Eventually, I gave in and turned around as well. The house hadn't changed. Malachi was lost in his own mind. It was a talent of his. His IQ might not have been higher, but his brain worked in a different way. He could make connections that I couldn't. He didn't need all the pieces to see the picture. It was very annoying to do a jigsaw puzzle with him or Sudoku. He would say the same about me and crosswords or word searches.

After a long time, long enough for my feet to go numb and my legs to start to tingle from the cold, I shrugged and looked up to the taller man that resembled Death. His face was still turned towards the house, the cigarette had burned out between his fingers. I wondered if he was having some sort of episode.

"Hey, I give, what do you see?" I asked Malachi.

"Huh?" He looked at me like I had just appeared. "Oh, not much. For all the studying and profiling and hours dedicated to him, I still don't understand him."

"I'll let you in on a secret," I motioned Malachi close, as if I were about to give him the secret cookie recipe that would make him rich and famous. He leaned in. "Patterson is slightly crazy. Not like psychopath crazy, but like the elevator stops a few floors short of the penthouse crazy."

"I'm not sure I understand the analogy," Malachi whispered back to me.

"That sucks, because I'm not sure I can explain it." I cocked my head to the side and looked up at Malachi. "Okay, let's try this. I'm a sociopath with an anxiety disorder. The two are not compatible. In no way, shape or form should I have an anxiety disorder, but I do. Why? Because I do not actually have one, my mind just manifests one as a way to cope with not feeling anything. That's kind of crazy and not like normal crazy, but special crazy. Patterson's a psychopath, so you imagine that he has the same range of emotions you do, but the disorder effects everyone slightly different. Also, you never had to justify eating people. The man can butcher another human, but passes out when he cooks a steak. You only seem to see the psychopath, I see the man with serious issues beyond being a psychopath and as I said, the elevator is not travelling to the top floor."

Malachi looked at me like bugs had just crawled out my nose. For a moment, I had to fight the impulse not to check. Surely, I would feel bugs crawling out of my nose.

"You are a genius," Malachi said.

"Well, duh, but we knew that already. What are you blabbering about?"

"I never thought of Patterson as anything other than a psychopath. As such, his movements should have been predictable. But he isn't just a psychopath, he's a psychopath with issues. That's why I can't figure him out."

"Glad I could give you a 'eureka moment.'"

"You have no idea how much of an epiphany that was."

"Maybe you should have asked me about it a week ago. I figured it out when we were hunting August."

"Speaking of which, perhaps we should rally the FBI agent and tally forth to Kansas City," Malachi started walking away. I stared at his back. People thought I occasionally said some off the wall things, like my recent interest in calling Gabriel "Kemosabe." At least that had a rational explanation. I had never seen an episode of the *Lone Ranger* and one weekend, Gabriel had shown up with snack food, take-out menus, and the box set. We watched every episode of the old TV show. I'd been randomly addressing him as "Kemosabe" since that weekend. However, why Malachi had suddenly decided to start talking like a 19th Century

British nobleman was beyond me. We all had quirks.

Twenty-Six

I was back at the hospital. It took time to set up a prisoner transfer and let Patterson get wind of it. Setting traps was akin to playing Russian roulette, sometimes it worked in your favor, sometimes you shot yourself in the head. I was hoping we weren't getting ready to shoot ourselves in the head.

Monitors beeped, machines whirred, and the entire room was still ugly. Flowers, balloons, and cards littered the available surfaces. I moved my card, complete with gift card to the very front again. The gift card was to Amazon, she'd be off work for a couple more months. She was going to get bored, maybe. Nyleena didn't lead the shut-in life that I did.

A book sat on the stand next to her bed. A bookmark was tucked between the pages. I picked up the book and looked at the title; *Storm Front* by Jim Butcher. I hadn't read *The Dresden Files*, but I'd loved the TV show. I was sure I would picture Paul Blackthorne as Dresden and probably not love the book as much.

This was one of my mother's books. She loved urban fantasy fiction. While I hadn't seen it on a shelf at her house, it didn't take a genius to figure it out. She still hadn't moved to the age of eBooks.

I began reading. Reading aloud wasn't my thing. It required me to read slower and my brain would disengage from time to time. When it did get distracted, my mouth would continue to move, working on autopilot, while it thought of other things. This kept me from getting interested in most books that I was reading to my comatose compadre.

Storm Front was no different. I'd read a handful of pages when my brain disengaged and my mind tuned out what I was reading. Instead, it focused on Malachi Blake.

Malachi was an odd duck, to say the least. His need for me was mirrored by my need for him. It wasn't exactly the same sort of need, but it was similar. If I could look at him, I could reassure myself that I wasn't that far down the rabbit hole. There was something to be said for that. Maybe not much, but something.

For a moment, I understood how Dr. Frankenstein felt. Malachi was a monster, but he was my monster. In many ways, he was my creation, I kept him in control by not letting him have control over me. It was a circular logic, but there wasn't a better way to explain it.

My mind never stayed focused on Malachi for very long. It always found a new subject to explore. I didn't know the reason behind it. Some sort of mental block kept me from thinking about him too intently, perhaps it was afraid of what I would find behind the mask that he wore.

"How's she doing?" My mother's head appeared in the door. Her voice was soft, harmonious.

"The same," I told my mother. Mom entered the room, closing the door quietly behind her.

"How are you doing?" She asked.

"It would be better if she were awake and Patterson were in custody. Unfortunately, I only get to control one of those things."

"How very confident of you," my mother frowned and I got the impression that "confident" was not the word she had wanted to use.

"But?" I asked her.

"Don't be too quick to believe that you control the situation with Patterson."

"You know him," I looked at my mother with a new feeling.

"Sort of, I've met him, once. After your brother did what he did. Patterson came by the house, not as himself, but as a friend of the family. However, his eyes. Your father had those same eyes, as do you. We spoke for maybe twenty minutes and I realized that your father had been concerned for no reason. Eric might have been like Patterson, but you weren't. You would never follow in your grandfather's footsteps. You have too much heart."

"I do not have much heart," I told my mother.

"No, you don't think you have much heart, but you do. Look at you here, reading to Nyleena or running all over the state with Malachi attempting to catch a serial killer. If you were heartless you wouldn't do those things. Same for Malachi. We've been trying to explain that to the both of you for ages. While you may not feel what I feel, or even what your dad felt, you do feel Aislinn, both of you do and you can both love. You love me, Elle, the kids, Nyleena, your SCTU team members, even Malachi. You may not think of it as love, because it's more familial than romantic, but it is still love and that's a powerful emotion."

"So is hate," I told my mother.

"True, but how many people do you honestly hate? Callow? You can't even hate your own serial killing grandfather."

My mother had a point. I didn't hate my grandfather. I should have. He was a serial killer, after all, and I'd been staring at his carnage for over a week. But hate required a lot of effort. Long ago, I'd learned I was emotionally lazy as well as emotionally challenged. As such, I only had enough energy to hate one person at a time and that hate was still focused on Callow, despite his death.

Strange that death didn't really change my opinion of him. If I could resurrect him and kill him all over again, I would. Multiple times. I'd just spend the rest of my life resurrecting him and finding new ways to kill him. As such, I didn't have room to hate anything else in my life.

It was probably what kept me sane. Since I only had the ability to hate one person, I couldn't hate the rest of the world. Bizarre, sad, and pathetic, but true. My encounter with Callow had changed me and for the first time, I saw exactly how it had changed me. It had saved me from myself.

In turn, I had saved Malachi from himself. A twisted form of paying it forward, my act of kindness and acceptance, had kept him from giving into his urges. As we aged, my unwillingness to let him control me, like he did everything else in his life, kept him intrigued by things that weren't born of the darkness inside him.

My mother's voice brought me out of myself. It was soothing, rhythmic, and soft as she read to Nyleena from the Jim Butcher book. As she read, I couldn't help but notice the resemblance between her and Nyleena. There were definite differences, but they had the same blue-grey eyes. The same smile. Looking at the two of them, I could see Nyleena as my mother's daughter.

She didn't look much like my father's side of the family. Until recently, I had assumed she had looked like her mother, a woman I had never known. I had met her a few times, but like everyone else time had faded her features. She had disappeared one day, either the victim of something tragic or simply a women seeking escape from the chaos of her life. Either was possible. Nyleena hadn't mentioned her in a long time. I think she had given up on finding her, dead or alive. She spoke of her in past tense.

For just a heartbeat, the green-eyed monster reared its ugly head. In that heartbeat, I had wondered if my mother loved Nyleena more than me. It was a ridiculous thought. My mother loved just about everyone. She'd accepted the damage members of the SCTU just as she had Malachi. Even if Nyleena hadn't been her biological daughter, she would have loved her like one.

That was my mother's greatest strength and greatest weakness. I felt almost no love and she felt only love. She could love anyone, forgive anyone, and accept anyone. It seemed surreal that this woman filled with love had spawned a mass murderer and me. It made sense that she would give birth to Nyleena and my sister, Isabelle. They were good people. In a world where the genetics was still part of the equation in what made a monster, my parents were an interesting sample.

"Stop pacing," my mother snipped between lines in the book. I looked at her, unaware that I had been pacing. My feet stopped moving. "Now, you're glaring."

"Sorry," I looked at my feet. The boots made my feet look small and round. I wasn't often aware of any of my body parts and staring at my feet was strange. It was like seeing my reflection, I knew they were mine, but my brain felt disconnected from them.

"Why don't you go help Malachi?" My mother suggested.

"Because at the moment, Malachi does not need my help. He is a more convincing liar than I am."

"That's true," my mother began reading from the book again. I sat down in another chair, putting my feet up in the final, empty chair. My eyes closed as Harry Dresden argued with a character I hadn't caught the name of. My body relaxed. It was a side effect of being around my mother. It was hard to stay on high alert all the time, especially with my mother's library voice reading aloud.

I drifted off to sleep. Not my normal fitful sleep with deranged dreams and haunting serial killers, but a deep sleep free of the dreadful terrors my mind could conjure. Few people put me at ease like my mother. It was strange that she could do it, I felt the need to protect her and yet, with her around, I felt like no evil could touch me. This conflict raged in me only when I was awake. My sleeping mind instead created images of fields full of butterflies hunting for nectar among the wildflowers while a large, lazy dog panted steadily in a patch of sunlight.

Twenty-Seven

Several Marshals had their guns drawn, held down near their legs, ready to be brought up and put to use in the space of a heartbeat. Two walked in front of us, two walked behind us and there was one on each side of us. It was a standard protection formation when dealing with a prisoner of high risk. Malachi and I held my great-aunt Gertrude between us.

The protection formation was great, unless there was a sniper around. If there was, Malachi was screwed, he towered over the rest of the Marshals. On the other hand, I disappeared among them.

We were nearing our destination and yet, there was no sign of Patterson. I tried to stop my mind from jumping to conclusions about choosing the wrong target. It screamed that we should have moved August, not Gertrude. That part of my brain was irrational and I wouldn't give into it. I knew that August would not elicit the response that Gertrude would. Patterson had tried to kill the man before, but he hadn't tried in Columbia. That meant there was something else to his end game and the logical part of my brain told me it was Gertrude.

One hundred feet between us and the courthouse. At the door, we'd have to hand her off to the courthouse Marshals. All capable, trained federal officers, to be sure, but I didn't like the idea.

Fifty feet. My gaze scanned the crowd in between the bodies of the Marshals. A large group had assembled to watch us walk the mother of the Columbia Cannibal into court. This moniker, earned in the last two weeks, was incorrect. August wasn't a cannibal, telling that to the press was a lost cause though and I knew better than to argue with the press. We didn't have good history.

Forty feet. Still no signs of the older man with the elaborate cane. Malachi made eye contact with me briefly, then returned his own gaze to surveying the crowds. His height gave him an advantage over me.

Thirty feet. My hand wanted to grab my own gun. I fought the urge. It hung loose at my side, but only through a sheer effort of will.

Twenty feet. I'd been bait before. I'd never been so jittery about it though. The calm that kept me alive hadn't come over me. The darkness that I depended on to keep me in control was absent.

Ten feet. I took a breath and held it. My feet moved automatically. My hand tugged at the arm of Gertrude Clachan, ensuring that she moved with us. Our pace had to be agonizingly slow for Malachi. The doors of the court house opened. Gertrude pinched me. I didn't look at her. If I were in her shoes, I'd be relieved.

Hand off. The two Marshals in front took up positions to the side. Malachi and I both let go of Gertrude, handing her to the new Marshals. Both men took firm hold of her. They moved forward. Malachi and I, determined to see her in the court room, followed.

A flash of black hair. My gaze caught the head for just a second, then it was gone, lost in the throng of Marshals and court house attendees. The press had been allowed into the hallways. Cameras flashed, someone took a picture only a few feet from me, blinding me for a moment.

"He's here," Malachi answered, pushing forward. I followed, shoving past the Marshals.

"Get down!" I shouted, pulling my gun on the small, elderly man with black hair. He raised his hands as he sunk to his knees. The hallway went silent. An echo of something metal hitting the floor rang loudly off the walls and floor. There was blood on one of the hands. I looked up. Gertrude sagged between the two Marshals. Blood gurgled out of her mouth and streamed from under her chin.

Malachi's gun was also aimed at the small man. Malachi faced him. I could only see his back. My need to see his face was overwhelming. I carefully stepped around him, moving in front.

He looked nothing like the identi-kit sketch. My father's face flashed in my memory. They looked a lot alike or would have, if my father had aged. The same small nose with its sharp point, the same smile with full, almost pouty lips. He wasn't ugly. Actually, for an older man, he was very attractive. He also didn't look a day over sixty.

However, it was his eyes that caught my attention and held them. My father had dark eyes, like milk chocolate. Patterson's weren't the same color as my father's. They were the same color as mine, a little lighter than milk chocolate with a tinge of darker brown around the edges. Technically, it was too dark to be considered hazel, but the ring was rare in people with brown eyes, so they were often mistaken as hazel.

"Hello Malachi," Patterson looked at my friend before turning to me. "Hello granddaughter." A ripple went through the crowd. Flashbulbs instantly began going off. I was going to be on the front page tomorrow.

"Patterson," Malachi said. "Put your hands behind your back."

"Of course," Patterson moved, putting his hands behind his back. We had caught The Butcher, but only because he had wanted to get caught. I pursed my lips together trying not to show my anger. There was no way I could put a bullet in Patterson Clachan, there were witnesses. Besides, despite his status as a serial killer, he was still my grandfather. If I needed any proof, it was there for the world to see. I looked like my father, Donnelly Clachan, and he, in turn, looked like his father, Patterson Clachan.

"Marshal Cain?" Someone spoke my name very quietly behind me. I turned to look at them. A Marshal, covered in blood, was speaking to me. His lips moved, his voice could be heard, but his words seemed to be in a foreign language.

"Are you okay, Marshal Cain?" Someone else asked me.

"Fine," I shook the fog that threatened to overtake me.

"You're shaking," the first Marshal whispered. "Let's get you out of this room."

"I'm fine," I looked down. Blood was pooling on the floor. "We need to get the reporters out of here. The last thing we want is my aunt's bleeding corpse on the front page."

"Ok, but only if you agree to sit down," the second Marshal said to me.

I took a step. My knee buckled. It collided with the marble floor, sending a shockwave of pain up into my hip. Confusion set in and with it, the darkness. My mind slowly replayed the events. Gertrude pinching me as I handed her off to the court house Marshals. My hand went to the fleshy area of my side, just above the waistline of my pants. Wet, warm liquid was soaking into my shirt. The bitch hadn't pinched me, she'd stabbed me. I'd been so focused on Patterson, I hadn't realized it.

"Aislinn!" Patterson shouted my name. "Get off me, get off me! What's wrong with her?" His voice carried over the noise of feet being ushered away. I stood up.

"There's nothing wrong with me," I looked at him.

"You're bleeding," Patterson told me.

"Just a nick," I told him, feeling myself get angrier. Malachi walked over. He leaned in close to me.

"It's more than a nick. Let me see," Malachi tried to pry up my shirt.

"You are not a doctor," I snipped at him, while my fingers touched the wound. There was something hard in it and small. I slowed my breathing, trying to slow my heart rate.

"Don't be difficult," Malachi snipped back.

"You just want to see what's under my shirt," I told him, feeling myself grow unsteady again.

"You are not all right," Malachi grabbed hold of me. "Let one of the other Marshals look."

"Fine," I yanked my shirt up.

"Oh shit," Malachi said, suddenly pressing something over the wound. "Medic, we need a medic, now."

"What is it?" I asked.

"Honestly?" Malachi frowned.

"I have been stabbed before," I reminded him.

"With an ink pen tube?" Malachi asked.

"No, that's new." I admitted.

"You're actually spewing out blood." Malachi put more pressure on the side. "I don't know if she hit an artery or a vital organ, but I can't believe how much you're bleeding."

"Figures," I sighed. "I never make it through a case without getting injured. Never."

"Get off me!" Patterson shouted again. A collective grunt followed it and Patterson was suddenly at my side, hands grabbed at him.

"Leave him for the moment, maybe he can help." Malachi looked at Patterson. "Well, any suggestions?"

"I should have killed her outside." Patterson sighed. His head fell.

Someone grabbed hold of his cuffs and this time, he let them. For the first time, he looked close to his age. His face had fallen, lines creased it. I realized it was concern and defeat on his face. He was convinced I was going to die.

"I'm not going to die," I snapped at him. "Just follow their orders. I still owe you for shooting Nyleena."

Patterson smiled at me. Malachi did as well. Neither of their elevators went all the way to the top.

"Where are the medics?" The first Marshal to notice there was something wrong with me shouted.

Like Moses parting the Red Sea, a gurney with two burly looking paramedics appeared. I wondered if they were used to dealing with psychopaths and not injured Marshals. It wouldn't surprise me.

The paramedics helped me onto the gurney. One of them began applying bandages. Malachi stood over me, looking down at my face, concern flickering in his eyes. I frowned at him.

"You realize this capture was as anticlimactic as the serial killer in Nevada." I told him.

"What?" Malachi asked.

"The artist that was killing people with mercury. He accidentally killed himself. It was a very unsatisfying end. Now, after nearly fifty years, The Butcher just walks into a court house and turns himself in."

"Well, he did kill your aunt." Malachi said.

"She deserved it," I closed my eyes. "An ink pen tube of all things. Where did she get it? You should figure out which Marshal lost an ink pen and tell Gabriel to deal with it. I'd tell you to do it, but you'd end up killing them."

"Ok, I'll see you at the hospital."

"Hey, if I have to have surgery, put me in Nyleena's room after recovery."

Twenty-Eight

The ink pen tube was plastic. The end had been chipped and sharpened. It had taken time to create, this ruled out the possibility that my now deceased great-aunt had taken it off a Marshal. It also raised questions about how she'd managed to get it into the transport vehicle.

I wasn't really surprised that she had tried to kill me with it. She'd never liked me, but more than that, people didn't like being dangled as serial killer bait. She'd known Patterson would kill her. Taking me with her was a last act of defiance. I couldn't really blame her for that. If I had been in her shoes, I probably would have tried to kill me too.

An audiobook played on Xavier's iPod. The words cast into the room through special speakers that he had also loaned me. At least they had put me in Nyleena's room. We could be recovery buddies.

The tube had hit my kidney. After learning this, I had demanded a shower. I'd had to settle for a sponge bath. All the warm, wet liquid hadn't been blood and the thought of urine leaking from my side was gross. I was amazed I hadn't smelled it.

But then, I hadn't been thinking about smells. I had been concentrating on people's faces. This was a difficult task for me. There was a vague memory of the scent, but I had thought it was coming off my great-aunt. Being used as bait could easily have made her a little leaky in the pipework's department. Plus, she had been old. Old people occasionally just leaked. It was one of the problems with getting old.

Besides, urine was one of those human smells that you get used to, like menstrual blood. I could always tell when a woman standing near me was menstruating and the smell was slightly different than regular blood. There were other smells you learned to ignore just because they were common, human smells. Like a sweet, tangy scent on someone's breathe when they have a sinus infection or the smell of decay when they have a bad tooth.

Most people didn't know or understand that I smoked to help control the olfactory onslaught that I dealt with every day. Smoking masked some of it, kept me from being overwhelmed by the sensory information. I could still tell if someone smoked, was wearing a scented deodorant or had drank a cup of coffee recently.

My kidney wasn't in danger, at least that's what they said. They stitched the hole closed, in both the organ and the flesh. It hurt, but it was a dull, aching pain that affected my back more than my side. A catheter ran out from under the blankets and attached to the bed. In the three hours since I had awoken from surgery, they'd already had to turn down the IV. I was always well hydrated. The IV just made me retain more fluid and my hands looked pudgier than normal.

So pudgy in fact, that I'd had to give up on exploring my new toy. Malachi, in an attempt to be nice, had decided to load up some new books on my Kindle. Somehow, he had dropped it in a puddle of water. I was still fuzzy on the details. However, he'd immediately gone out and replaced it, not with a Kindle, but with a tablet.

The tablet was a little bigger than the Kindle and it had more reading apps. The surgery had taken about an hour and I'd spent another two hours in recovery before getting to my room. It was during these hours that

Malachi had ruined my Kindle, bought the replacement, and loaded it with reading apps. Unfortunately, with the pudgy fingers, I was having trouble typing in any of my passwords to access my book collection.

Which brought me back to what I was doing. They had given me the ink pen tube. It had been cleaned thoroughly and it wasn't needed for evidence. They'd found the missing bits in Gertrude's jail cell. If I wanted to keep it, I could. There was a morbid fascination with keeping it. I'd never been given the opportunity to keep a weapon that had been used in an attempt to kill me.

Lucas would have plenty to say about my keeping it. However, I couldn't bring myself to pitch it. Part of me found it hard to believe that this little piece of plastic had almost brought me down. It was like Batman finding out that his suit didn't protect against Tasers.

There was a second container as well. This one was a small round dish with a lid on it, a specimen jar. Inside, nearly invisible through the clear plastic walls, were tiny plastic splinters. Pieces of the tube that broke off as it entered my skin and kidney. Those, I were not going to keep.

"Have I been sucking on salt cubes? My mouth is so dry," Nyleena spoke softly from the second bed.

"Forced oxygen will do that to you," I said. "Oh shit, you're awake!" I exclaimed and began frantically pressing my call button.

"Marshal, what do you need now?" A nurse, who looked very tired of me, came into the room. I pointed at Nyleena.

"Oh," she hopped into action. Several people began to fill the room. All of them were wearing either white coats or nurses uniforms. Someone set a clipboard down on my bed. Normally, I would have pitched a fit about this obvious disregard for me, but I let it slide. Nyleena was awake. The world could breathe a collective sigh for a few minutes as I stopped being my usual self.

Our room stayed full and busy for almost an hour. Tests were being done. The situation was explained. The longer they talked, the more tired Nyleena looked.

"Out, harbingers of gloom, let her rest a while and wrap her head around the situation." I eventually yelled. "It is difficult to come out of a coma." I spoke from experience. It was strange coming out of a coma. There was more than just lost time to contend with. Even as an emotionally-challenged person, I'd had a flood of emotions when I came out of mine. Plus, Nyleena had a hole in her face. It was covered, but it was still a hole. Even with stitches, I was always acutely aware of holes in my body.

"Thanks," Nyleena said. "Patterson put you here?"

"No, Patterson killed Gertrude, while she was in custody and then quietly surrendered. It was very unsatisfying. Gertrude did this to me. She stabbed me with the tube of a plastic ink pen. It lodged in my kidney and I didn't notice the leakage until after we had Patterson in custody and Gertrude was dead."

"Did you talk to him?"

"Only to order him to the ground." I told her. "Another day perhaps. I may decide to visit him while he's in The Fortress, but I honestly do not know what to say to him."

"Me either."

"You should shoot him in the face and ask him how it feels." I told her.

"I'm not really mad at him for it. I know Nina asked him too." Nyleena sighed. "I mean, she asked him to kill her, shooting me wasn't really the plan."

"How would you know that?" I asked.

"She told me, on the way to the restaurant. I didn't expect him to do it right that moment, but," Nyleena adjusted her bed. "I had the weirdest dreams about Ranger and the demon, Crowley. They aren't even from the same books."

"You always did have a thing for bad boys." I grinned at her. "By the way, Patterson killed one of your ex-boyfriends, the Jack-Ass, I cannot actually remember his name at the moment."

"Ah," Nyleena closed her eyes.

"Still tired?"

"My face hurts."

"Go back to sleep, it will hurt less when you sleep. I will turn on another audiobook."

"I think I've slept enough for a while."

"Well, you do not have to talk."

"How'd he kill Gertrude?"

"He took a really long hunting knife and shoved it through her chin, up into her skull. Then he yanked it out."

"Nina told me we're sisters, biologically speaking."

"That's what our DNA says. My parents gave birth to you. It does not change anything. You are still my friend and my cousin. We got a new person in the SCTU, it's a girl, her name is Fiona."

"Pretty name."

"Xavier says I'm going to hate her."

"That's ominous."

"I know," I told her. "I think I get out tomorrow, but I'll keep you stocked up in books and things."

"Thanks," Nyleena touched the bandage. "How bad is it?"

"I do not know, I have not seen it." I shrugged and the motion kind of hurt.

We settled into silence after that. Despite her protestations, Nyleena fell back asleep. Her soft snoring drifted to me, reassuring me that she was alive. I put the ink pen tube back in the baggy and stared at the ceiling.

My mind searched for something to think about and decided to think about Patterson. I hadn't lied to Nyleena, I had no idea what to say to the man. He might have been my grandfather, but aside from a few homicidal urges and the same ringed eyes, we didn't have much in common.

I pushed the button for the Demerol and was rewarded by the drug surging through my veins. This was why people became addicted to drugs. It stopped the brain from thinking. Mine turned off as it started working on the chemical receptors in my brain. I closed my eyes and let Nyleena's snores take me off to sleep as well.

Mazes

The test run had been only mildly successful. The strain not nearly potent enough, not contagious enough. This new strain though, showed promise. If history had taught her anything, it was that sometimes, a virus or bacteria suddenly became very contagious and suddenly started wiping out huge populations.

The new strain was antibiotic resistant. She'd stolen the rats years ago from a university lab, keeping the bacteria alive by keeping a fresh supply of rats and mice for the fleas to breed upon. She wasn't a scientist and could only guess that she had made it resistant to antibiotics by partially treating some of the rats.

At the moment, she had roughly four hundred rats, running around in a giant maze in an out building. Rats were easy to catch, she was an exterminator for the city of Dallas. Which was good, because it took about two weeks for the rats to die. The mice were another story though. She was finding the mice population, while most certainly infected, weren't showing as many symptoms and took a lot longer to die. This was both helpful and problematic.

The fleas that carried bubonic plague wouldn't leave their host until the host died. In the rats, this meant a transfer every couple of weeks. In the mice, it took a whole lot longer.

Her plan was simple, infect the rat population of a major city. At least, it sounded simple. She'd have to keep rats in stock that she knew had plague and she didn't exactly have the equipment to test every rat. She couldn't mix the rats and mice, the rats tended to kill their smaller cousins.

In Dallas, she could trap twenty or thirty rats a day and bring them back to the house. She'd put them in the tubes and wait for them to get infected, but unleashing small waves of infected rats didn't seem like a good dispersal method.

Dropping fleas on people was unrealistic. How would she get the fleas off the rats? These were problems for another day. She was tired. She'd think about it some more in a week or two. Maybe she could expand her tube system. If she did, she could hold more rats. Maybe if she could get two or three thousand rats infected and release all of them at the same time, it would work better.

With that thought in mind, she went to bed. Her pillow was soft. It cradled her head perfectly. All the years of torment and abuse were going to be repaid. That thought soothed her to sleep.

Epilogue

There was an impression of my butt on my couch. It was the first time I had actually noticed it. It glared at me, indicating that I sat in that one spot far too much. I'd owned the couch for a year and it was supposed to be a good couch. The accusation of it was too much. I threw a pillow in the spot and sat at the other end.

The other end wasn't nearly as comfortable. I shifted several times without much luck. My gaze drifted to the pillow. Screw it, I could always have Trevor buy me a new couch. I took the pillow off and plopped into my usual spot, ignoring the implications.

I'd been home for four days. Nyleena had been released yesterday. My team was due back in about an hour. They'd caught their killer. Mine had quietly surrendered. Well, maybe not quietly surrendered, since he had killed someone in the process, but he'd surrendered without a fight. My face, along with Patterson's, had been splashed on newspapers for the first two days after the capture.

My front door opened. Heavy footsteps crossed the threshold and entered the living room. Malachi's long legs appeared and he fell into one of the recliners with the ease that only a cat could exhibit. I would have made it look epileptic, he made it look graceful.

"How's the side?" He asked.

"Fine," I told him. "What's up?"

"We are getting ready to go out on a case, but I thought you might like to see this first," he passed me a baggy. Inside was a piece of paper with dark brown smudges. The ink had run in several spots. The paper was yellowed.

Hey Boss, I killed her. I enjoyed it. The whore had it coming. I stopped reading and passed it back to Malachi.

"A copycat with the decency to at least do some serious copying," I said to him.

"We tested the ink, it's an iron mix. He even used authentic ink."

"Who was it sent to?" I asked.

"Me, I'm the 'boss' in the letter. He even included a piece of kidney from a prostitute in New York City that was found murdered a week ago. Not only is the ink authentic, but the paper isn't paper, it's vellum. However, it's been artificially aged."

"So, you're looking for a printer or antiquarian forger."

"That's my thought. Most people don't know what vellum is or how to age it and they certainly don't know how to make ink. What are your plans for the evening?"

"Oh, I do not know, I thought about plucking out the hair on my toes and watching *Alien vs. Predator* for the umpteenth hundred time."

"Sounds fun. When you finish with your toes, you might do your eyebrows, they're a little bushy." He stood up in a single, fluid motion that made me momentarily hate him. "Patterson's been asking to see you."

"I have no interest in seeing him."

"You can't hide from him for forever, Aislinn. You'll have to see him eventually."

"Eventually, I will. Maybe in court."

"Whatever," Malachi shook his head at me and left. I read maybe half a book when my door opened again. I waited for Malachi to walk back into the room. Instead, it was Gabriel. He was sporting stitches on his cheek and a cast on his arm.

"Never again." He flopped into the seat Malachi had vacated. It lacked grace.

"Never again what?" I asked.

"You not going with us. That was freaking dreadful. I think Fiona is the only one that didn't get injured and that's because she doesn't break down doors."

"I thought Lucas broke down doors," I commented dryly.

"I'll rephrase, she doesn't go into serial killer lairs. She's truly a geek. She can use a gun, but she looks petrified when faced with real danger. Lucas broke through the back door, we all went in behind him and she stands in the yard, with the regular cops. Why? Because she doesn't do that sort of thing, it's in her contract."

"Sounds like a problem."

"Damn straight. Michael, and even John, went into the danger zone."

"Well, maybe she is interested in living a long life. You have to admit, following you is not a great way to stay alive."

"Obviously not. Following you seems to be better. I heard you got stabbed with an ink pen."

"Yep, one of those clear hard plastic tubes to the side where it entered my kidney and leaked piss all down the side of me without me realizing it because I was sure Patterson was going to be a problem. But he just gave up, after killing Gertrude. Now, what happened to your face and arm?"

"Well, the arm was broken when a big, mean son-of-a-bitch grabbed hold of my wrist and snapped it like a twig. Then he grabbed hold of Xavier and threw Xavier into me, which is when my face got cut on Xavier's jacket zipper. Lucas Tasered him, but he might as well have shot him with a rubber band. Eventually, Xavier spider monkey climbed up him and put him in a choke hold while Lucas took a crowbar to his hip."

"Why didn't you shoot him?"

"We're trying a new 'non-lethal approach.'" Gabriel raised his eyebrow as he said this. "Something about too many dead bodies in our wake."

"Pity Christmas has passed, I'd get you all Tasers like mine." I told him. "I guess there's always Valentine's Day."

"Wouldn't it be weird to give us Valentine's Day presents?"

"Nope, I love all of you and it is not like I have a romantic interest in my life. I can probably get the company to ramp up a few more and pass them our way. Where's the new policy coming from?"

"Above my pay-grade, but killing a suspect now requires forms, a written essay on other possible choices, and several visits with a shrink that isn't Lucas and the turning over of your firearms while the shrink goes through your head."

"Is this just us?" I frowned.

"Nope, VCU is also being subjected to it, but because it's the FBI, they have to do everything in triplicate." Gabriel stood up.

"Does your broken arm mean we have time off?"

"Nope, we're just waiting on a call. They figure if you can work after being shot in the head, I can work with a broken arm. Besides, the cast provides me with another, non-lethal weapon. VCU got sent a kidney by a Ripper copycat. That means the next case is ours. I'd guess two days, maybe three." Gabriel stared at me for a moment. "Patterson gave himself up because he wants a relationship with you and Nyleena."

"And Eric," I agreed. "I do not know how I feel about him at the moment. Neither does Nyleena. So, he'll mostly be bonding with Eric."

"Well, Eric will be his closest neighbor."

"Yeah, maybe they can share a cell block."

"They are. They have adjacent cells. Patterson's already plead guilty and asked for sentencing. He was transferred yesterday, which is giving the Department of Justice, the Department of Corrections and the Marshals Service some serious things to consider. August is also at The Fortress while he awaits trial. Someone put forth the theory that Patterson surrendered to get to August. That's why they put him in the same block as Eric. He'll have the fewest opportunities to attack August. But they can't move Eric either because he poses a risk to other inmates."

My brother, Eric, wasn't known for playing nicely with others. Since going to The Fortress, he'd killed three other inmates. Like Patterson, he was suspected of having a hit list. That apple hadn't fallen far from the tree.

Unnatural deaths were rare within the walls of the fortified maximum security prison, corruption among the guards was kept to a minimum by changing out the Marshals every six or nine months. Once in a while, they were suspected of turning a blind eye when the serial targeted cops specifically, but otherwise, their record was nearly spotless. The inmates that were a threat to other inmates were segregated into a special cell block.

However, punishing a killer in The Fortress was a lot like shaking your finger at a kid. It didn't do much. They were all lifers. Special privileges were offered as incentives to be good and those privileges were removed when someone broke the rules. There was also an area of special confinement, but again, like shaking your finger at a kid. Most behaved simply because it made life more interesting.

Unfortunately, neither Patterson nor Eric particularly cared about life being more interesting. They would find trouble, probably together. I didn't envy the powers that be or the Marshals in charge of keeping them from the rest of the population.

Hadena James

I've been writing for over two decades and before that, I was creating my own bedtime stories to tell myself. I penned my first short story at the ripe old age of 8. It was a fable about how the raccoon got its eye-mask and was roughly three pages of handwritten, 8 year old scrawl. My mother still has it and occasionally, I still dig it out and admire it.

When I got my first computer, I took all my handwritten stories and typed them in. Afterwards, I tossed the originals. In my early twenties, I had a bit of a writer's meltdown and deleted everything. So, with the exception of the story about the raccoon, I actually have none of my writings from before I was 23. Which is sad, because I had a half dozen other novels and well over two hundred short stories. It has all been offered up to the computer and writing gods as a sacrifice and show of humility or some such nonsense that makes me feel less like an idiot about it.

I have been offered contracts with publishing houses in the past and always turned them down. Now that I have experimented with being an Indie Author, I really like it and I'm really glad I turned them down. However, if you had asked me this in the early years of 2000, I would have told you that I was an idiot (and it was a huge contributing factor to my deleting all my work).

When I'm not writing, I play in a steel-tip dart league and enjoy going to dart tournaments. I enjoy renaissance festivals and sanitized pirates who sing sea shanties. My appetite for reading is ferocious and I consume two to three books a week as well as writing my own. Aside from introducing me to darts, my SO has introduced me to camping, which I, surprisingly, enjoy. We can often be found in the summer at Mark Twain Lake in Missouri, where his parents own a campground.

I am a native of Columbia, Missouri, which I will probably call home for the rest of my life, but I love to travel. Day trips, week trips, vacations on other continents, wherever the path takes me is where I want to be and I'm hoping to be able to travel more in the future.

http://www.facebook.com/hadenajames

hadenajames.wordpress.com

@hadenajames

CPSIA information can be obtained at www.ICGtesting.com
Printed in the USA
LVOW10s1451071215

465787LV00020B/1087/P